Revenge

of the

Assassin

✝

Book II of the Assassin series

Russell Blake

First Edition

ISBN: 978-1480238305

Published by

Reprobatio Limited

INTRODUCTION

Most of the events and people in Revenge of the Assassin are fictional. Many of the organizations and a few of the events are not.

The state of Tamaulipas in Mexico, bordering Texas, has had numerous mass prison breaks over the last few years. It is also largely considered to be out of the control of the Mexican government.

The Bureau of Alcohol, Tobacco and Firearms was recently embroiled in a massive 'gun walking' scandal where thousands of weapons were shipped into Mexico from the U.S. while the American authorities turned a blind eye. No coherent reasoning was ever offered, and the matter quickly disappeared from the public eye after a Congressional investigation that went nowhere – much as the Iran/Contra hearings never yielded any real meat.

Submarines are regularly manufactured out of fiberglass in Colombia for the trafficking of cocaine to Mexican waters, where the drugs are either offloaded to Mexican boats or left submerged with sea anchors for later pick up by Mexican craft.

The tunnels under the border in most frontier towns are a matter of regular news coverage each time one is discovered, which occurs with considerable frequency.

Massacres carried out by the Los Zetas cartel are well documented, and their descriptions in this novel are true.

The Sinaloa, Juárez and Los Zetas cartels are very real, and are now the most powerful drug-trafficking and organized crime syndicates on the planet.

CHAPTER 1

Midnight, six weeks ago, Mexico City, Mexico

The pounding from the front door of the high-rise condo echoed in the entryway as the strident ringing of the kitchen phone matched its insistence. Captain Romero Cruz of the federal police flicked on the hallway light as he pulled a bathrobe over his naked torso. The phone stopped its trilling as he shuffled down the hall and then peered blearily through the peephole. Satisfied there was no obvious threat, he fumbled with the deadbolt and opened the door.

A man in the distinctive blue uniform of the *Federales* saluted, ignoring the disheveled hair of his superior officer. He shifted nervously as he stared into space at some neutral point a thousand miles beyond his commander's shoulder. Cruz ignored the circumstances and gestured for him to speak up.

"*Capitan.* I'm sorry to intrude. But you wanted to be alerted as soon as we had confirmation on the Tijuana situation. We've been calling for half an hour, but there was no answer…"

"That's fine. I'm sorry. I had the bedroom door closed, and this phone isn't very loud. I must have slept through it. What's the update?" Cruz asked, cinching the robe ties around his waist as he shook off his grogginess and became more alert. Unlike when he'd been younger, now that he was in his mid-forties it took a while for him to fire on all cylinders, especially since he'd only gotten to sleep two hours earlier.

"We received word that five hundred kilos arrived at the suspect warehouse this evening, to be transported tonight or tomorrow morning at the latest. That means if we want to catch them red-handed–"

"I get it. Do we have sufficient assets there to go in on a frontal assault? And can we be ready in an hour?"

"Yes, sir. I already took the liberty of putting out the word." He hesitated. "We have a jet standing by to get tactical leadership there by three in the morning, worst case," the officer confirmed.

Cruz paused and considered the alternatives, and then nodded. "Then we go in. I'll put on a pot of coffee and be ready to get to headquarters shortly. Have my car ready for me. I'll run the operation from there." Cruz studied the man's face, hardened from years on the force and strained with fatigue. "It's going to be a long one. What time did you come on duty today?"

"I got in at ten this morning, *Capitan*. I was going to quit by eight tonight, and then we started getting chatter from our sources, so I decided to stay on for a little while."

"No good deed goes unpunished. Do we have any idea whose dope this is? Or do I even need to ask?"

"Sinaloa."

"Ahhh. Well, let me take a shower and get ready, then. I'll be downstairs in forty-five minutes. That's all," Cruz said, and waved off the officer's parting salute as he closed the door.

Five hundred kilos of cocaine. Now that was worth getting out of bed for.

"*Corazon?* Who was that? Is everything okay?" a female voice called from the bedroom once the front door had slammed closed.

"It's fine, *mi amor*. But I need to go into the office. I'm sorry. I'll probably be getting back around the time you're up for work," he apologized as he moved into the bedroom. "It's an emergency. Go back to sleep. I'll be as quiet as possible," he reassured the woman peering at him from the far side of the bed, beautiful even with no makeup and roused in the middle of the night. He padded over to her and gave her a fleeting kiss. "Close your eyes, Dinah. I need to get a uniform out of the closet."

ও~ও

3:27 a.m., six weeks ago, Tijuana, Mexico

Monday nights in Tijuana were usually calm, the weekend's lunacy and tourist rush having ebbed, leaving the town worked, but marginally wealthier. The weather was chilly in late March, in the low sixties, with a light drizzle having clogged the poorly drained streets with refuse and murky runoff. The industrial row of warehouses along the border wall was a no-man's land in the best of daylight hours, and after midnight, only the foolhardy, the desperate or the suicidal ventured into the menacing district.

Junkyards and body shops dotted the area's mean streets, with decrepit buildings and darkened half-completed construction punctuating the rows of tin-roofed shacks and wrecking yards. An occasional car prowled along the unlit thoroughfares, bass-heavy reggaeton booming from the lowered chassis as the shady occupants crept about their nocturnal business. Near one of the larger gray cinder-block edifices, a bony stray dog rooted through bags of refuse dumped on the sidewalks for morning collection, its furtive movement ample evidence that, even for scavengers, danger was a constant.

One of the armed guards standing watch outside the ten-foot-high, broken-glass-topped walls of a compound at the end of the cul-de-sac flicked his cigarette at the mutt, causing it to bolt from its paltry find. He grinned to himself and wiped a sheen of moisture from his brow, then glanced over to the other two men lurking at the far end of the wall, also toting weapons and on the alert. The rain had stopped twenty minutes earlier but there was still a pall of humidity mixed with raw exhaust and the reek of overflowing sewage pipes that coated everything with a noxious film. The smell of the tobacco offered slim relief from the ever-present stench that was part of the duty of guarding the complex.

The roar of heavy vehicles tearing up the street shattered the gloom, then the guard was blinded by spotlights mounted on the turrets of the BTR-70s. He fumbled for his two-way radio while simultaneously raising his M4 assault rifle and barely barked out a warning before he was cut

3

down by a stream of silenced rounds from the leading truck. The other two sentries met with the same fate, though one managed to get off several bursts of sub-machine-gun fire before being hacked to pieces by the muffled shooters in the vehicles.

Within thirty seconds, the sidewalk in front of the wall was bristling with black-clad marines in full combat gear, augmented by federal police carrying Heckler & Koch UMP45 machine pistols with specially-fitted sound and flash suppressors. The leader of the squad made a curt hand gesture to his lieutenant, indicating the security camera mounted near the gate – a well-aimed volley from his weapon shattered the device.

An armored assault truck slammed through the steel-plated gates, and four dozen armed commandos followed it through. The percussive burp of machine guns strafed from the largest of the three warehouses as the defenders inside engaged their attackers. Several of the marines uttered cries, cut down as they ran, their body armor slim protection against the armor-piercing rounds spraying from the windows.

Three of the personnel carriers rolled into the yard and focused their gun turrets on the main building, unleashing a devastating volley of lethal fire, the neon orange of tracer rounds illuminating the windows as they streaked to their targets. A federal police sergeant ran in a crouch under the cover of the shooting, and rolling to the side of one of the large, partially-open steel doors, tossed a grenade inside before ducking away from the volley of shots that greeted his silhouette. A muffled explosion blew out the glass from the windows above his head, and he quickly threw in two more grenades, shielding himself by hugging the concrete foundation as the detonations hurled shrapnel throughout the interior.

The squad leader watched helplessly as another of his men had his throat torn out in a bloody spray by gunfire coming from the roof, and he ducked behind the relative safety of one of the BTR-70s as he barked commands into the radio. Thirty seconds later a helicopter shredded the air above the building with its rotors and rained destruction down upon the shooters on the rooftop.

One of the cartel gunmen swiveled around at the sound of the approaching chopper and methodically fired three-round bursts at the craft's silhouette, as he'd been trained to do when a marine himself only a few years earlier. He watched with satisfaction as his M16's fully-jacketed slugs punctured the front window and the pilot's chest exploded in a red pulp. His glee was short-lived as the helicopter gunner directed his last salvo of large caliber rounds at him, cutting his torso in two before he could throw himself flat against the roof.

The chopper spun giddily in the night sky before plunging into the side of the neighboring building and exploding in an orange fireball that momentarily blinded the assault team. A second detonation erupted from the shattered hulk and a cloud of sooty smoke redolent of burning flesh belched into the dank breeze.

The leader fired through the haze at the few remaining defendants, and then held up three gloved fingers and murmured into his com line. The shooting gradually subsided, replaced by an uneasy silence. The blast from the copter crash and the booming of the turret guns still echoed in the team's ears as they waited cautiously for direction. Seeing no further fire from the main building, the leader made two hand signals. His men divided up and raced for the warehouse door that the advance man had pitched the grenades through.

After a few moments of hesitation, the men dropped night vision goggles into place and tore through the opening, weapons ready to cut down anything that moved. The bodies of the defending gunmen lay strewn around the floor near the windows, where the brutally effective onslaught from the BTR-70 guns had cut any resistance short. The goggles illuminated the gloomy depths of the warehouse with a distinctive green glow, and it quickly became apparent that nothing remained alive to threaten them.

The squad leader crept into the area, and once satisfied that all danger was neutralized, he motioned to one of his men to hit the lights. The team members flipped their goggles up, and an officer at the entry threw the breaker into the on position.

The overhead bulbs flickered to life, revealing a tableau of carnage. Corpses littered the floor in pools of blood alongside pallets of cardboard boxes accumulated in haphazard piles. Studying the scene, the leader approached an ancient forklift that sat idle in a far corner, in front of a crudely-formed cinderblock room with a steel roll-up door. That had to be the elevator they'd been told about.

A sound caused him to whirl around. A man lay on the ground, his arm and half his torso blown off by a grenade, along with much of his face. His one good eye regarded the interloper as his breath gurgled in his chest, and then he groaned and lay still. The leader paused to consider the now lifeless carcass, and then returned his attention to the elevator. He gestured to his men, and three of them hurried to take position on either side, their weapons trained on the steel roll-up door.

On the leader's nod, the tallest of his men pulled it up, revealing a shaft twelve feet square. He cautiously shone a flashlight into the depths; its beam reflected off a steel platform four stories below. Glancing around, the leader summoned a group of his fighters and conducted a hurried discussion. A sweating marine trotted out to the vehicles and returned with three bundles of rappelling line.

Five minutes later, six commandos stood deep in the earth below Tijuana, peering down a long tunnel with an elaborate rail car system. One of the soldiers activated the low voltage lighting that ran the length of the excavation and noted that it stretched on seemingly forever. Wood and cement blocks supported the walls and ceiling of the passageway, ten feet wide and seven feet high. The rails of the electric trolley gleamed in the light. It was obvious that the system had been in place for some time and was well used.

A storage room sat just adjacent to the shaft, and when a technician cut the lock off with a welding torch, five hundred and thirty kilos of cocaine sat neatly packaged in orange plastic, with a distinctive scorpion logo stamped on the outside of each bundle. The room was large enough to accommodate ten times that amount, and there was no question in any of the men's minds that this was only a few days' worth of shipments waiting to make their way to the other end of the passage – a small, decrepit warehouse on the U.S. side of the border that ostensibly sold used automobile parts.

Further examination revealed an advanced ventilation system and numerous battery chargers to keep the trolley rolling, an additional indication that the tunnel was regularly used to move large amounts of contraband into the U.S. How long it had been in operation was anyone's guess, but by the looks of some of the debris, it had been years, not months.

The next day's newspapers on both sides of the border were quick to herald a victory for the anti-drug forces and skimmed over the casualties as well as the obvious fact that many thousands of tons of cocaine and heroin had been making their way across undetected. Nobody was ever connected to the U.S. warehouse, other than a pair of low-level brothers who claimed they only paid the property taxes and utilities and hadn't been to the building in half a decade. Their case was remanded into the system and would take over a year to be heard in the overcrowded courts. They would ultimately wind up spending less than six months behind bars, along with credit for time served, having no criminal records other than an unrelated burglary from over ten years before.

Twelve marines and federal police were killed during the assault, including the helicopter crew, and six more were wounded. A total of fourteen cartel gunmen died during the gun battle, with no survivors. Nobody claimed any of the cartel fighters' corpses, which were buried in a mass grave with no ceremony.

One month later, two more tunnels were discovered and shut down.

By the best estimates over twenty are in operation at any given time – an inevitable fact of life in an environment where a laborer who works to excavate the tunnel makes five to seven dollars a day, and a kilo of cocaine that costs two thousand dollars in Colombia wholesales for twenty-five to thirty on the U.S. side of the border.

☙❧

11:18 p.m., one week ago, 80 miles west of Ixtapa, Mexico

Six-foot swells with frothing white crests surged relentlessly from the northwest, driven by a frigid twenty knot wind. The cloudy night's crescent moon scarcely illuminated the inky water's surface, its roiling unbroken except for the battered steel hull of an aged seventy-five-foot shrimp boat lurching against the waves' pounding.

El Cabrito had departed Mazatlán two weeks before and had plied her way down the Pacific coast at a dismally slow eight knots, under way twenty-four hours a day until she arrived in the warmer waters off the coast of Zihuatanejo. There, she'd worked the nets, accumulating what she could by way of catch as she waited for her true cargo to arrive.

Her gray paint was ravaged by sea salt; patches of rust bled through along the waterline, signaling that soon it would be time to haul her out and weld new steel plates where corrosion had taken its toll. The topsides were slick from the windy spray, and the crew was inside below decks, waiting for the signal that they were needed. The captain, Mario, a thirty year veteran of the coastal waters, puffed on a hand-rolled cigarette as he watched the waves moving in a steady procession, the red illumination of his primitive gauges and the ancient radar unit bathing the pilothouse in a warm glow.

The diesel engine chugged quietly, driving the old single screw with just enough power to make headway against the building seas. They were in position, the handheld GPS unit near the throttle confirmed that the waypoint marking the rendezvous spot had been reached. The instructions were to hold position – for days, if necessary – while they waited. It was usually easy duty, but the squall that was eighty miles southwest of them was beginning to cause problems. Reports of fifteen to twenty foot swells had come in a few minutes earlier over the radio from a cargo ship making its way north. It was just a matter of time until the six footers doubled in size, and then it would get rocky.

Comfort wasn't the concern. Rather, it would be impossible to transfer their cargo in huge waves with the boat pitching uncontrollably. Under normal circumstances they'd have been in four to five foot, gently rolling swells, the undulations of the surface easily timed. But with confused conditions and a tropical depression looming further out in the Pacific, all bets were off. If their contact didn't show up soon, it could be days before a handoff would be practicable again.

Mario scanned the ocean's murky form, searching for a beacon, as he had every fifteen minutes since the black of night had fallen. The rolling didn't make it any easier. Worst case, he had his second radio tuned to a frequency that was rarely used, and he hoped that the captain of the other vessel would avail himself of the channel discreetly. One never knew who could be listening, and in a high-stakes game, there was no such thing as being too careful.

His first mate, Julio, mounted the stairs from the crew quarters below, two cans of Tecate beer clenched in his left hand as he steadied himself with a series of practiced grips on the handrail. Mario took one from him, and they toasted.

"It looks like it's going to get snotty soon," Julio remarked, before savoring a mouthful of cold brew.

Mario peered into the blackness outside. "There's a big one blowing from the west. I figure we have maybe three more hours before we need to break off and head inland some. If the storm turns towards us, we don't want to be here in sixty knot winds if we can help it."

"How late are they?"

"A day. Smart money says they'll be here tonight. Sometimes shit happens en route."

Julio nodded.

They watched in silence as the cresting water rushed to meet the bow of the boat, the steady throb of the diesel engine a reassuring constant.

The radio crackled to life, and after a few terse exchanges, Julio slid back down to the crew quarters to rouse the men. It was show time. Their rendezvous was on.

Out of the gloom, a long tubular form rose from the depths, two hundred yards from the bow. Mario throttled the engine up and the boat surged forward towards the shape. Within a minute they had pulled alongside it, where two deckhands threw lines to the four men who had materialized on the top section of the darkened craft. After a short struggle they secured the pair of vessels together until the two rose and fell as one. After hurried greetings between the crews, plastic-wrapped rectangular packages began making their way from the bowels of the newcomer to the men on *El Cabrito*'s deck, who passed them into the shrimp hold to be squirreled away under the catch.

The submarine had been crafted in the jungles of northern Colombia and had been traveling for twelve days to make the meet in Mexican waters. Equipped with two nearly silent diesel engines that charged the battery-driven electric motor, the handmade fiberglass vessel could do fourteen knots and submerge comfortably to a depth of twenty-five feet. Forty yards in length, she was equipped with primitive climate control for the crew, was virtually invisible to radar, and carried twenty-five hundred kilos of pure cocaine, with a street value of seventy-five million dollars, uncut. Once it was adulterated, the precious cargo would bring more like a hundred million. Wholesale cost in Colombia had been a cool six million dollars. The sub had cost seven hundred thousand dollars to fabricate and equip, with the crew costing three million. All told, the trip was a ninety percent profit margin transaction, even after all costs were factored in.

The loading took four hours of spirited loading. By the time the Colombian vessel was empty, the seas had built to nine footers. The crew of the sub hurriedly placed explosive charges along the craft's hull, and once they were aboard the fishing boat, the captain depressed a transmitter and the submarine's waterline ruptured. The sub crewmen stood on the back of the fishing boat and watched as their conveyance sank beneath the waves, then quickly moved into the pilothouse and down into the ship's bunk room. After almost two weeks submerged in cramped conditions they were ready for showers and drinking. It was the kind of trip you only made once or twice in a lifetime, and then you were done.

Mario checked the radar and noted that there were no other ships within twenty miles. With a grunt, he spun the wheel and pointed the struggling bow north, on a course that would get them closer to the less turbid shore within a few hours – if their luck held out. From there they'd be two days to Mazatlán, maybe three, where their cargo would be offloaded to other craft for the trip up the Sea of Cortez.

Commander Villanuevo watched the blip on his radar screen with interest. It had remained stationary for a full day, and now was moving in their direction at a snail's pace. By his calculations, they'd be within striking distance in six hours at the current course, assuming that the Durango-class offshore patrol vessel Villanuevo captained stayed immobile.

That wasn't the plan. His ship could easily hold twenty knots in any sea conditions, which would put them alongside *El Cabrito* in a little over three hours. Villanuevo barked a series of orders to his second in command and advised him to ready the men. They'd move on the boat at flat-out speed and call in the helicopter when the patrol boat was twenty miles away so the fishing boat didn't have time to jettison its cargo or prepare in any way.

A team of ten marines were standing by at the military base outside Manzanillo, ready to board the chopper and move on *El Cabrito*. It could reach the fishing scow in a little over two hours, which would work out perfectly. Villanuevo radioed the coordinates of the ship and told the assault team to scramble the helicopter. It would be airborne within half an hour and in a holding pattern over the destroyer by six a.m. Once they were ready, he'd send the team in, and within a few minutes the shrimper wouldn't know what had hit it.

Villanuevo gave the signal and the patrol boat rocketed forward, impervious to the chop as it cut through the waves. At two hundred forty feet, with a crew of fifty-five and another twenty marines below decks, there were few vessels that could outrun or outfight the *ARM Sonora*. By his calculations, they could be boarding their target by seven a.m., with the mission hopefully concluded shortly thereafter.

They'd received the tip on the drug shipment a week before, with surprisingly detailed information. If it was even close to correct, this would be one of the biggest seizures in his career, and a major blow to the Sinaloa cartel, which was the purported trafficker of this particular load. The new administration wanted to send a message to the Mexican people that it wasn't going to be business as usual, and this interception would be critical in establishing the tone of the next six years in office. Of course, the information had likely come from a competitive cartel looking to cause maximum discomfort to its competitor, but that wasn't Villanuevo's concern. His job was to stop the shipment, and that's what he'd do. The politicians could fight over who got the credit.

Villanuevo checked his watch and pushed the button that activated the stopwatch function. If all played as he hoped, it would be a very bad morning indeed for the crew of *El Cabrito*.

Mario jolted awake from his brief slumber. His first mate was shaking his shoulder. Julio's eyes were wide with a look he'd never seen during the sixteen years the man had been his second in command: terror. Mario quickly shook off the sleep stupor and bolted upright, then turned to the pilothouse window to be faced with an image that was his worst nightmare.

A Sikorsky helicopter in full battle regalia bearing the colors of the Mexican Navy hovered a hundred yards away, the side panel open and a fifty caliber machine gun trained on the shrimp boat. Inside, a group of grim-faced marines in assault gear were grouped behind the weapon.

Waiting.

Dawn had broken a few minutes earlier, but even in the meager light of the new day it was glaringly obvious to Mario that this was a full-scale disaster. The massive blades of the chopper churned the water below; its downdraft from the buffeting whipped the sea into an angry froth.

Mario throttled back to near idle. Keeping his eye on the aircraft, he barked at Julio, "What the…when did they show up?"

"They came out of nowhere. There was nothing on the radar, and then suddenly, there they were."

Mario grimaced. "Shit. They must have been flying at a high altitude, which is why we didn't pick them up."

He was interrupted by an amplified voice from the copter.

"Put the engine in neutral and stop. Prepare to be boarded. Get your crew on deck where they can be seen," the voice boomed across the water as the helicopter closed the distance, now no more than sixty yards from the boat.

Julio glanced around wildly. "You think this is some kind of a drill or random inspection?" he asked, panicked.

Mario shook his head. "I'm afraid not. Look at them. They're geared up for a small war. No, I'd say we've been sold out."

"Dammit," Julio spat. "What do we do?"

"Look at the radar. See there?" His grubby finger jabbed at the screen. "That's a huge ship, and it's moving very fast."

Mario had to make a quick decision. They had several automatic assault rifles on board, but they would be no match against the entire Mexican navy. His mind raced over alternatives, and then he shook his head again.

"We're finished. Get the men on deck and tell them to keep their mouths shut. The last thing we want is a gunfight with the marines on the open sea," Mario said.

"So we're going to just give up?"

"Do you have any better ideas?" Mario seethed. "We've got a ship bearing down on us, and that chopper has enough firepower to blow us to Japan. Do you really feel like dying today? I don't. We can always let our lawyers deal with the fallout from this." He shook his head and sighed. "It's better than the alternative…"

Julio took a deep breath and wordlessly descended the stairwell to where the crew was asleep after a mini-*fiesta* following the loading.

A few minutes later, the men filed onto the deck with their hands in the air or behind their heads, and watched as the distinctive outline of the warship moved towards them. The chopper held its position, fixing the boat with its full attention as it waited for the *Sonora* to get within range.

Mario caught movement in the pilothouse as he squinted at the horizon from the deck; upon seeing the source, he dropped his arms and began gesturing wildly with his hands. The crazy Colombian submarine captain had stayed below, and now peered through the doorway with an AK-47 pointed at the helicopter.

"Noooo–" Mario screamed, but it was too late.

The captain emptied the weapon at the chopper. Julio and Mario watched in horror as the slugs tore into the side of the aircraft, cutting down several of the armed marines. The fire was answered by the staccato high-speed chatter of the big .50 caliber gun as it issued forth a broadside of rounds that riddled the fishing boat, annihilating the foolhardy submariner in a rain of lethal fury.

The last thing Mario saw before his world went black for good was the stream of tracers from the chopper shredding the deck around him, mangling his crew in a rain of death as the spooked marines opened up with everything they had. A few of his men tried to find cover from the slaughter, but there was nowhere to hide. It was finished in a matter of a few seconds, and when the shooting stopped, nothing remained on the shrimper but corpses.

When Villanuevo arrived on the *Sonora* twenty minutes later, the drifting boat was awash in blood, the slug-torn bodies of the hapless crew scattered across the deck. The marines rappelled from the helicopter and moved cautiously over the boat before descending to the lower compartments, wary of another attack. After a few minutes, the leader emerged from the pilothouse and shook his head.

"There's nobody left alive."

An hour later, Villanuevo radioed in one of the largest drug busts on the high seas in Mexican history – a triumph owed entirely to an anonymous tip from parties unknown.

In the end, *El Cabrito* was only one of many shipments that made its way from Colombia every month, and even though it was a large seizure, there were infinite amounts of both criminals and drugs from where it had originated. Submarines continued to be fabricated in the hidden depths of the guerrilla-controlled jungle, and men desperate to make one big score that would set them up for life remained eager to pilot them north. As it had been for decades, and as it would remain for generations to come.

ॐॐ

6:04 a.m., yesterday, Los Mochis, Mexico

The yard of the paint supply company's storage facility was particularly well fortified, with gleaming new barbed wire and hurricane fencing to keep trespassers at bay. Several ill-tempered Rottweilers prowled the grounds, further dissuading potential thieves from picking it as a target. Four armed sentries sat positioned at the corners, where they remained every night until they were relieved at eight a.m., an hour before the yard opened for business.

It was still dark out, but the first orange rays of dawn were beginning to seep over the hills to the east of town, providing tentative illumination of the road that led to the facility. At the far end of it, three military Humvees swung onto the pavement and raced towards the gates, followed by two trucks loaded with soldiers. The security men, alerted by the roar of the engines, hurriedly discussed their alternatives. They were there to protect the building – not take on the Mexican army. The head of the sentry detail told his men to stash their weapons where they wouldn't be found, and one of the four ran to the far end of the yard where an old pickup truck sat on blocks, its engine long-ago dismantled for parts. He pushed the Kalashnikovs under the seat and was just moving back to the group when the vehicles pulled to a stop in front of the gate.

A federal police officer wearing a bulletproof vest eyed the men dubiously from the safety of the lead truck's cab, and satisfied that there was no imminent danger, swung his door open and stepped onto the hard-packed dirt. He approached the obvious leader of the security guards and held out a piece of paper.

"Open the gates. I have a court order to search this bodega," he announced perfunctorily.

The leader read the document, taking his time, and then nodded.

"I'll be happy to, but I need to call the owners first and get their permission."

The officer shook his head. "That's not what the order says. It says you let us in, now, and shut up until I say it's all right to call anyone," the cop explained menacingly.

The leader's eyes narrowed, and then he shrugged. "Suit yourself. But the owners are very powerful, and they won't appreciate their property being trampled without any notice. I just work here, but I'm glad I'm not in your shoes."

"Your concern is noted. Now open up."

The leader glared at the cop and the soldiers, who had deployed from the trailing vehicles and now had their weapons trained on his men. He sighed, then fished in his pocket for the key to the massive padlock that held the gates closed.

Two hours later, eighteen tons of marijuana had been discovered in two shipping containers at the far end of the storage facility, along with ninety kilos of Mexican heroin and several crates of automatic weapons. The *Federales* clamped a lid on the bust until they could round up the owners, who were going to jail for a very long time. The guards were charged with being accessories, but the police knew that would be a tough charge to make stick, given that they'd cooperated and the seizure had taken place without bloodshed – an anomaly in the ongoing war against the cartels.

The following week, all four security men were found beheaded, stuffed in the back of an abandoned Chevrolet van on the outskirts of

Hermosillo. The leader's wife, sister, and three children were also found in the vehicle, beaten to death with a tire iron that still bore traces of their blood and hair on it, tossed casually on the floor of the passenger side of the cab. The local papers published lurid photos and made much of the grisly details, but within a few days the incident was forgotten, yet another in an endless parade of cartel violence that showed no signs of abating, regardless of the government's rhetoric to the contrary.

CHAPTER 2

The president's security team was in place hours ahead of time in Tampico, where he was scheduled to make an appearance at a local hospital. It had been a lousy week for his entourage, as the president had insisted in venturing out of Mexico City to show that he was a man of the people, unafraid to visit his constituents.

It would be a welcome break from the bureaucratic grind that was his typical fare. The burdens of running Mexico were considerable, especially having only taken office a few short months before, during a time of upheaval. Infighting from political foes, the routine duties of being a head of state, jockeying to compromise on the host of campaign promises he had no ability or intention of keeping – all added up to a momentous pressure load, but one he gladly shouldered.

The exiting administration had looted the country's coffers, as had each administration before it, so one of the most pressing items he had to deal with was rebuilding the nation's finances. This was problematic, as the windfall staple that had been responsible for much of the country's prosperity was becoming harder to pump out of the ground – or sea, in this case. Once flush with oil revenues, over the past years the amount of energy required to extract a barrel of oil had skyrocketed as the oil fields matured and the low-hanging fruit had been picked, demanding ever greater effort for each subsequent year's production. Simply put; in the past, a field would yield a hundred barrels of oil for one barrel's worth of energy to extract them. Now they were lucky to see four barrels to one. To make matters worse, Mexico's internal consumption had almost reached the point where it wouldn't have any oil left to export within a few years – one of its largest sources of revenue.

His other overwhelming problem was that the U.S. wanted Mexico to fight its war on drugs by pursuing the cartels at every turn, and it paid substantial foreign aid to Mexico in order to continue the nation's criminalization of trafficking. The reality was that drugs were largely decriminalized within Mexico, and the population consumed them at whatever rate it felt like, without much fanfare or violence. Measures had been floated numerous times to make them legal, in an attempt to end the unprecedented bloodshed that had accompanied the rise of trafficking by the Mexican cartels, when they'd taken over from the Colombians as the transportation arm of that nation's enterprise.

The president's security detail was chartered with performing advance reconnaissance of any area he would be visiting, and today he was scheduled to first fly from Mexico City to be at a new social security hospital ribbon cutting ceremony in Tampico, and then jet to Guadalajara to spend an hour at an orphanage. Both events were photo ops, nothing more, but much of the role of being president involved kissing babies and feigning interest in the mundane. Nonetheless, the challenges involved with safeguarding him in an environment of constant danger and violence were significant, and the men chartered with doing so were professionals of the highest caliber.

Once the day was done, the plan was to fly into Durango before dark for a few days of relaxation at a massive ranch the president's family owned. As with all presidential visits there, a helicopter would wing the president to the rural compound, bypassing any travel on roads. The highways were too much of a question mark, even with a massive military presence, so whenever possible the president eschewed motorcades in favor of air travel. The security detail tried to keep his arrival low-key, however that was generally impossible, and by evening the airport would be temporarily closed down and ringed with army troops to discourage any sort of an attack.

Major Luis Cena headed up the group of special forces troops assigned to presidential protection duty – the most prestigious posting in the nation, and one that carried with it significant pressure. He preferred when the president remained in Mexico City under rigorously controlled conditions, and hated these junkets for the risk they posed.

He was agitated this morning because the route from the airport in Tampico to the hospital was riddled with security problems, which he was handling to the best of his abilities but which introduced substantial uncontrollable variables. The president would be there within a half hour, and even after posting men along the way and closing off the streets, he was apprehensive. The president's new offensive against the cartels had caused consternation at the highest levels and retaliation was a given.

Tampico was a problem area due to the high concentration of cartel cells in the region – always the case around any of the ports where drugs could be smuggled in and distributed. Cena had argued against the foray to the hospital, but the new president was still trying to earn the support of the people even though the campaign had been won – a fool's errand, and a dangerous one, Cena thought.

Still, his job wasn't to second guess the boss, but to protect him, which is why he was in crisis mode. It was days like today that drove him crazy. Not one, but three visits, all of which had to be viewed as very real brushes with danger for a man who acted as though the whole world loved him.

The short-hop presidential jet touched down at General Francisco J. Mina International Airport amidst a stoppage of flights for half an hour, in order to accommodate the entourage and security precautions. As the Gulfstream III rolled to a stop at the far end of the runway and taxied to a secure area, it was circled by army vehicles. Cena quickly deployed his men, who formed a protective perimeter. A fleet of gold-toned armored Chevrolet Suburbans waited, and when the stairs lowered from the plane's fuselage, the security detail notably bristled. Traffic on all roads approaching the airport had been stopped with roadblocks, as had the frontage access-way, to reduce any likelihood of attack. A small group of specially selected reporters obligingly took photographs as the president descended the steps, waving to a non-existent crowd for the cameras.

Cena's six plainclothes bodyguards surrounded the president as he made his way from the plane to his motorcade, and the group moved cautiously to the waiting vehicles. The five Suburbans sat alongside six military Humvees, Cena's men manning the heavy machine guns mounted just behind the roofs. In Mexico, there was no pretense of civility when it came to law enforcement – the sight of heavily-armed soldiers in combat readiness was a daily occurrence and drew no raised eyebrows. The reporters crammed into the last SUV, and the convoy was ready for departure.

Cena exhaled a sigh of relief as he climbed into the lead vehicle and gave the signal to get underway. At the airport security gate, six motorcycle police and three federal police trucks joined the convoy and took the lead, with another two bringing up the rear for the four mile drive to the new hospital.

The vehicles wound their way from the centrally-located airport along a pre-planned route to the hospital. Unfortunately, braving the city streets was the only way to reach the site. There was no available area to land a helicopter in the limited parking area adjacent to the hospital without inviting a rocket attack from one of the surrounding buildings, which had been deemed an unacceptable risk. To make matters more difficult, a large crowd had gathered there, along with another group of reporters. It was free entertainment, and the president didn't visit every day. Even though everyone in the vicinity had been searched as a condition of attending the momentous event, Cena still was nervous. He hated crowds because of the potential variables that came with them.

Twelve minutes after departing the airport, they arrived without incident at the large, new medical facility. The governor of Tampico stood beaming, waiting for his ally, the president, to make his way to the ceremonial ribbon. The city's mayor and a host of minor dignitaries also stood patiently by, insistent on being proximate to the seat of power. The governor had been a strong supporter of the president's election campaign, and was an old friend, which accounted for the visit. Chits had to be paid, and it was questionable whether the president could have carried the election had it not been for Tampico. Normally, a hospital opening wouldn't have rated his time, but the party had developed a strong bed of support in the state, and it never hurt to solidify sentiment. There was always the next election to consider.

The governor shook hands with the president, and then gave him a warm hug. After greetings were exchanged, the speeches began, promising a new era of prosperity and national pride. There were no surprises, and forty minutes after the ceremony had begun, it was over. Ripples of applause followed the waving of the dignitaries as they hastened to depart, their media circus having come to an end.

Cena's precautions had paid off. The president was still alive and ready for the flight to Guadalajara for his afternoon appearance. The entourage moved back to the cars, and the motorcade prepared for the return trip. Cena radioed ahead to alert the waiting commandos to prepare for their passage back.

ॐॐ

Juan Ramon was sweating, even though the temperature was moderate and a breeze blew through his partially open bedroom window. He peered at the roofs of the buildings that were forty yards in front of his dingy apartment complex, and noticed that the soldiers lining the sidewalk had stiffened within the last few minutes, presumably in anticipation of the return of the president's motorcade. He'd watched as it had made its way down the two lane street on its way to the hospital, noting the number of Suburbans.

A warble interrupted his thoughts – he snatched the cell phone from the table by his side.

"Yes."

"He left in the second car, but it looked like they switched the order once they were out of the parking lot, so it could now be the fourth," the voice reported, sounding harried.

"What? How the hell is that supposed to help me? It's one or the other. Think, man. Which is it? Second or fourth?" Juan Ramon seethed into the phone.

"I don't know. Like I said, they did some shuffling in the staging area, and I couldn't see from so far away. Too much of a crowd, and the security looked like it was on unusually high alert."

"You know what happens if we screw this up."

"I know. I'd say go with the fourth truck. That's my best guess. They left exactly ninety seconds ago. Should be within range in three minutes," the voice advised.

"Your best *guess*? Fine. It's your funeral if your *guess* is wrong," Juan Ramon warned, then hung up. He checked his watch, then slid the small, black plastic radio transmitter nearer to the window sill. He raised a pair of camouflage binoculars to his eyes and watched for the first motorcycles. The timing would be easy, but the ambiguity over the president's position within the convoy was a problem.

❧

Cena's buzz of agitation hadn't diminished since they'd left the hospital. If anything, it had grown worse. There had been warning indicators that the cartels were unhappy with the president's aggressive offensive against them since taking office, and this was one of the first expeditions from the capital since he'd been inaugurated. Perhaps it was professional paranoia, but Cena had the sense that something was brewing, and he felt out of control, even though nothing had occurred.

So far.

They rounded a curve onto the primary thoroughfare through town, and Cena studied the myriad buildings along the route. The Suburbans had bulletproof glass and armor plating, so any danger from a sniper was moot. The president was in far more danger when he'd been standing in the open than in his coach. At least that part of the ordeal had gone off without incident.

A massive blast tore through the line of vehicles as one of the storefronts lining the road exploded, and the third and fourth Chevrolets flipped over from the force, their armor providing slim protection against six mounds of Semtex coated in three-quarter inch steel ball-bearings – the claymore mine-like bombs favored by the cartels. Once the orange eruption had done its work and the trucks were immobilized, an anti-tank rocket streaked from an apartment window four hundred yards away, the laser guidance system directing it unerringly to its target. The Suburban exploded in a fireball, and it was several seconds before the surviving detail opened fire on the apartment, directing a barrage of bullets at the already vacated window.

Smoke and fire belched from the devastated SUV, and sirens wailed through the downtown as emergency vehicles raced to contend with the effects of the attack.

Juan Ramon was two miles away by the time the special forces commandos stormed the building from which he'd fired the rocket, motoring towards the edge of town on his motorcycle, the pizza delivery box on the back rendering him anonymous as the army clamped down on the area in a vain attempt at containment.

The evening news reported that thirty-seven lives had been lost in the savage attack, including six reporters, a host of soldiers and police, and four of the president's elite personal guard. Fortunately, the president had escaped unharmed, the explosion having narrowly missed his vehicle at the front of the motorcade.

All public appearances were cancelled until further notice, pending a full investigation. Cena was out of the hospital within a week, the damage to his left arm and part of his face requiring two additional surgeries over the next three months, but the prognosis for a full recovery guardedly optimistic.

Juan Ramon disappeared shortly thereafter, and his remains were discovered in a car crusher in a junkyard near Mexico City two weeks later, the only clue to his identity his dental plate, his hands and feet having been removed while he was still alive.

CHAPTER 3

Spring in Argentina was mild, the days warm and the nights only somewhat chilly, at least in Mendoza. Sometimes the wind would blow from the towering Andes mountains down into the valley and make things unseasonably miserable, but thankfully this year there had been none of these unexpected surprises. Seasons in South America, like in Australia, were the reverse of the northern hemisphere, so April was in reality autumn for the region, which enjoyed a kind of Indian summer during that period, before plunging into a cold and snowing summer that was in reality the region's winter.

The young man pulled his pea coat around him as he made his way past the small markets and cafés on one of the main arteries, stopping at his favorite to buy coffee and a breakfast roll. Groups of high school students loitered across the street, smoking and talking loudly as they waited for their classes to begin. Leaves blew down the sidewalks and into the deep storm drains that bordered every street, acting as a kind of informal network of tunnels for the region's stray dogs. The man paid the smiling cashier and shouldered past the line of waiting patrons, all in a hurry to eat and run, the business day about to start for the offices around the stock exchange building, to be followed a few hours later by the retail shops at the street level.

He passed in front of the Park Hyatt hotel and meandered through the large park that was a central feature of the downtown tourist area. Groups of Rastafarian-inspired hippies were laying out blankets on the park sidewalks to display their handcrafted wares, consisting mostly of leather wallets and beaded necklaces, with the ever popular multi-colored friendship bracelets a staple. An odor of marijuana lingered over the bunch, and the man hurried past them lest one try to engage him in conversation.

The park denizens were largely friendly and cheerful, in spite of their living in near poverty conditions in a nation that was bankrupt fifteen times over. The papers were predicting more power shortages and gas rationing for the year, and the unofficial exchange rate put domestic inflation at twenty-five percent, even as the government number was more like three. Nobody took the official utterances seriously, just as nobody took the tax system seriously. If a small business didn't cheat early and often, it wouldn't be in operation for very long. The official tax rate was so high that it rendered most types of commerce impractical, creating a booming secondary economy that operated on an all-cash basis.

The man took in the grandiose buildings of the downtown pedestrian promenade as he sipped his coffee. Mendoza was an odd town – strangely prosperous due to the surge in demand for the region's excellent wine, while the rest of the nation languished, but with a frailty just below the surface that was uniquely Argentine. Nobody believed that lasting prosperity was possible, which was a direct function of the looting of the country for decades, culminating in the 2002 financial collapse that wiped out much of the nation's middle class and gutted its economy.

He paused in front of the small storefront two blocks from the park and set his coffee down on a planter as he fumbled with a key ring. After a few moments, the steel grid that protected the plate glass window slid up into its housing, and he found himself staring at his reflection. Longish dark brown hair with sun highlights worn in a *laisser faire* style, a perennial three day growth of dark stubble, high cheekbones and piercing, nearly black eyes staring out of a light brown complexion. A pair of non-prescription horn-rimmed eyeglasses completed the look, which for all appearances was that of a scattered young academic, or perhaps a painter or sculptor who'd met with moderate success.

He studied the result with satisfaction. The man looking back at him bore little resemblance to the cold-blooded international cartel super-assassin known as '*El Rey*' – the King of Swords – made infamous by his leaving a tarot card bearing the image of the seated king at the scene of his executions. No, that man was thinner, younger, with black hair and a differently shaped face. The only photographs of him known to exist were from his construction security pass when he'd been part of the crew building a convention center in Baja, and he'd taken care to alter his image for that shot. Foam padding stuffed in his cheeks had created marked jowls, short-cropped ebony hair parted on the side and a bushy moustache with a chin beard beneath it had sculpted a classic Mexican laborer look, as had the skin dye that had darkened his complexion by three tones.

The only thing that man had in common with the aristocratic young proprietor of the shop was a frigidity to his gaze. There were some things you couldn't change. The slightly tinted Dolce and Gabbana eyeglasses were sufficient cover, though, given that he was an unknown in Argentina. He'd considered contact lenses, but discarded the idea as unnecessary. After all, he was on the other side of the world from his hunting ground in Mexico and was now a respectable business owner dealing in curios and knick knacks for the tourist crowd.

He'd bought the business for a song from the old woman who had owned it for a decade, and even though it barely made enough to cover the rent and his lone employee, Jania, he was happy with the bargain. It gave him something to do, without placing any demands on him. Jania took care of the sales and bookkeeping, which were simple, and he frittered his time away in an innocuous pursuit. Most of his day was spent in his comfortable little back office, and it was relatively rare that he had to deal with customers – a strong positive from his standpoint because interacting with patrons was the one aspect of the business he disliked.

He unlocked the glass door and glanced at his watch. Still two hours before the shop would be open, which meant that Jania would be there within an hour and forty minutes. She was always punctual, along with being very attractive and conscientious, making her the perfect employee. At times, he sensed she would be receptive to a more intimate relationship, but he didn't want to mix business with pleasure. His life was fine with the bevy of dancers at the strip clubs he frequented. Those relationships were simple and efficient, and nobody probed too deeply into his life. Which was how he liked it. Clean, with no baggage or explanations required; everyone lying as part of the transaction and nobody surprised or concerned about it.

He relocked the door and made his way to the back office, where he reclined in his executive chair and savored his rich cup of brew. He had developed a number of bad habits since relocating; coffee being one of the vices he'd taken up and red wine another. It was impossible not to drink both in Mendoza, so he'd adapted, although strictly limiting his intake to two cups of coffee per day and one glass of wine. He offset these by spending two hours at his gym, an hour spent on hard cardio and another on isometric exercises and weight training, and he'd joined a martial arts studio, where he attended classes four times a week. It was a somewhat tedious routine, but he'd resigned himself to it as necessary, especially since he was number one on the Most Wanted list in Mexico for an attempted execution of the former president. Better to be a dull boy than to invite unwanted scrutiny. He was fully aware that Interpol had circulated a bulletin with his photo on it, and even though he had three passports in different names issued from dissimilar countries, he was still on guard, regardless that almost a year had gone by since his narrow escape and with each day the likelihood of pursuit diminished.

Antonio, as he was known in Mendoza and in his Ecuadorian passport, powered on his computer to check on the markets. He'd invested most of his twenty million dollars in a basket of commodities, from silver and gold to copper and iron ore, as well as some currencies that showed promise, such as the Chinese Yuan and the Aussie dollar. He was now up seventeen percent in under a year, and he fine-tuned his holdings once a week based on trends he perceived. He'd even made an easy ten percent playing the Mexican Peso, buying a million dollars' worth when it hit fourteen to the dollar, and selling them when it hit twelve six. He'd shown a knack for all things financial, just as he'd done well at anything to which he'd applied himself, and he found the challenge of prospering by being ahead of international trends to be engaging enough to keep him occupied.

He pulled up the Mexican national news and saw more coverage on the unsuccessful attempt on the new president in Tampico. That had all the earmarks of a cartel operation, judging by the massive overkill and collateral damage. He shook his head. When would these guys learn that careful and surgical yielded superior results every time? A part of him itched to get back into the game, but he didn't need the money, and he recognized that Mexico would be too hot to go back to for many years. After his last sanction there, he'd have to stay away for the duration. To return would be foolhardy. It was best to watch the carnage from afar.

He checked on the action in the gold and silver markets, and jolted when he heard the front door chime sound. His watch told him that he'd lost almost two hours online, so that meant it was Jania.

"*Hola. Señor* Antonio? Are you here?" Jania called from the front of the shop.

"Yes, Jania. Good morning. I thought I'd get a jump on the day. How are you?" he called from the back room.

Jania pushed the partially open door ajar and greeted him with a smile. She was twenty, slim, with long, dirty-blond hair and an appealingly fresh face.

"Good morning to you, as well. Is there anything special you need me to do before we open?" Jania continued to beam at him, seemingly unaware of the multiple ways the invitation she was extending could be taken.

He paused, then returned her smile. "No, we can do the inventory tonight after we close. You've been keeping track of our sales, right? It's probably time to reorder some of the top sellers."

"The corkscrews are moving well and so are the bone-handled steak knife sets. I think we'd be wise to stock more of those."

"Noted."

"Oh, and my uncle Gustavo will be by at eleven. He says you promised to let him beat you at chess today," she announced, then spun perkily to attend to the small showroom.

Gustavo came by every few days, and Antonio allowed him to hang out and kill time at the store. Gustavo presented a welcome diversion

28

and got him out of the shop. They would sit at one of the numerous outdoor coffee shops adjacent to the entry and play chess for hours, shooting the breeze and watching the world go by. Normally anti-social, he'd made a measured effort to appear friendly since moving to Argentina. Socially adept people were not regarded with suspicion, whereas recluses were. And the last thing he wanted to do was attract attention.

"I'll look forward to his arrival." He checked the time again. "Might as well open the front door, since we're both here now," he called after her.

Gustavo was a character – a retired bureaucrat in his early sixties living on a pension, who always seemed to have plenty of money to throw around. He drove a new BMW and lived in one of the most expensive areas of town, which had struck Antonio as out of character with his means. When he'd probed the topic with Jania, she'd simply responded that her uncle was the black sheep of the family and always had his hands in something lucrative. Antonio took that to mean that he was involved in the black market that was ubiquitous in Argentina, and without which the economy couldn't function. As far as he was concerned, what the old man did to make ends meet was none of his business.

He finished up his online chores and then heard the chime again, followed by Gustavo's distinctive baritone from the front. He quickly powered down the computer and, after doing a scan of his desk to ensure he hadn't left anything sensitive out, closed the office door and moved into the shop. Gustavo was chatting with Jania, examining the tango music CDs on the countertop display.

"Ah, good morning, my friend. So today is the day where I finally win a game against the *maestro*?" Gustavo boomed in greeting, holding his boxed mini chess set aloft in his left hand.

"It's a time of hope. One never knows what little miracles will be bestowed upon the fortunate," Antonio replied with a grin.

"Shall we?" Gustavo gestured at the door.

Antonio nodded.

They made their way to the French bakery a few doors down and claimed one of the sidewalk tables. A waitress emerged from the shop and took their order as Gustavo carefully set the pieces on the chessboard.

"How's business, my friend?" Gustavo asked.

"Oh, you know. Slow. It could be better." The truth was that business was dismal, not that Antonio cared much.

"It's the damned government. Did you know that Argentina was the eighteenth richest nation in the world at the start of the twentieth century?" Gustavo commented.

"What happened?" Antonio asked politely, having heard the story before.

"Back at the end of the Eighties, the president, Menem, started privatizing all the industries in Argentina that were part of the collective national worth. That's the polite way of saying that he took anything of value and sold it to foreign banks for two cents on the dollar, in return for massive bribes. That's why everything costs so much here. Argentina produces oil, and yet there are chronic gasoline shortages, and the price is higher than most non-producing countries. Same for power. The electric rates are among the highest in the world. Even the airline got sold, and it was wildly profitable at the time – and yet it went for less than the value of the assets, much less the revenue."

"Well, the rest of the world is starting to get the same treatment by the same banks. The population gets screwed while the banks and the government get rich," Antonio observed.

"Is it any wonder that the rule of law is breaking down? Society is a contract, between the people and their government. If the government doesn't honor the deal, and lets special interests rob them, and inflates the currency till savings are worthless and prices go through the roof, then the population walks away from the deal. That's how things are in Argentina," Gustavo concluded.

"I'm not here to judge. I'm here to get beaten at chess. You do what you have to in order to get by."

"A wise philosophy, my friend," Gustavo said, nodding. "So how are you getting on with Jania?"

"She's perfect for the job. I couldn't ask for a better person," Antonio replied neutrally.

"I think she's rather fond of you."

"As am I. Like I said, she's the perfect person for the job," Antonio repeated, preferring not to go down the road Gustavo was trying to steer towards.

"Ah. Just so." Gustavo moved his opening pawn and eyed Antonio warily. "Your move."

∂∽∮

Gustavo had always perceived that, with Antonio, there was more going on than met the eye. He considered himself a good judge of character, having spent years doing handshake deals as he built his network in the Argentine underworld while he was one of the directors of the secret police. He wisely vacated his position after his role in the mass executions and death squads of the 1970s came into question, and he faded into obscurity before being recruited for the new regime, which was equally brutal, a few years later.

He'd leveraged his power in the newly-created intelligence apparatus to solidify a slavery and drug distribution network in Buenos Aires that survived to the present, albeit with younger men in the active positions. Upon his final retirement from public service twelve years earlier, Gustavo had moved first to Patagonia, and then later to Mendoza, to be as far from the scene of his crimes as he could get while still remaining in the country.

He wasn't sure what Antonio's situation was, but he did know one thing after spending a few months chatting with the man and playing chess. He claimed to be from Ecuador, but his accent said differently. It was oddly neutral, almost in a practiced way, but Gustavo thought he detected Mexico rather than South America. Whatever the case, he knew that a young man of brilliant capabilities such as he'd displayed with the chess board didn't appear out of thin air in Mendoza to operate a money-losing trinket shop unless there was something else going on.

Gustavo's natural curiosity had been aroused as he'd gotten to know him, and he'd put out feelers to see if he could figure out who he was dealing with. As a career criminal, he sensed an opportunity potential with Antonio. Perhaps young Antonio could be of use in his ongoing Buenos Aires operation, or maybe he had contacts with the Colombians or the Mexicans that could help in solidifying new suppliers for the drugs that were so in demand in the Argentine capital.

Whatever the case, Gustavo smelled rat all over Antonio, and it wasn't in his nature to let that go without rooting around and finding out what the real story was. If he'd learned anything during his time on the planet it was that information was power, and he could no more help his drive to discover more about his current chess adversary than a salmon could help swimming upriver. It was part of his wiring – what made him who he was.

He'd made some calls over the past week, and his former colleagues on the police force and with the Argentine intelligence network had agreed to check in Mexico and Central America for any young men who were wanted for serious crimes. It was a shot in the dark, but Gustavo had time on his hands. This was a project he could get interested in, and his instincts were piqued whenever he sat with Antonio. There was more to him than met the eye, and as a predator himself, he recognized the same qualities in others when he saw them.

And make no mistake. Antonio was a predator. Of that, Gustavo was sure.

Once home, he turned on his computer and began downloading the thousands of photos and rap sheets his network had come up with through Interpol. It would be a painstaking and potentially fruitless chore, but he was infinitely patient and loved a project. And there was a point of stubborn pride in the equation. Gustavo's nose was never wrong.

Now, it was a matter of discovering where and what young Antonio was running from, and then they could have an altogether different discussion than one revolving around chess. Which Antonio had beaten Gustavo at today, yet again, for the seventeenth straight time since they'd begun their irregular matches.

Gustavo was more than intrigued.

The files finally loaded, he began paging through the photos.

At three a.m., as he finished the bottle of local Malbec he'd opened at midnight, he came across one that stopped him. There were striking similarities, and yet the face was different.

He made a few notes and resolved to make a call in the morning to get some more information. Gustavo wrote down the sparse details on the file and yawned, beyond tired. He'd do a web search for more tomorrow. For now, he was exhausted.

If Antonio was the man described in the bulletin, he might be just what the doctor ordered for messy contingencies, as his subordinates grew bolder and deferred to Gustavo less and less over the years. It could never hurt to have a pit bull on a chain.

Especially one that loved the taste of blood.

CHAPTER 4

Mexico City, Mexico

Captain Romero Cruz walked with a slight limp to the kitchen, hurriedly buttoning his federal police shirt. A plate of eggs and chorizo sat steaming on the small dining room table, a cup of coffee at its side. He sat down, and Dinah, glowing as ever in a fitted dress and colorful purple blouse, emerged from the attached laundry room and placed her hands on his shoulders, leaning in and kissing his cheek. She was stunning, as always, with wavy black hair and huge eyes and a face that was as beautiful as the most famous starlet to him.

"You're going to be late, my love," she warned playfully.

"They have to wait for me. I'm the boss," Cruz responded, swallowing a forkful of eggs before grabbing her arm and pulling her closer to him. He kissed her neck and, with a minor adjustment, her lips.

"Good eggs," Dinah said, pulling away and moving to the counter, where a glass of orange juice waited for her with a much smaller plate holding two pieces of toast.

This had been their regular routine since she'd begun staying at Cruz's modest new rental condo, courtesy of the *Federales*. Ever since he'd been kidnapped by the head of the Sinaloa cartel, he'd been under twenty-four hour armed surveillance, and likely would remain so until he left his position with the police. Cruz was the head of Mexico City's anti-cartel task force, which effectively made him the head of the national effort as well, given that DF, as Mexico City was called by the locals, was the largest city in Mexico, containing thirty percent of the nation's population. He'd also developed somewhat of a reputation after a near miss assassination attempt on the last president was foiled by his team's actions, which accounted for why he still had the job now that a new administration had taken office for its six year stint at running the country.

Usually, when an administration changed, the key positions went to new blood as payback for favors, but Cruz's position was too critical to play politics with. Or alternatively, and more likely, nobody else wanted the job of tackling the most powerful and rich narcotics trafficking groups in the world. It was a position that wasn't great for extended life expectancy, and Cruz believed that he was still heading the group because there wasn't anyone foolhardy enough to take it. During his tenure, Cruz's wife and child had been kidnapped and brutally murdered, he'd been shot in a bloody ambush that nearly cost him his life, he'd been kidnapped by the most powerful cartel kingpin in the world, and his life had been threatened by virtually every organized crime syndicate in Mexico.

This was a world where the most prominent people in the ongoing war against the cartels had a suspicious habit of crashing in aircraft accidents, or getting gunned down in heated assaults, so being the poster boy for the government's push to eradicate narco-trafficking was slightly below lion tamer or Russian roulette gambler in terms of safety.

Cruz was used to it. He'd long ago reconciled himself to the idea that he would live as long as he lived, but that he'd do everything in his power to bring the groups that had butchered his family to justice in the meantime. He was brutally effective, and though his methods were controversial, nobody argued with the results.

And he was the only one willing to strap on a bull's-eye every day and go into the office, wondering if today was the day a bomb or a sniper snuffed out his existence. That ensured a certain job security, if that phrase could be used to describe the circumstances in which he lived on a daily basis.

Dinah and Cruz had become an item following his recuperation from the shooting, and she'd taken to staying with him most nights for the last few months, going so far as to move in two large suitcases full of clothes. Cruz had mixed feelings about the situation at first because of the constant threat of danger surrounding him, but Dinah had shrugged it off.

"You have the best protection in the world ensuring you don't even trip on a crack in the sidewalk. This is probably the safest building in all of Mexico," she'd reasoned.

It was hard to argue, and truthfully, Cruz didn't want to do so with any real enthusiasm. This was the first time he'd had a female companion since his wife had been torn from him, and it felt good. Nothing could ever replace his lost family, but if healing was possible, he'd done so, and had resolved to move forward and focus on the future, after having spent years dwelling on the past. Every two months, the department rented a new condo for him, in a different building in a different area of town; his possessions appeared at the new address as if by magic. It wasn't an ideal situation, but it was the one that was keeping him alive, and so both he and Dinah had reluctantly grown accustomed to the disruptive grind.

Cruz admired Dinah's curves while she stood in the kitchen, wolfing down her breakfast as she rushed to be at her job on time. She was a teacher, and she couldn't be ten minutes late for work like Cruz could. The class wouldn't wait, and it was policy that everyone had to be on campus fifteen minutes before school started. At the rate she was going, she wasn't going to make it. It would be a miracle if she could get across town before the opening bell.

Cruz slurped his coffee and then rose from the table, his breakfast only half done. He approached Dinah and put his arms around her waist, nuzzling her neck as she finished her juice.

"Do you know what today is?" he asked.

"Monday. Now I have to run, *Corazon*. I'm already way too late."

"It is indeed Monday, but no, I was thinking more that it's been exactly six months since you began staying with me," Cruz nudged.

"*Ah*. Has it? It really only seems like yesterday…"

Cruz fumbled with his shirt pocket and extracted a small black velvet box, moving it over her shoulders and positioning it on the counter next to her plate.

"Wha…what's this?" Dinah asked in a whisper, suddenly serious.

"Go ahead. Open it."

Dinah reached forward with trembling hands and pried the small case open. Inside sat a platinum band with a solitary one carat diamond. Dinah drew in a sharp intake of breath, and lifting the box, turned to face Cruz, who still held her waist, smiling.

"Is this…?"

"I love you, Dinah. It's time. I'd like you to marry me. I know I'm not perfect – I certainly have my faults, but…"

Dinah's eyes welled with moisture as she silently removed the band from the box and slipped the little velvet square back into his shirt pocket. She slid the ring on her finger and smiled through the tears.

"It fits."

"Yes. I measured one of your other rings. Actually traced the interior circumference and took it to the jeweler. He said you're a six. Looks like he knew his stuff," Cruz explained nervously.

She shushed him with a long kiss on the mouth. Beads of joy trickling down her flawless cheeks, she gazed into his eyes and smiled. "*Capitan*, I accept your offer." She kissed him again.

They'd come a long way since Cruz had met her while investigating *El Rey*. He'd have never thought it possible when he'd first seen her, hair gleaming in the sun, radiantly beautiful in the shabby little pawn shop lobby where Cruz and his partner had been waiting. And yet a kind of small miracle had taken place, and she'd been attracted to him, and now, ten months after first setting eyes on her and six months since their first full night together at his place, the most beautiful woman in Mexico was going to be his wife.

❧⚬❧

Once Cruz had been transported to the office in the armored BMW 760 Li that was now his official vehicle, the usual crush of reports and urgent requests buried him. One benefit of his line of work was that there was never any shortage of events – the cartels were always up to something – so it never threatened to be boring or uneventful. He probably coordinated at least one major raid per week on a cartel stronghold or suspected drug or arms storage location, and while his group's success rate wasn't stellar, it was better than anyone expected. In a hierarchy that was historically riddled with corruption, Cruz's group was considered above reproach – one of the very few clean organizations in a nation where their adversary wielded enormous financial resources they couldn't hope to match.

The entire budget for the Mexican army was a billion dollars a year, and the army worked alongside the *Federales* to battle drug trafficking. The budget for the entire Mexican federal police force was thirty-five billion, but that included all duties – only ten percent or so was spent on anti-cartel activities. The rest went to personnel and administration and general law enforcement, and in the way that large government bureaucracies were always inefficient, the *Federales* were no different than, say, the Pentagon, where hammers cost two hundred dollars and trillions could go missing with a shrug.

The actual money that made it to the street level battle against the cartels was a laughable few billion. Contrasted against the estimated eighty to a hundred billion of wholesale value drugs moving through Mexico – cocaine, heroin, methamphetamines, marijuana – the army and law enforcement was perennially outgunned and outspent. If the cartels expended twenty percent of their profits on battling law enforcement, the government's efforts were dwarfed by a factor of six or seven.

The sad reality was that Mexico would never be able to spend sufficiently to curtail the cartels, certainly not as long as its huge neighbor to the north was the largest market for illegal drugs in the world. Everyone knew it – Cruz, the government, the cartels, the American DEA. But that didn't mean that there couldn't be successes along the way. Over the last few years, a sustained clampdown in Tijuana, one of the largest gateways for drug smuggling, had devastated the Arellano Felix cartel there, leaving a power vacuum. So wins could happen. Of course, the ultimate futility of the victories was simply that another cartel would step in and take over the territory – in this case, the Sinaloa cartel had radically increased its hold in Tijuana, and nothing much changed except who the money stuck to at the end of the day. Shipments continued unabated, supply in the U.S. was constant, and the cash flowed like champagne in a rap video.

It was easy to get demoralized, but Cruz considered his job as much like that of a doctor. Patients would come and go, and yes, everyone ultimately would die – nobody escaped that final outcome. But in the interim, if he could save some people, or extend their lives, then he counted it as a success. True, one could view the entire exercise as futile – after all, the patients always succumbed eventually – but that perspective wasn't useful. Everything if viewed in that light was pointless, and nobody would ever get out of bed and do anything if they thought about it too much.

No, better to stay focused on the small, sustainable victories and leave the big picture to its own devices.

Cruz hurried into his private office, trailed by his younger lieutenant, Briones, now fully recuperated from the shooting that had almost taken his life during the confrontation with *El Rey* at the G-20 financial summit. Cruz tossed his satchel on his desk, then plopped down behind it, eyeing Briones warily.

"What's the damage today? What have we got going on?" Cruz asked.

"The tip we got yesterday about the construction supply bodega seems to be panning out. We've had it under surveillance all night, and there's a surprising amount of traffic for a storage facility that supposedly closes at six," Briones reported.

"Out towards Toluca, right?"

"Near the airport. Four different SUVs, all luxury, visited between nine p.m. and midnight. Then nothing more until this morning, when what looks like three night guards were relieved by a day shift of two. The strange thing is that they were all heavily armed. I wonder if that means anything?" Briones asked rhetorically.

Cruz held back a smile. "Considering that gun possession is a felony in Mexico, you may be on to something. Seems like a lot of firepower to keep some kids from stealing a few bags of cement for beer money."

"That was my thinking," Briones said, smirking. They both knew that the bodega was likely a distribution point for the Sinaloa cartel. "Has it seemed to you that we're getting an awful lot of luck thrown our way lately against the Sinaloans? I mean, I'm not complaining, but over the last few months, I'd guess that ninety percent of our leads have been Sinaloa deals. That's almost the polar opposite of how last year went."

Cruz nodded. "My guess is that the other cartels are trying to move against them, so they're rolling over whenever possible. I'd say this is just a routine power play. Same as it ever was," Cruz opined. "The continued war of attrition – survival of the fittest."

"Maybe you're right. I just thought the timing was odd. It's like someone flicked a light switch, and it became open season on Sinaloa, whereas in the past they've been untouchable."

"Does it really matter which scumbags we put away, at the end of the day? There will always be more to take their place. For now, it's Sinaloa. I say good. About time they started going down." Cruz smiled at his secretary, who had entered with a cup of coffee for him. "What do you think, Raquel? Do you think it matters whether we arrest more Juárez, Sinaloa, Knights Templar, or Los Zetas cartel this month?"

She just shook her head before departing unobtrusively.

Cruz took a cautionary sip and then put the cup down to cool. "Let's keep an eye on the bodega and have a tactical squad standing by for whenever a delivery gets made. It's probably coming in as a shipment during business hours, and then the distribution takes place at night. Make a list of all the suppliers that show up, and let's look for the oddity. I don't want to take the place and wind up with my dick in my hand. If we're going to move on it, let's make sure there's something there. Clear?" Cruz instructed.

"Yes, sir. I'm way ahead of you. We'll maintain surveillance for a week, and then once we've established a pattern, especially on the night visitors, we'll go in. We've got nothing but time. They have no idea we're on to them."

"Very good. What else do we have? Any progress on the Operation Fast and Furious weapons?" Cruz asked.

Fast and Furious was a notorious international scandal where the American Bureau of Alcohol, Tobacco and Firearms had allowed thousands of weapons to be purchased in the U.S. and smuggled to cartels in Mexico, which were then used to murder countless people, including cartel members, American border patrol agents, Mexican policemen and soldiers, as well as the usual scores of innocents who were unlucky enough to be in the line of fire. The ATF had allowed the weapons to be shipped to Mexico for years, knowing full well who the customers were, and had lied to Congress about the program.

Briones shook his head. "Most of the weapons have been traced to the Sinaloa cartel, but from there it's a black hole. Some of them have been recovered, but the majority are still floating around on the street. We got a lead on a warehouse that was supposed to have a few hundred weapons stored, but as you may recall, that turned out to be a false alarm – or the guns had been moved by the time we made it in," Briones recounted bitterly.

"That's the chicken ranch, right?" Cruz asked.

The weapons had been reputed to have been stored at a farm that raised roosters for chicken fights. The only thing that their raid had yielded was hundreds of combative birds and a disgruntled owner. Someone had tipped the press, and the laughable image of heavily-armed *Federales* toting assault rifles juxtaposed against a backdrop of protesting birds in pens had circulated in the papers for weeks, embarrassing everyone concerned, including Cruz, who had authorized the raid. Briones had led the strike that day, and for the second time in a year, been the public face of law enforcement run amok.

"How can I forget? My cousins gave me shit about being a chicken molester for a month," Briones muttered.

"All right. Are we done for now? I have a mountain of paperwork I need to catch up on here. Do you need anything? Maybe a warrant to detain and body search some poultry?" Cruz inquired innocently.

"No, sir. But thank you for the support. I'll let you know as circumstances change on the bodega. Oh, and we got an international inquiry circulated our way on *El Rey*. Routine. We were flagged automatically on the distribution list."

"Haven't heard that name for a while. I suppose we're the experts on him now that the task force got dismantled…" Cruz observed.

Since the assassination attempt, the three-year-old task force, which had proved completely inept at anything but burning money while delivering zero results, had been closed down, and its responsibilities incorporated into Cruz's organization. He had two officers who worked part time on the *El Rey* case whenever the name came up, as opposed to the thirty full-time staffers upstairs who'd been employed at the task force's peak. The notorious hit man had vanished without a trace after the unsuccessful attempt on the former president and hadn't been heard from since. Perhaps that was for the best, Cruz reasoned.

"It was just a routine inquiry, looks like. Wanted more information on him. Nothing more," Briones confirmed. "The probe came through Interpol, and we sent the usual package of data back – the photo, a few of the better sketches, and his dossier. Maybe he's in South America now? Taken up cattle ranching?"

"As long as he's not here making our lives miserable. Although I have to admit that aside from his hits on politicians, he was doing the world a favor executing the cartel targets. Some would argue the same about targeting the politicians, too…" Cruz mused.

Briones smiled. He shared his superior's disdain for elected officials.

"All right. Thanks for the briefing. Let's get together this afternoon and compare notes. Please close the door on the way out and spread the word that I'll shoot anyone who interrupts me before lunch," Cruz ordered.

Briones paused at the door. "Did you ask her?" he inquired softly on his way out.

Cruz grinned lopsidedly. "She said yes."

"I knew you were in trouble when I first set eyes on her," Briones finished. "Congratulations."

"Thanks. And you were right about being in trouble. But listen. Keep the news of our engagement to yourself. I don't want to be the subject of any gossip, and you know how word spreads…"

There were also safety concerns. The image of his family's heads showing up in a box was still fresh in his mind, and he didn't want to make Dinah any more of a target than she already was.

"Of course. Congratulations all the same."

CHAPTER 5

Mendoza, Argentina

"Jania – what's wrong? What is it?" Antonio asked, as her voice trembled over the phone. It was morning, and she was calling twenty minutes before the shop was supposed to open. A first for her. She'd been as reliable as the rising sun…until now.

"It's my uncle. Gustavo. He's been murdered." She choked on the final word, unable to go on.

"Murdered! Good Lord, Jania. What happened? Are you all right?"

"The police found him this morning and called me as next of kin. Someone broke in last night and killed him in his home office. Stabbed him with a letter opener. It's horrible. The officer wouldn't go into detail, but…"

"Oh my God. That's unbelievable, Jania. I'm so sorry. Is there anything I can do for you? Anything you need?" he offered.

"No. I don't think so. It's just…I mean, he was just an old man. What kind of sick bastard would kill a helpless old man?" Jania seemed confused by her question. Antonio knew better than to try to answer.

"Do they have any leads?" He stopped. "Is this kind of thing common in Mendoza?"

"No. I mean, there are robberies, of course. Just like anywhere. But a vicious murder like this in a good neighborhood…it's very rare. I've never heard of anything like it," Jania explained.

"So it's a robbery gone wrong?"

"That's what the police think. The officer was very nice on the phone. I'll know more once I go down to the station. They want to take a statement from me. I don't know how long that will take. That's one of the reasons I'm calling – I don't think I'm going to be in today. This is such a shock, and I have no idea what's involved in claiming the body, or dealing with the police…" Jania stuttered to a halt.

"Don't worry about anything here. I can look after the shop in your absence. Take as much time as you need, and don't come back to work until everything's settled on your end." Antonio paused. "I'm so sorry about Gustavo. He was a wonderful man."

"Thank you. You don't know how much that means to me."

"Take care, and do what you need to do. I'll be here when you're done."

Antonio carefully placed the handset back into the cradle and considered the front door of the shop, which was still locked.

So the police had found Gustavo murdered with a letter opener and suspected a robbery gone wrong.

Just as he'd hoped when he'd plunged the spike through the bastard's chin and up into his brain, after kindly old uncle Gustavo had invited him over for a chat and a glass of wine. The topic had taken a turn for the worse when Gustavo had revealed his research into his true identity and concluded that he was an internationally notorious assassin hiding in Mendoza. The old man had laid out the evidence and given Antonio an ultimatum: either work for him in taking care of some problems in Buenos Aires with his criminal syndicate, or be exposed and the target of a manhunt.

At first he'd pretended surprise and shock, but the old man had been relentless. Ultimately, Antonio had agreed to do as Gustavo wanted after being assured that nobody else knew what he'd discovered. He had done his level best to appear amenable. It sounded like child's play, actually, to terminate the chieftains who were skimming from Gustavo's take. The only real problem was that he didn't respond well to blackmail, or to anyone knowing his identity, even if Gustavo was an outwardly gentle soul who was just trying to get his needs met. And so *El Rey* had palmed the letter opener when Gustavo had sealed the arrangement with a proposal of a glass of rare Cobos Reserve Malbec and had leapt across his desk and skewered his brain when he'd swiveled around from the credenza to the desk with the bottle – which he'd caught with his free hand and had taken home with him, to be savored as an after-dinner treat.

He'd made short work of wiping Gustavo's computer of any incriminating files and had painstakingly cleaned the handle of the letter opener, still protruding from the old crook's chin, his eyes open in shocked surprise, staring off into oblivion as if regretting his ultimate misjudgment.

El Rey's pulse hadn't increased from the effort, nor had he been particularly upset over having to terminate his friendship so abruptly. It was nothing personal, just as the uncle's researching his past hadn't been personal. He'd done what he'd felt compelled to do, and *El Rey* had responded in kind. That was how the world worked. If you played with vipers, you shouldn't be surprised when one bit you. It was the law of the jungle *El Rey* lived by, and the incident only served to reinforce why it was a good idea to never get too close to anyone, or too attached to any place or thing. Relative peace and safety could turn dangerous in a heartbeat, and it was foolishness to drop your guard.

Gustavo had been working on his project for over a week – he'd seen from the e-mail dates. Which meant that if he'd been telling the truth, he'd known, or suspected, for almost that long. *El Rey* could only hope that he'd kept the information to himself, which he believed was strongly likely. Anyone else knowing would have compromised the old man's hoped-for hold over *El Rey*, and he was sure that Gustavo had leveled with him about his problem in Buenos Aires. His only miscalculation had been in believing that he could control the assassin and force him to do his bidding.

It was a pity – it was hard to find friends these days. But it was also unavoidable.

El Rey now had two choices. He could disappear, hoping to elude any pursuit, or he could stay put and see what happened. But he didn't want to trip any alarms and a sudden departure immediately after the murder of his chess partner might trigger the exact sort of manhunt he was hoping to avoid. After much thought, he decided to wait and see rather than running. He liked Mendoza more than anyplace else he'd been, and he wasn't anxious to leave if he didn't have to. So he'd gathered up his passports and double-checked his escape kit, which he'd stowed in the large safe behind a paneled section of his home study, and resigned himself to being patient and waiting it out. Nothing was ever gained by making rash moves.

Jania had sounded genuinely surprised and shocked, so Gustavo hadn't told her anything. That was good. He would have hated to have to kill her over that sort of indiscretion. On balance, then, it wasn't a bad start to the day. She would get to live.

He hummed to himself as he walked to the glass front entry, silently debating not opening, and then dismissing the idea. Better to go about his business as though nothing had happened – which in a way, it hadn't. His shopkeeper's uncle had been the victim of a failed burglary attempt, or alternatively, had been killed by some of the unsavory elements from his murky past. Either way the police looked, they'd encounter a dead end. There was no trail to him, or the shop, to follow.

He flipped the sign over from closed to open and unlocked the door. If today was like any other weekday, he'd be lucky to see five customers before dinner time.

El Rey brought his notebook computer from out of the back office and settled in behind the counter on the high padded stool where Jania spent most of her time. Peering at his watch, he mentally calculated how many hours he'd be on this lonely duty and sighed resignedly as he moved the cursor to his favorite web browser to surf the web.

El Rey closed at two o'clock for the customary two hour lunch break that all of Argentina took. Sometimes it was extended to three hours on slow days, which today, given the two customers so far, he felt qualified as such. He walked a block to his favorite lunchtime restaurant, a small Italian place on one of the main streets, and ordered a salad and some duck ravioli. Following his meal, he opted for an hour and a half at the gym.

Refreshed from the exercise, he stowed his gear in the locker he rented by the month and made his way back to the shop. The usual sprawl of students was lounging around, carousing on the promenade in front, but other than that, he saw nothing of note. He grudgingly opened the door, propping it open to lure tourists in, and remounted the stool, waiting for closing time to come.

At six, two men in trench coats entered, removing their fedoras, and Antonio instinctively stiffened, their bearings unmistakable. The taller of the pair approached him – a rough-looking man in his early fifties whose baby face had long ago succumbed to the effects of wine and gravity, and whose day-old stubble was laced with gray.

"*Señor* Balardi? Antonio Balardi?" he asked officiously.

"Yes. How can I help you?" Antonio answered in a modulated, quiet voice.

"I'm Detective Rufio Starone, and this is Detective Franko Lombardetti. We'd like to ask you a few questions," the taller man responded.

"Certainly. Would you mind showing me some identification?" Antonio asked reasonably.

The request seemed to annoy the two men, but they flipped out their badges, which Antonio studied over the rims of his glasses and then nodded.

"What can I do for you?" he asked.

"We're investigating the murder of Gustavo Peralta Malagro. We got your name from his niece, Jania."

"Yes. She called this morning. A shocking crime. He was a wonderful man. But I'm not sure how I can help you…"

"We're following up with everyone he knew, to see if there was anything suspicious or worrisome about him in his last days. Let's begin with you telling us how well you knew him," Starone said.

"Not particularly well. He and I would play chess a few times a month. I've only known him for maybe four months, through Jania. He'd come by, we got to talking, and it became somewhat of a ritual – a way to kill time," Antonio explained.

"When did you last see him?" Detective Lombardetti asked.

"Oh, it must have been four days ago. We sat over at the little French bakery and played a game of chess, as was our custom."

"Did he seem preoccupied or concerned? Did he mention anything worrying him?" Starone inquired.

"No. Not unusually so. I mean, he would complain about things sometimes, but just routine stuff, nothing dramatic. Why? I thought Jania said that this was a burglary? Isn't that the case?"

Starone ignored the question. "What kind of routine stuff? Give me some examples."

"Well, let's see. He griped about the cost of gas and energy a lot, and about international banks robbing the country blind, and about how the economy sucked and the government was incompetent…"

"Basically what everyone in Argentina talks about," Starone remarked.

"Yes. That's what I mean about routine."

"Did he ever mention his past?" Lombardetti interjected.

"His past? No, not really. He mentioned that he had been with the government, but he made it sound like a bureaucratic function. All due respect, I wasn't all that interested. He was a nice old man I played chess with. I wasn't thinking about dating him," Antonio explained.

"Yes, well, he was a little more than a low-level flunky. He was actually fairly high up in the intelligence service for much of his career. He made a lot of enemies, I'm sure. Those were difficult times for our country. Dark times." Starone paused, studying Antonio's face. "So what's your story, Antonio? I see by your records that you have been in Argentina for eight and a half months. What brought you to Mendoza?"

"Oh, you know. I was tired of living at home, in Ecuador, and wanted a change of scenery. I inherited a little money when an uncle died, so I decided to see the world. I wound up staying here after falling in love with the place. I'm hoping this business takes off and I can make a go of it. Things could be better, with the economy still in the toilet and tourism off so much," Antonio complained, convincingly, he thought. But he didn't like the direction the questions were turning.

"Yes. It's been a tough few years. And what did you do in Ecuador?" Starone probed, while making a few notes in a small pad he'd extracted from his coat. "What part are you from?"

Antonio launched into his carefully rehearsed cover.

"Quito. The capital. I helped my parents with a little store off the *Plaza Grande*, by the cathedral. Cell phones and consumer electronics. But there's not a lot of opportunity there, and I got bored, so I set out for somewhere new once I got some money. I love Mendoza, and I'm hoping I can succeed with my business here," he gestured at the shop.

"Who's president of Ecuador now? I don't follow those things," Starone asked.

"Rafael Correa. He's on his second term," Antonio said without hesitation. He was getting really uncomfortable, but outwardly his demeanor didn't change, and he continued to project polite concern and worry over Gustavo.

"Isn't he ex-military?" Starone countered.

"Mmm, I don't think so. He's an economist. Economic reforms are the basis of his government, and he pissed-off a lot of the country's creditors when he declared the national debt invalid due to having been accrued due to corruption. Argentina could learn from that and take a page from his playbook," Antonio fired back.

Apparently satisfied, Starone closed his little book and gave a smile that was more a grimace. "Can you think of anyone who would want to hurt your friend, Gustavo? The reason I ask is because in our routine discussions with the neighbors this morning, one thought she saw a younger man with longish hair. Very much like yours. Do you know anyone like that?" Starone delivered the body blow with quiet sincerity.

Antonio's mind raced, but he didn't even blink. The cop was probably bluffing, doing some fishing, otherwise he wouldn't have said anything. He was almost sure of it. Almost.

"Everyone seemed to like him, but as I said, I didn't know him beyond playing some chess a few times a month. But I hope you get the bastard who killed him. Too bad this haircut is so popular – that description only narrows it down to a third of the males in Mendoza. But if I think of anything, I will absolutely give you a call. Do you have a card?" he replied.

The detective's eyes narrowed, just a little, and he fished a business card out of his pocket and put it on the counter as he looked around the small shop. "What do you sell the most of?" he asked conversationally.

"The steak knives are very popular, as well as the leather goods. But it's a tough time of year. Nothing's moving as much as I'd like," Antonio lamented.

"Well, you're not alone in that. Please do call if you think of anything." Starone appraised him. "Have a nice day."

The two policemen shuffled to the door and disappeared into the fray. Antonio considered the discussion and felt a tingle of alarm. He didn't think the taller detective had bought his story, or rather, the cop seemed to sense something off about him. That might have been stylistic – a technique to make potential suspects squirm – but it hadn't had any visible effect on 'Antonio'. Still, a small part of him elevated his threat level assessment up a notch. He hadn't anticipated a visit in Gustavo's killing. That was stupid, and lazy.

His brief days of relaxed, worry-free existence were officially over, all thanks to the meddling old man. It wasn't a crisis yet, but if they really did have a witness, it could be difficult. He hadn't worn his glasses that night, and his clothes had been unremarkable, but it was an unknown, and he didn't like unknowns.

Perhaps it was time to move on to somewhere even more remote than Mendoza. A pity, but things changed, and a smart man changed with them.

CHAPTER 6

When *El Rey* closed up that night he took his laptop with him in its shoulder bag, along with a few items from the store that might come in handy. He wasn't sure he'd ever see it again; he was back to his old self now, no longer Antonio – and *El Rey* always expected the worst, and planned for it.

Reality was that he'd been borderline delusional believing he could ever live normally – whatever that meant. Like a shark, he needed to keep moving, or he'd die. There was no point in wasting any time wishing things were different – his life to date had been extraordinary, and he'd just need to continue down whatever path he found himself on. Gustavo had set a course in motion, and he'd reacted in the only way that made sense – he'd neutralized the threat. Now the police were sniffing around, and while there probably wasn't anything to worry about, *probably* wasn't good enough. *Probably* got you caught, or killed. *Probably* was for others.

As *El Rey* pulled down the steel grid security door he surreptitiously scanned his surroundings. He knelt and padlocked it into place, noting that there were a lot of people on the promenade – so it was hard to be sure he was clean, but what he was looking for was anything atypical – something that didn't belong. He didn't immediately detect anything, but that didn't mean he was safe – taking the long way home would indicate whether there was a problem.

He ambled slowly towards the park, moving with the flow of the pedestrian traffic, mindful of potential surveillance without giving any outward appearance of being on guard. He stopped abruptly across the street from the stock exchange building and examined a jacket in a display window – its reflection revealed a figure fifty yards from him had stopped to tie his shoe. It would have been innocent, except that with an eighth of a second glance he confirmed that the man's laces were still tied. Sometimes it was the small things that gave you away.

Confident he was being followed, he now needed to decide how to deal with his pursuers. He didn't think it was police. They would have no reason to sneak around. Rather, they'd walk through the front door, as they had earlier, and pick him up. No, this was someone else, which was worse. Probably Gustavo's crew. Perhaps the old man hadn't been entirely truthful with *El Rey*. Yet another of life's small disappointments. Sometimes people weren't completely honest.

⁂

The shoelace tier resumed his casual following once the target made for the street that separated the park from the pedestrian thoroughfare and murmured into his cell phone, "He's crossing into the park. If you get into position on the far side, you'll be able to pick him up as he exits. He's wearing a dark blue long coat and has longish hair and glasses. Black pants. I'll stay on him, but lay back. He's all yours. But remember. He's extremely dangerous, so be careful."

He watched as his quarry jaywalked, a car honking angrily as it narrowly missed him. The target seemed unfazed and picked up his pace past the street vendors at the park entrance. The light turned green, and he joined the crowd in crossing to the verdant expanse, trying to maintain a fix on the target's trajectory.

The young man was now a good hundred and fifty yards ahead of him, and he watched as the distant figure cut through a line of people waiting to enter the small underground theater that was the central hub of the park. He could just make out the lights and distinctive white façade of the large hotel across the far street and knew his men would take over once he'd crossed that street. If the man made a right or a left,

52

they could still track him, but it would be more obvious. It wasn't a perfect scenario, but it was the only one they'd been able to improvise on short notice.

A few lights glimmered dimly in the area he was walking towards, which could work well for them. The target seemed to have no idea he was under surveillance, so it would be straightforward enough to corner him. He wished he could still see him, but the theater crowd was now in his line of sight as he moved past the massive fountain.

He wasn't worried. It would be over shortly.

El Rey could just make out the pair of shadows lurking beneath one of the large tree trunks twenty yards from the path he was on. A pair of teenage lovers lay sprawled on a darkened park bench, exploring each other's charms with single-minded intensity, oblivious to anything but their passion as he hurried past. An old woman moved out of his way, clutching her purse tightly as if afraid he'd assault her. He nodded as he walked by, offering a non-threatening look.

At the street, he made a split-second decision, and instead of crossing straight over as he normally would, he instead moved diagonally across the empty thoroughfare to the far block. He registered the two shadows beneath the tree begin their pursuit and considered the desolate sidewalk he was now on. There were a few construction projects over the next two blocks he'd noted while wandering the neighborhood, one of which was a large remodel of a turn of the century building. That could provide exactly the cover he was looking for.

He slowed to give his followers a chance to get closer, and judging the timing, turned the corner onto the smaller street – empty now that the business district had closed down. He spotted the building he'd remembered and smiled to himself. The old habits came back easily. Like riding a bicycle.

The pair watched as their quarry rounded the block and momentarily disappeared from view. They exchanged worried glances and increased their speed. The last thing they needed was to lose him now that they were this close. One of the men pulled a stun gun from his jacket pocket in preparation for taking him down. With any luck it would be over within a few minutes, on the outside.

They turned the corner and found themselves on an empty street. There was no sign of him.

The shorter of the two hastily stabbed at his cell phone and muttered into it, "We should be on top of him, but when we made the turn, he disappeared."

"Could he have entered one of the buildings? Maybe he lives there."

"Anything's possible. What do you want us to do?"

"Keep walking and see if you can spot him on the far street. Worst case, if you can't, watch the buildings for a light going on in one of the windows. He couldn't have gotten too far, so either he ducked into one of the buildings or he ran for it. I think we can assume he spotted you. Get moving. No need for subtlety now," the shoelace tier instructed. "I'm right behind you, maybe forty-five seconds. Move."

They increased their speed to a near jog. As they passed the construction site, a shadow burst from the depths and hurtled past them.

The first man clutched his midsection in disbelief, as though he could hold his organs in with his hands now that his stomach had been slit open, sliced below his ribcage through the abdominal wall. He crumpled as his intestines spilled out onto the sidewalk in a wet puddle. His partner collapsed simultaneously, dropping the stun gun to the ground, the femoral artery at the top of his leg severed, the outpouring of blood causing an immediate drop in blood pressure. He quivered as he feebly pushed against the gash in his thigh, consciousness fading almost instantly as his life seeped from him.

El Rey kicked the stun gun into the darkness and then silently moved back into the bowels of the gutted building, carefully avoiding the blood that his interaction with the first two had created. He listened for footsteps and was rewarded by the clumping of shoes approaching from around the corner, which stopped, as anticipated, in front of the two dying men. He slid out of the far side of the building and circled back soundlessly on his pursuer.

The man never saw him coming. The next thing he knew, a bloody straight razor was at his throat, millimeters from severing his carotid.

An eerily calm voice whispered in his ear, tender as a lover, "Who are you?"

The man swallowed and allowed his body to go slack, signaling submission to his assailant.

"Please. Don't kill me. I'm here from *Don* Aranas. He sent us to bring you back. He needs your help."

Aranas? The name instantly caused a flood of images. The head of the Sinaloa cartel was as legendary as he was elusive. He was as much of a ghost as *El Rey* and had defied decades of concerted manhunts to bring him to justice. *El Rey* had never met him, but he'd performed hits for his syndicate, taking sanctions against the Gulf and Juárez cartels. He'd delivered flawlessly on the contracts, and Aranas had always been punctual in payment. But how...?

"I need more than that. How did you find me? You have five seconds to convince me not to slit your throat."

"There was an inquiry through Interpol from the Argentine secret service. One of Aranas' contacts in the *Federales* alerted him, and we traced the origin to a man in Mendoza. A man who was found murdered this morning. Our sources in the police department here gave us the list of possible suspects. You were one of the names."

"How did you know it was me?" *El Rey* whispered.

"We didn't. I have five other men in town – now that these two have been taken out of the game. They're watching other targets."

"That doesn't explain how you knew I was your likeliest objective."

"You don't look that much different than your photo, if you know what to look for. It's a good disguise, but nothing's foolproof. You should know that."

El Rey felt the man's pockets for weapons. He had a pistol – a Remington 1911 R1 .45 caliber, no silencer. *El Rey* took it and removed the razor from his neck, pausing to wipe the blade on the man's jacket.

"Turn around. Slowly. Face me, and then back into the construction site so we can have some privacy. Don't make a sound or you're dead. We don't have a lot of time, so do exactly as I say."

The man did as instructed, raising his hands over his head and moving into the shadows. *El Rey* trained the gun on him, the barrel steady, almost casual.

"What does Aranas want with me? Why search halfway around the world for someone who's gone out of his way to disappear?"

"Aranas has an offer for you – a job. He was insistent. Money is no object to him, and he wants the best."

"I've retired."

"I don't think so. With all due respect, if Aranas wants you that badly, it's time to come out of retirement just this once. You know the power he wields. *Don* Aranas is not a man to refuse. I mean no disrespect in telling you this."

El Rey thought about it. This was a very strange situation, and not at all what he'd envisioned. He'd been expecting almost anything, but not a job offer. He regarded the man, who was clearly extremely tough. This was a man who had faced death many times, you could tell. He was afraid of *El Rey* killing him, but he was also resigned to it, if that was how the night would end. Better dead than to let down his master. *El Rey* knew the kind. He gestured with his weapon.

"I'll consider it. Give me a phone number to call, and when I'm ready, I'll get in touch," *El Rey* instructed.

"My orders were to have you accompany me. We have a Gulfstream V waiting at the airport that can hit Mexico without refueling. I urge you to reconsider."

"I don't care what your orders were. I'm retired. If I decide to meet with *Don* Aranas, it's out of respect for his position, not because of any orders. Give me a number, and if I decide to, I will call and arrange a meeting within a week. It will be just the two of us. Nobody else. And the price will be very high. Twenty million U.S. There will be no negotiation. That's what it will take to bring me out of retirement if I choose to do so. If I decide not to, I won't call, and you can tell *Don* Aranas that I have respectfully declined." *El Rey* motioned with the gun. "You're still alive for one reason. I want you to take that message back to him. If you're unwilling to, say so, and I can arrange for you to join your men in the gutter."

The man nodded and then slowly reached into his jacket pocket for a pen and a scrap of paper – a parking stub. He watched *El Rey* studying him, and then, after considering it for a few moments, scrawled a number on the back of the ticket. He replaced the pen in his jacket and then held the slip out to *El Rey*.

"Place it on the ground and then turn around and walk out of here. Keep walking until you get to the main street and then cross into the park. Walk to the far side, and from there, do whatever you want. But be assured of one thing. If I ever see you, or any of your men, again, I will kill you like a dog, without hesitation. Nothing personal. You know how it is," *El Rey* said, speaking softly, as was his custom.

The man nodded. "I'll take him the message."

He bent down and placed the parking ticket on the concrete floor and then turned as instructed. *El Rey* slammed him in the base of the neck with the heavy steel pistol, and he tumbled to the ground. Picking up the stub, he calculated that the man would be out for at least fifteen minutes – plenty of time to get to his apartment, grab his gear, and disappear forever.

☙❧

When the man came to, he was being shaken awake by a uniformed police officer. A blue glow flickered on the street from the roof lights of the squad cars. A harsh glare illuminated the building's battered façade from the headlights of the four gathered cars. A huddle of cops stood outside by the two corpses, which had been covered with a tarp. *El Rey* was gone.

He told the police that he'd been assaulted and mugged, and that the last thing he remembered was being told to move into the building. He knew nothing about the two dead men – perhaps they'd happened along and tried to help him. He didn't know. He'd been unconscious throughout whatever had happened and vaguely remembered a pair of large men, rough-looking, perhaps homeless – he struggled to give as

57

good a description as he could muster, but it was all blurry and had happened so fast.

Unfortunately, he didn't have his wallet – not surprising, given that he'd just been robbed; but he could get his passport brought to him with a phone call to a colleague at the airport. The officers took him into the precinct and processed his statement, and a doctor checked him perfunctorily. No concussion – just a sore neck and a bad headache. He was allowed to make his call, and within a few minutes the shift chief got a phone call from the head of the Mendoza police force.

Four hours later, the Gulfstream lifted into the night sky and banked north, paralleling the Andes on its way up the coast.

CHAPTER 7

Mexico City, Mexico

Cruz sat with his advisory team in the conference room, Briones seated by his side, as they strategized on how best to take down the bodega, which they'd been watching for a week. It was obvious to them that the facility was being used as a distribution point for drugs and arms, and the only real questions that remained were ones of timing and logistics.

Briones glanced at his notes. "As suspected, the contraband comes in during the day, apparently from two suppliers, both of which are small construction supply companies that don't have any other customers. We haven't been able to get close enough for hundred percent confirmation, but it appears that one of them is dropping off crates of weapons, and the other, drugs. Most likely meth, because the vehicles that are arriving to pick it up at night are well known local meth distributors who specialize in trafficking in the barrios. Could be some marijuana, too, but that's not a big concern. Guns and meth are," Briones summarized.

Cruz stood. "We need to coordinate taking down the two vendors as well as the bodega, preferably all at the same time. I'm not nearly as worried about the individual dealers making the pickups. There will be ten more to replace them when we drag them off the street, so the overwhelming priority has to be the supply. Cut off the supply, and most of the problem goes away." He turned his attention to Briones. "Let's talk about defenses."

"It's relatively low-key. At night, there are only three security men, and we haven't seen any inside, so neutralize them and it's a clean sweep. There are usually more men there during the day – workers and legitimate delivery people, so the odds of collateral damage increase with a daytime strike. I'm recommending going in just before dawn, when the night shift will be the most tired, and doing a stealth take-out of the sentries," Briones concluded.

One of the men at the table shook his head. "It's not going to sit well with the press if we just gun down the guards with no warning or opportunity to allow them to surrender."

Cruz nodded. "I'd normally have a problem doing so, but these men are carrying automatic weapons that are illegal in Mexico and are playing host to known cartel street dealers. Our last operations involved considerable police and army casualties, and I've about had it with our men being butchered to give these animals a chance to lay down their arms. They almost never do, and all we are doing is giving them warning so they can dig in and kill our forces. I'm done with that. If you're carrying around an AK-47 and distributing drugs that are killing kids, you don't need a warning. You need a coffin. That's going to be our new policy. Zero tolerance."

The man persisted. "Will the attorney general buy off on that? Doesn't it violate their rights?"

"On this mission, we will be presenting it as a *fait accompli*. It's better to ask for forgiveness than permission. If you have a problem with that, then you can be the one to go visit the families of the dead officers when these bastards gun them down after they've gotten their warning, and explain why the killers deserved a chance. We've identified all three as low-level enforcers for the Sinaloa cartel – men who are vocational killers. These men are butchers. We know it. I'm saying we cut them down before they can do more damage. If you're uncomfortable with that, I can have you re-assigned to a different group. Make up your mind," Cruz warned.

The man backed down, shaking his head. "I just don't want any fallout that could hurt us later."

"Let me worry about that. Now, Lieutenant Briones will take over and go through the plan for the attack. We'll hit it tomorrow morning and then get the area cleaned up so that we can take the day crew captive and arrest the delivery trucks as they arrive with their cargo."

❧❧

A drowsy rooster crowed in the distance, sensing that dawn was approaching. The guards at the bodega lounged around the back of the building, weary after yet another long night of inactivity, their weapons by their sides as they sat playing cards. Only two more hours to go, and then they'd be off until eight the next night for another eleven hours of tedium.

Two hundred yards away, a pair of marine snipers stealthily moved through a vacated junkyard to a position where they'd have a clear line of fire. Their weapon of choice for the exercise was the M16 rifle, with an accuracy that was perfect at such a range. They had the guns set to single fire, confident in their ability to dispatch the three men sitting around a white plastic Pacifico beer table near the bodega's main entry.

Their ear bud com lines crackled and a quiet voice told them to be ready to fire if the men moved for their weapons. They steadied their rifles against an old Dodge Dart's rusting fender and prepared to engage.

A loud voice boomed from the public address system of an armored federal police truck that roared around the corner on the dirt road that led to the bodega, followed by three police cars with their lights off.

"Do not move. Do not attempt to reach for your guns. This is the federal police. We have you surrounded."

The men froze momentarily, then dived for their rifles. The first man's head exploded in a froth of blood and brains, spackling the wall behind him. The second man's chest shredded in seconds, peppered by smoking holes, the dark stain of exsanguination spreading before he hit the ground. The third guard made it to his weapon as the slug intended for him missed by scant millimeters, and taking cover, fired a burst in the direction of the police truck before a sniper round tore his esophagus apart, taking most of his C3 vertebrae with it.

The assault was over almost before it started. The three corpses lay immobile in the sticky dirt. Briones got out of the lead vehicle, approached the lock with bolt cutters, and made short work of the chain securing the gate in place. A squad of combat-equipped *Federales* jogged into the storage yard, followed by the coroner's van. The instructions were clear. Photograph the carnage, then get the bodies out of there and clean away any trace of the battle so the day crew had no idea there was a problem until it was too late.

Half an hour later, the scene had been sanitized, and the only evidence of the slaughter was the hanging gate chain and the line of police vehicles preparing to pull away. A small group of curious locals had gathered up the road, drawn by the gunfire, but the officers quickly dispersed them, warning them to stay away from the area. Most were night watchmen at other buildings, although a few lived in the ramshackle hovels that were a perennial on the periphery of any rural industrial area in Mexico – squatters whose desperation had forced them to construct meager shelters from discarded or pilfered materials, and who lived without the benefit of water, electricity or plumbing.

The human flotsam shuffled back to wherever it called home, driven by the warnings of the police. Nobody wanted to bring any more trouble down on their heads than the universe had already visited upon them, so their curiosity took a back seat to self-preservation.

One man, a security guard at a plumbing supply warehouse a block from the yard, made a surreptitious call on his cell as he made his way back to his lonely watch, murmuring a summary of what he'd seen into the phone before terminating the call.

The day crew never appeared that morning, and neither did the delivery trucks.

As the day wore on, it became obvious that the raid had somehow been leaked to the higher-ups in the scheme, who had taken appropriate measures to cut their losses and terminate operations. It was always a risk for the police, in any incursion, because the industry was always on guard and lived with the expectation that it would have to fold up its tent and move to greener pastures at any moment.

In the end, Cruz and Briones were both stymied by the exercise because while they'd seized thirty-five kilos of methamphetamine, two hundred pounds of marijuana, eighteen automatic Kalashnikov AK-47 assault rifles and twelve FN Five-seven pistols, they'd failed to stop the driving force behind the operation – the cartel lieutenants who had set up the bodega in the first place. And so, within a few days, the operation would switch to another warehouse somewhere close by where more of the insidious cargo would be distributed, and aside from a few dead enforcers, nothing had changed.

It was frustrating, but all part of the job, and both men tried to keep it from getting to them. They had achieved a good outcome – they'd stopped a local drug and gun distribution scheme with zero police casualties, and dealt a blow to the forces of evil. All in all, not a bad day's work, although when Cruz made it home that day he'd seemed somewhat dejected to Dinah. She'd sensed his frustration and suggested dinner at one of his favorite restaurants, followed by a bottle of passable Mexican cabernet from the Guadalupe Valley.

As they sat on the floor in front of their small fireplace upon their return, holding each other while savoring their wine, Cruz again silently remarked to himself that he was extremely fortunate to have found such a beautiful and wonderful companion to share his life.

Sometimes all you could do was live to fight another day and cherish the good around you.

Sometimes that was enough.

CHAPTER 8

Costa Rica, Central America

Three miles off the Caribbean coast, *Gato Negro*, a two hundred forty-eight foot super yacht with its own helicopter, cruised north at fourteen knots, its stabilizers working to ensure that the passengers were not troubled by any rolling. There wasn't much chance of that in the four foot waves – the ship's forty-two foot beam and aluminum construction made her as stable as an oil rig in all but the worst conditions. A staff of sixteen full-time crew worked diligently to ensure that she was always ready for use, year round, whenever her owner decided to take in some salt air.

She flew a Bahamian flag, registered there by a corporation specifically formed for that purpose, whose shares were held by a Panamanian trust, which was in turn the asset of a Hong Kong corporation. Ownership of the Hong Kong entity was murky at best, with its shares technically owned by a bank, whose owners in the Isle of Man were not a matter of public record. A team of highly specialized attorneys worked full time to ensure that the dizzy network of intertwined entities remained impenetrable. The Byzantine web of structures was one of the more powerful financial conglomerates in the world, counting dozens of casinos, real estate holding companies, hotels, pawn shops, nightclubs, hedge funds and two insurance companies in its stable of assets.

Especially useful were the groups of casinos on Indian land in the western United States, whose receipts were colossal even in times when the massive parking lots were empty. Apparently, some things were recession-proof businesses, and between the gambling establishments and the nine hundred motels that sat forgotten by American freeways, staggering quantities of dollars made their way to the related credit unions and banks that processed the syndicate's money.

Some of the top finance graduates from prestigious universities devised impossible to follow schemes to obfuscate the moving parts of this improbable empire, the magnum opus of the top narcotics boss in the world – *Don* Carlos Aranas. Aranas had been a man of vision, having taken a page from the Italian mafia's playbook and worked towards sanitizing his income from the drug, human trafficking, murder-for-hire and kidnapping trades, by diversifying into legitimate businesses. Now, decades after having taken over the Sinaloa cartel when 'The Godfather', Miguel Angel Felix Gallardo, had gone to jail immediately following his dividing Mexico into the current decentralized scheme of smaller regional cartels, Aranas was a man with no home, who divided his time between Mexico, Honduras, Guatemala, Costa Rica, Panama, Colombia and Venezuela.

Not surprisingly, well-publicized efforts to bring down the number-one drug lord in the world had all failed. Aranas was incredibly resilient, having even escaped from a maximum security prison when he'd been apprehended in the early Nineties. While details were murky, as were most facts surrounding him, legend had it that Aranas had co-opted everyone in the prison, from the head of security on down, and on the day of his escape had simply hidden in a laundry cart pushed by the director of the guard shift, who had been thoughtful enough to then drive him to a nearby dirt airstrip, where a twin engine prop plane had winged him to points unknown.

The total revenue of the Mexican drug cartels was a hotly disputed topic, with no agreement. For understandable reasons, hard numbers were difficult to come by. Some estimates placed the number at twenty billion. Others at fifty billion. Reality was that both numbers were laughably low, and that between all the cartels the real revenue number was closer to a hundred billion a year, wholesale.

Officials in the U.S. tried to downplay the number, as they did with virtually all statistics, preferring to massage them for their own devices. Just as unemployment was officially pegged in the eight percent range through elaborate sleight of hand, and the GDP number was inflated by accounting hijinks, so too was the scale of the illegal drug business. Most experts privately agreed that the true ultimate retail value of all drugs that passed from Mexico into the U.S. was closer to three hundred billion dollars a year, with two thirds of that sticking to the American side as the drugs were cut and distributed from the large wholesale distribution points and passed down to the street level dealers. Regardless of whose numbers one believed, the glaringly obvious fact was that, for whatever reason, the top man in the world was invisible to all law enforcement authorities and passed across national borders without hindrance.

Three deck hands cleaned the hull of one of the larger ship's tenders – a thirty-two-foot Cabo Express Aranas liked to use for fishing, which was mounted across the rear of the yacht's second-story deck, leaving the first free for entertaining. A massive crane swung the boat over the side and into the water whenever he was in the mood to use it to explore shallower waters for elusive game fish.

Aranas was almost sixty years old, which made him ancient in the drug business. Most of his rivals and peers had long since expired or had been incarcerated, and yet *Don* Aranas enjoyed glowing good health and virtually limitless prosperity. The ship was furnished with a fully-equipped gymnasium, and Aranas made a habit of taking an hour of exercise at least five days a week. What was the point of becoming one of the wealthiest men in the world if you threw it away with a sedentary lifestyle and poor habits? His intention was to live to a ripe old age, confounding his enemies and pursuers in the process. So far, the odds favored him. No photograph existed that was more current than twenty years old, and he no more resembled the images circulated of him than did his captain – a state of affairs he encouraged.

His nephew, Javier, approached him in the lower salon, where he was watching a DVD on the seventy-five-inch flat panel television, and wordlessly handed him a small cell phone. He stared at it momentarily, and then nodded to Javier, who discreetly departed. Aranas muted the volume and paused the film, and the only sound was the almost imperceptible hum of the twin diesel power plants two stories below him.

"Yes," he said into the phone.

"*Don* Aranas. I apologize for terminating several of your men in Argentina. I did so before knowing who they were or what their errand was."

"It is of no consequence. They should have been more careful."

"Yes. Well, I have given your request considerable thought, and I think it would be worth meeting to have a more meaningful discussion," *El Rey* said.

"That's a problem. I don't meet. Anyone. Ever."

"I understand, however I don't come out of retirement *ever*, either. If you want me to do something I never do, I think that we all need to be prepared to make concessions. Wouldn't you agree?"

Aranas' anger flashed to the surface for a moment, but he quickly won the struggle to control it. He needed *El Rey*. These were unusual times. Perhaps flexibility was in order.

"What did you have in mind?"

"Did you receive my message about my fee?"

"Yes, yes. I have no problem with it, although for that amount of money, success had better be guaranteed. I heard about your adventure in Baja. That sort of outcome isn't an option," Aranas warned.

"That was the only instance of a failure in an otherwise exemplary career, and frankly it would have been rectified if the client had still been around to pursue it. As things worked out, it wasn't a priority any longer, so it seemed more prudent to remove myself from the equation," *El Rey* explained.

"You insist on a meeting. Again, what do you have in mind?"

"It must be only you and me. Nobody else. Just as you value your privacy, so do I. And it won't be for three weeks. I have other matters that must be attended to before I can meet. I'll call this number again on the twenty-fifth, at this time. Then we can arrange to get together somewhere both of us can be assured is safe. Will that work for you?"

"I still don't like it."

"Yes. I understand. The alternative, of course, is that we don't meet, and you never hear from me again. I trust you'll still be able to solve whatever problem that is so pressing you needed my services above all others?" *El Rey* suggested.

"You're playing a dangerous game, my friend," Aranas warned, his patience at an end.

"That's all I do, *Don*. I mean no disrespect by my conditions. But that stipulation, as well as the fee, isn't negotiable. Will that be a problem?"

Aranas sighed. Why was everyone competent a prima donna? He'd been cautioned by his associates that *El Rey* didn't intimidate easily and was scrupulous in all aspects of his trade. If one wanted him, one expected to meet his terms. That's just the way it was.

"I accept. But I will warn you. Anything that jeopardizes me will bring down the weight of the world on you, and there's nowhere remote enough to hide from me. And why do we have to wait so long? I have a strong sense of urgency to this contract."

"I completely understand and would expect no less. But I'm afraid that I can't make it any sooner. Hopefully that won't be a problem." *El Rey* waited for any protest, and when none came, continued. "I will call at the agreed upon time and propose several meeting spots. I shall leave the final choice to you. We'll need no more than half an hour. Thank you for your consideration in this," *El Rey* said, and then the line went dead.

Aranas stared at the cell phone in his hand, and then stabbed the power off and resumed watching his film. One of his favorites. Bruce Willis was up against a diabolical terrorist, tackling impossible odds while taking names and kicking ass. They just didn't make movies like that anymore. His nephew re-entered the salon upon hearing the film resume.

Aranas handed him the phone. "Remove the battery and lock this up. On the twenty-fifth, charge the battery and bring it to me. I'll be expecting a call." He fixed his nephew with a hard look. "Javier, don't forget this. It's extremely important. Put a reminder in your phone or computer or whatever, but make sure I have that phone charged and ready on the twenty-fifth, or there will be hell to pay. Don't disappoint me," Aranas instructed.

Javier swallowed nervously. He knew that if the *Don* said it was important, failure wasn't an option. He nodded and went to do as instructed. He'd program reminders in every device he had and probably wouldn't be able to sleep for days before the big date.

The *Don* had that effect on people.

Gunfire erupted from the speakers as Willis again demonstrated that he was impossible to kill. Aranas smiled with delight.

He loved that part.

CHAPTER 9

Rio de Janeiro, Brazil

Rio was a noisy symphony of sound and color, and as the taxi cruised along Atlantic Avenue past Copacabana beach the world appeared to be a nonstop parade of tanned skin and fake breasts ensconced in miniscule strips of fabric. *El Rey* watched the crush of nubile humanity move along the promenade, its distinctive wave design famous all over the world.

They pulled to the curb in front of the Palace Hotel and the driver exited the cab and opened the trunk. A uniformed attendant rushed to retrieve the single Tumi travel bag as the young man paid the fare, offering a generous but not memorably large tip. He wore a white linen short-sleeved shirt and tan lightweight cargo pants, and his hair was pulled back in a ponytail, revealing a tanned complexion and appealingly symmetrical features. He looked like nothing so much as an international playboy arriving in town for a taste of the city's renowned pleasures – an image he would do nothing to deny.

Once in his room, he watched the sea of tourists ambling along the iconic beach and checked his watch. His appointment was in an hour at the exclusive private clinic he'd been directed to, giving him just enough time to unpack his bag, walk down the strand a ways, and then snag a taxi at one of the numerous other hotels. He knew from his research that the clinic was ten minutes away, and traffic was light at this hour so he had no fear of running late.

The cab pulled up to a discrete contemporary edifice in an upscale neighborhood with a mirrored-glass lower floor as street frontage, and a small sign announcing the Rodrigo Caleb Surgical Center. *El Rey* tried the front door, but it was locked. He noted a chrome button on the side of the doorjamb and pressed it. A few seconds later a low-pitched buzz vibrated through the frame, and he pushed the door open.

The lobby area was all stainless steel and black leather furniture: ultra-modern, and obviously very expensive. Several large aerial photographs of Rio adorned the otherwise barren walls, illuminated by halogen spotlights. A breathtakingly beautiful nurse sat behind the severe reception desk, eyeing him neutrally.

"I have a noon appointment," he announced, approaching her, his Portuguese passable but obviously not fluent.

"Please fill out this form, and the doctor will be with you shortly," she replied in perfect Spanish, guessing his mother tongue by his pronunciation, and held forth a clipboard and a Mont Blanc pen. He was liking the clinic's style so far. "Would you care for some water? Pellegrino? Fiji?"

"No, thank you. I'm good."

He busied himself scribbling an invented medical history, and after six minutes returned the form to the nurse, whose only reaction was one eyebrow shifting upwards a scant millimeter. He wondered how much of her was surgically augmented and decided that it really didn't matter – the net effect was absolutely riveting, even in a town full of beautiful women.

Everything about the clinic said extremely expensive, which was exactly what he was hoping for. The last thing he wanted was a botched job by an economy hack.

The console on the reception desk trilled, and the nurse murmured into a Bluetooth headset before rising and gesturing to him.

"The doctor will see you now."

Normally not one to spend a lot of time focusing on female charms, even he had to admit that the way she filled out her uniform would have been the envy of any men's magazine in the world, and would have sold out an edition with her on the cover. He was getting a very good feeling about the doctor's skill level.

He followed her back to a large room with a desk, couch, and an examination chair much like a dentist's. A man in his early fifties wearing a white physician's coat rose from the desk and approached him with his hand outstretched.

"Ah, *Señor* Guitierez. Nice to meet you," he said in fluent Spanish with no trace of a Portuguese accent. "I am Doctor Caleb. Has Nina been attending to you satisfactorily?"

"Yes. Everything's good. Pleased to meet you."

They shook hands as the nurse left, closing the door behind her.

"What brings you to my establishment?" the doctor asked, studying the young man's face.

"I want to change my look. Alter my nose and give it a thinner shape, and perhaps a chin implant?"

"Come sit in the exam chair, and let's see what we have here. Would you like me to make suggestions, or do you have a very specific idea in mind?"

"No, I just want something new. Definitely a change to my nose. I've always hated it. I got the idea for a chin implant from the television…" *El Rey* did his best to sound hesitant. "And if I don't like the effect of it, I suppose I can always have it removed."

"Well, it's not quite so easy, but let's see if we can come up with a plan that will accomplish what you want."

They spent a half hour going over possibilities and agreed on a nose alteration, chin implant, and cheekbone augmentation.

"We should do the procedures a week apart, at least," the doctor advised.

"No. I don't have unlimited time. I'm only here for a few weeks, and I want it all done at once so I can go home looking different. And I'll need an apartment with full-time care – do you have something like that?"

"Yes, we have a full suite upstairs. Yours isn't an unusual request. Many wish to remain sequestered while the bruising and trauma is attended to. Although I'll caution you that it's quite expensive to go that route…"

"The money isn't as important as a quality outcome and discretion," El Rey assured him.

"Ah, then...just so. It's against my best advice to do the procedures all in one sitting, however, it can be done. You run more risk of a longer recovery time required and increase the possibility of complications. But if you'll be availing yourself of our inpatient services, I think we can reduce the trauma to a minimum..." the doctor paused. "Now, to the matter of price. The nose will be four thousand U.S., the chin implant thirty-five hundred, the cheek implants three apiece, and two weeks of round-the-clock care in our suite will be sixteen thousand dollars, for a total of...call it twenty-nine thousand dollars, plus any special requests. Will you be paying by credit card?"

"Cash. Half in advance. Half upon completion."

"Well, we can work something out. We ordinarily get a hundred percent of our fees up front, however, if you are willing to pay for the surgery in advance, we can bill for the suite on a weekly basis, with the balance due before checkout," the doctor advised.

"That will be fine."

"We can do this within the next two days. During the interim, avoid any aspirin or alcohol." The doctor studied the information on the pad *El Rey* had completed. "You don't take any medications? No vitamins? No, er, recreational substances?"

"No."

"Alcohol?"

"No."

"Coffee? Tea?"

"No."

"Very well, then. When would you like to have the surgery and begin your stay?"

"Tomorrow works for me. The sooner the better."

They arranged the payment details for the following morning. *El Rey* was advised to avoid any food or water after midnight, to reduce the likelihood of any complications from the anesthesia. The doctor went over to his station and took a digital photo of him, and then made modifications based upon the suggested procedures. *El Rey* stared at the new him, and while he looked similar, the difference was substantial – he was instantly reminded of the film actor from a movie that had been playing on the flight from Santiago, Chile, after he'd driven across the border from Mendoza. Something about buccaneers in the Caribbean.

He supposed if he was going to change the way he looked, he might as well improve things to the extent it was possible. So celebrity pirate it would be. He just hoped that the healing would be faster than the doctor had indicated. No point in wasting any more time than necessary.

☞∞☜

When he came to after the surgery he was groggy, with his entire face wrapped in gauze. Nina and an equally stunning young woman were attending to him. Nina explained that they would be there for him twenty-four hours a day, staying in the en suite apartment in shifts to attend to his every need. For now, he'd need to take anti-inflammatory medication along with pain relievers and antibiotics in his IV drip, so he could expect to be out of it for the next few days. Ice would also be regularly applied to reduce the swelling and subcutaneous bleeding.

The doctor came in four hours later and said, "You'll look like you lost a fight with a bear for the first week, but within ten days you'll be mostly better, and within three weeks or so, a new man. I'll check back with you today before I leave for the night, and the girls will be here round the clock. Anything you need, any discomfort you feel, just let someone know, and we'll deal with it. No point in this being any more unpleasant than necessary," he assured his patient, and then with a wink at Nina, he departed.

El Rey slept most of the day, except for a few trips to the bathroom. The following morning, the doctor removed the gauze to change the dressing, and indeed, he looked like he'd been in a head-on collision. It was to be expected, but still, wasn't pleasant to see.

By the end of the first week, the swelling was receding and the deep purple circles under his eyes and around his chin were fading. The small sutures from the implants were removed, and by day ten, he was looking human again, the bruising now diminished to yellowish-tinged skin that the doctor assured him would look normal within another few days. The doctor spent time with him inspecting his new features, pointing out the delicate nuances he'd created for a more natural look. *El Rey* had to admit that the surgeon was a truly gifted artist – it was a remarkable and natural-appearing transformation.

The face looking back at him when he shaved every few days was similar to the one he remembered, but different enough to be another person – albeit a better looking one, which he supposed had been the doctor's intention.

On the sixteenth night, as *El Rey* stepped over the doctor's lifeless body on his office floor to clear all traces of his surgical procedure from the computer, he was actually sad that a valuable resource like the physician had to be terminated. But in his business he couldn't take any chances, and there was no point in dwelling on collateral casualties.

Nina's corpse lay upstairs in the suite, and all that remained after the computer scrub was for the second nurse to arrive at nine p.m. After attending to her, he'd be done with Rio for good. He'd already erased the security camera footage, which was stored on a tape backup and a hard drive in a maintenance room, so once the second girl was dispatched he was good to go. Standing in the office, *El Rey* studied the doctor and debated pulling the Mont Blanc pen out of his eye socket and then decided to leave it in place.

He extracted the hard disk from the computer and then painstakingly sorted through the file cabinet for any paper records of his stay. Once he'd located them, as well as the attached before and after photos, he busied himself with burning them in a metal garbage can near an open rear window and then settled in to wait for his final victim to show up. He had nothing against the night nurse, just as he'd borne Nina no grudge, but what needed to be done wasn't a matter of like or dislike.

By his calculations he could be in São Paolo by midnight after a short private plane ride, and then tomorrow he would be winging his way to Venezuela – his next stop before meeting with the elusive kingpin, *Don Aranas*. If all went well, he'd call in a few more days and be ready to meet within a week.

CHAPTER 10

Zihuatanejo, Mexico

Don Aranas sat alone on the beach, watching as the water reflected the twinkling lights of the boats anchored off the pristine stretch of sand. He was the only patron of the luxury resort's oceanfront restaurant, which had closed early to host a private party – for one. As agreed, his bodyguards had stayed away, although two watched Aranas sipping a Bohemia beer at the small white plastic table on the strand, peering at him through the scopes of their sniper rifles from the hotel looming behind him. If his guest arrived and harmed the *Don* in any way, they were instructed to blow the man's head off – a reasonable precaution, Aranas felt, even if it technically violated his agreement with *El Rey*.

He glanced at his watch in irritation – the meeting had been for nine p.m., and the assassin was now ten minutes late. Aranas was not a man who liked to be kept waiting, no matter who it was. He vowed to give it another five minutes, and then he'd finish his beer and leave – and *El Rey* would have bigger problems than just the Mexican government trying to hunt him down.

A small girl, perhaps six years old, approached him from the darkness of the beach on wobbly bow legs and held up a small hand-carved turtle with a bobbing head. Aranas waved her off. He was in no mood for trinket buying. The girl was insistent and placed the turtle on the table before running off down the spit into the night. Aranas took a final pull on his beer, then noticed a slip of rolled-up paper protruding from the turtle's head. Looking around but detecting nothing unusual, he carefully extracted the note and unfurled it, reading the few words before nodding and pushing to his feet.

He took his beer and walked to the water's edge, where the gentle lapping of the surf was almost lake-like in its lack of intensity, and began walking towards the town a mile or so away. Three minutes later, a fishing *panga* pulled up a few yards from him, beaching its bow in the wet sand, and the pilot gestured to Aranas to climb aboard. Once he had scowlingly done so, the boat backed off the beach, its engine frothing from the reverse thrust before it cut around in a circle and headed towards the open ocean, rapidly becoming invisible in the moonless night.

"Sorry for the drama, but I didn't like the looks of the scopes trained on you from the hotel. I thought I was clear about this," *El Rey* said, throttling back the large outboard when they were a thousand yards from shore.

Aranas studied the man's dim outline at the stern, a baseball cap pulled down low over his brow and a week-old beard masking most of his lower face. He was completely unremarkable, which Aranas supposed was the point. He noted the night vision scope on the bench next to him, along with a black waterproof nylon bag that was ominously long.

"My security head wanted some options if you gunned me down on the beach," Aranas replied, shrugging.

"Out of courtesy, I didn't kill the snipers, however I'd prefer if we could operate with a little more trust. I've done work for you before, always satisfactorily, so you should have no reason to doubt me," *El Rey* said.

"Fair enough."

"Now that you have me here, what is this situation that requires me to come out of retirement? And why will nobody but me suffice, out of all the available contractors in the world?"

"Can't you guess?"

"For twenty million, of course I can. But I didn't fly halfway around the world to speculate. We have five minutes before I drop you off over at the *malecón* in town. It would be a more productive use of both our time if you simply told me what's required," *El Rey* said reasonably, his soft voice barely audible over the burbling of the outboard.

"The president has decided to renege on our arrangement. We had agreed before he was elected that we would continue to receive a certain preference, as with his predecessor, but once he was elected he seemed to forget who put him in office, and has been favoring interests that are hostile to mine. That is a material breach of our agreement, and it cannot be allowed to stand," Aranas explained. "If you follow the news, you'll see that quite a few of my group's shipments have been apprehended lately, whereas my adversaries, the Jalisco and Los Zetas cartels, are enjoying an almost magical bout of good fortune. I suspect they made *El Presidente* a better offer, but that's not how these things are supposed to work. You keep your side of the bargain when you make a deal with me. He has violated our trust, and I need you to extract an appropriate penalty."

"You want me to execute the president of Mexico," *El Rey* said dispassionately. "Do you agree to my fee?"

"I do. I believe on our last contracts you received half in advance and half upon successful completion of the sanction."

"Yes, I will require ten million dollars in advance, and ten upon successful completion of the hit. The botched hit in Tampeco has the security forces in a state of high alert, so this will be an almost impossible feat – which is why the fee is commiserate with the level of difficulty. You pay twenty million dollars, and in return, our president will be dead within sixty days – no later. At that point our business is concluded, and I will be in permanent retirement. Is that acceptable?" *El Rey* offered, not so much asking as stating.

Aranas smoothed his hair where the light breeze off the ocean had ruffled it.

"I can wire transfer ten million tomorrow to any account you want, anywhere in the world. Alternatively, I can arrange for you to receive it in cash, or in gold. Your preference. Just make sure you take the miserable shit-rat out – no mistakes or excuses," Aranas warned.

"I will call you tomorrow morning with wire routing instructions. I would prefer Swiss francs, if that is acceptable? I'm sure you have the ability to convert before you transfer. And don't worry, I will keep my end of the bargain. He will be dead inside of two months."

El Rey throttled up the motor and swung the boat back in the direction of the harbor, cutting through the small waves effortlessly at high speed. It was impossible to carry on any further conversation due to the wind and engine noise. Which was fine. There was nothing more to say.

The boat pulled up onto the beach in front of a string of open air seafood restaurants, and Aranas climbed over the bow and hopped agilely onto the sand.

"I'll await your call," he said, and the assassin nodded before gunning the motor and heading back to the dark waters of the open sea. Aranas watched as he disappeared and nodded to himself. If anyone could pull off this hit, it was *El Rey*.

Aranas fished his cell phone from his shirt pocket and noted that he had sixteen messages. He'd felt it vibrating non-stop in the boat, but part of his arrangement with the assassin was no phone calls, so he'd erred on the side of discretion. It was bad enough the man had spotted the two jackasses with the rifles – two of his very best men. He hadn't wanted to show any further bad faith.

Aranas punched the redial button and issued terse instructions. He wanted to be in the air within half an hour. His chartered jet was sitting at the airport, waiting for him and his security detail. He'd had about enough of this little fishing hamlet, between the beach and the boat ride.

After tossing his empty Bohemia bottle in a gray plastic trash receptacle, he moved up the shore towards the waterfront walkway, confident that his men would be there within a few minutes.

A group of five drunken *gringos* staggered past him, laughing loudly at some private joke as they moved down the strand in search of a party. Aranas eyed the two leggy teenage blondes, wearing miniskirts so short that they more resembled T-shirts than dresses, cackling with glee as they passed a fedora back and forth, their boyfriends' expressions already tequila-glazed. *Ah, youth. It was wasted on the young.*

Aranas ambled past the boat ramp and towards the pedestrian shopping area that was closing down for the night. As he trudged along, he reflected on his brief meeting with the assassin, the ephemeral *El Rey*, seemingly more phantom than human, judging by his miraculous string of successful executions. Twenty million dollars was a lot of money, but Aranas wasn't in a bargain-hunting mood, and in the scheme of things, it was loose change to the cartel kingpin. *El Rey* was absolutely correct in his assessment of the current situation – the disastrous attack on the motorcade had served to escalate the conflict, and now the president's security forces were in a state of agitated high alert. Meanwhile, every day, shipments worth many times the twenty million were in jeopardy due to the law enforcement focus on his cartel.

The man was right. It would require a small miracle to pull the hit off successfully. And these days, miracles cost.

It would be money well spent, of that he was sure.

Aranas spotted the two silver Suburbans his men had rented pulling along the beach drive and hiked in their direction. The assassin's reputation and legacy of kills notwithstanding, Aranas was certain of one thing after their brief encounter.

He was very glad that *El Rey* wasn't targeting him.

The following morning, a young man with almost impossibly attractive features lounged by the pool at a private beachfront villa in Ixtapa, taking in the breathtaking beauty of the pristine ocean while munching contentedly on a fruit plate. A porter in white linen stood a discreet distance away in the shade of the house, sensitive to the slightest indication that the guest required anything at all.

El Rey tapped a few keys on his laptop computer and then reached over to the small marble table for a wireless headset. He placed the fruit on the ground next to him and waved the man off – he needed privacy for the call he was about to make. The attendant bowed and scurried into the house, leaving the area empty except for a brave herring gull that had landed, eyeing the pool curiously.

After another series of keystrokes, the young man heard a distinctive ringing in the headset, followed by a now unmistakable voice.

"Yes?"

"Good morning. The funds should be sent to the following account, care of a correspondent bank in Germany." *El Rey* then slowly recited the wire information, listening attentively as Aranas repeated it.

"I have one other assignment I would like you to consider. Before you make your final arrangements for the discussed contract," Aranas said once he'd noted the banking details.

This wasn't part of the deal.

"I thought I was clear. I am retired. This is my final transaction."

"I know, and I understand. But if you'd like to make an easy five million, you might want to at least hear me out," Aranas dangled as bait.

El Rey sighed. Things were never simple with the cartel bosses. They were volatile and impetuous, he'd found. Still, five million was a substantial contract price if the job was straightforward. "What is it you wish me to do?"

Aranas gave him a name. '*Chacho*' Morenos, the head of the *Familia* Morenos cartel that was battling for control of Juárez.

"He has made my life uncomfortable in a critical gateway to the United States. For a man of your abilities, this would be an easy sanction. Almost beneath you. But for five million…"

"Very well. Transfer fifteen million today – the full value of the second contract plus the agreed ten – and I shall make it so within a matter of a few weeks, if not days. I'll need to nose around and get a feel for the lay of the land. Because of the last-minute nature of this, I will undoubtedly also incur higher expenses."

"I have no doubt. Which is why I am willing to be so generous. That, and it seems prudent to clean the whole house while I have a competent sanitizer…"

"I will get in touch once I've dispatched this secondary target. I'll look for the transfer," *El Rey* said and then disconnected.

He had put the call through an IP-masking software package that bounced his address all over the planet, so he was untraceable. The bank account the money was going to was in the name of a Lithuanian shell company with accounts in Luxembourg, and there would be two further transfers to an account in the British Virgin Islands, where his funds were ostensibly investment proceeds for a hedge fund registered there, and the trail would end within another week when that fund purchased a number of credit default swaps from a hedge fund in Ireland that would expire, worthless. The money would be effectively laundered, and once in Ireland, it was clean – the proceeds of legitimate investments in the unregulated centi-trillion dollar derivatives market. Nobody would bat an eye over a measly fifteen million.

El Rey shut down his computer and set it to the side, on the table, and resumed his fruit breakfast, pausing to sip some freshly squeezed orange juice and pomegranate nectar the staff had obligingly prepared for him.

By the end of the day, with his savings, he would be worth close to forty million dollars. Not bad. Not bad at all.

Now all he needed to do was take out one of the most heavily protected cartel bosses in the world and execute the president of Mexico.

He took a bite of pineapple. That had been one of the things he'd missed living in Argentina. Fresh pineapple.

It would be an eventful few months.

CHAPTER 11

The air in Ciudad Juárez, across the Rio Grande River from El Paso, Texas, stank of sour exhaust and raw sewage. The downtown was dilapidated and reeked of disrepair; the ancient school buses that were the public transportation belched toxic fumes into the atmosphere as they groaned past platoons of impoverished workers on their way home from long shifts in the *maquiladoras* plants that dotted the city. Trash choked every gutter of the broken sidewalks; colorful chip bags and ice cream wrappers mingled with cigarette butts and sludge that the pedestrians moved cautiously around, ever mindful of random ruts and holes awaiting the unsuspecting. If there was a sorrier sight than Juárez by day, it was surely Juárez by night.

Handcarts wedged between battered cars served all manner of food for the work crowd; the odor of hot dogs and frying mystery meat wafted like a cloud past the bus stop where the young man waited patiently, reading a newspaper by the storefront light while he kept a wary eye on the bar across the street – a known hangout of the enforcers who worked for the *Familia* Morenos cartel, and a poor choice to frequent unless suicide was high on one's wish list.

Juárez had earned the dubious distinction of being the most dangerous city on the planet that wasn't in an active war zone. Fully forty percent of the population had evacuated over the prior five years, while the Sinaloa cartel and the Juárez cartel battled over the trafficking hub that led into the United States. The murder rate was a minimum of eight deaths per day, with bursts of executions during an active conflict easily driving the number into the double digits.

The armed wing of the Juárez cartel, *La Línea*, comprised former police officers and military specialists from the Mexican Special Forces, as well as street gang members. *La Línea* was especially feared, even among the routinely savage Juárez crew, because of their penchant for decapitations and mutilation. They had borrowed a page from the U.S.-backed regime in El Salvador during the Eighties, which regularly left the mutilated bodies of its victims in prominent areas as a warning to would-be rivals, and to keep the population subdued with fear. Hardly a week went by without a grotesquely butchered corpse being left in a central location. The papers had grown so accustomed to the slaughter that there was a sense of boredom to the daily stories of slayings and beheadings – it took a significant event to make a dent in the jaded sense of apathy that floated over the doomed city like a haze.

For the past two years, Sinaloa had battled it out in the city streets with the Juárez cartel, culminating in Sinaloa having appeared to have won the war after a particularly bloody massacre that claimed the lives of over fifty people in a single day. But other rivals to the throne quickly threw their hats in and joined the killing frenzy in a bid for power, and the result was that the town had remained a death zone, with a population that didn't venture out at night for fear of armed onslaughts. The cartel factions also augmented their income by conducting kidnappings and murder-for-hire, as well as slavery, car theft, fraud, burglary…anything that could be done at the point of a gun for profit, making life in Juárez a kind of living hell for the innocent residents who were the natural prey for the criminal syndicates.

El Rey watched as groups of tired females clung to each other while waiting for their bus. In addition to all its other sins, Juárez had earned a position of disrepute for the serial murder of thousands of young women, attracted to the city by the promise of work in the multitude of factories that were the region's only saving grace.

Multinational conglomerates had discovered the value of assembling their North American products on the border, leveraging the dirt-cheap labor cost in Mexico to create windfall profitability – all part of the miracle of globalization. But the workforce, which was mainly young women, had drawn predators in the form of organized serial killing gangs, in which the police and the local power elite were strongly

84

suspected. Even after the official four hundred or so cases had been solved and attributed to bus drivers, street gangs and deviant killers, the unofficial estimate remained closer to five thousand, with mass graves their legacy. The government had been quick to proclaim the spree over seven years earlier, and yet women still disappeared with regularity, and the word on the street was that the killers were still active.

At one time, the city had boomed to an estimated two million population, but the constant violence had driven many from the region, and it had shrunk by seven hundred thousand. Blocks of abandoned homes and businesses abounded, mute testament to the impact of the cartel warfare that defined the area.

With the United States just across the river, Juárez remained a critical junction for drug trafficking, and so it was that new contenders continued to move into town to take on the entrenched players. The Morenos gang had appeared eighteen months before with a splash, and had immediately begun a campaign of systematic brutality that rivaled the most brazen and vicious in Mexico. The town was divided up into the equivalent of fiefdoms where the local warlords reigned supreme, with the most dangerous to Aranas' Sinaloa group run by *'Chacho'* Morenos, one of the most influential power players in the region, having forged a coalition with Aranas' sworn enemies in the Zetas cartel.

None of which particularly bothered the young man, who was himself one of the earth's most dangerous predators. *El Rey* had spent ten days in Juárez so far, plying the street criminals with cash to gain their confidence, buying drugs and a few weapons, which were both in plentiful supply. He'd maintained an aura of the underworld by claiming to be a high-end male prostitute for rich *gringos*, which his new movie-star features lent credence to, as did his choice of clothing, deliberately selected to maximize his flamboyant cover. He knew from experience that prostitutes were largely invisible in criminal circles, and so quickly had entre to many establishments that would have immediately questioned a young, fit male who wasn't in the cartel game.

He'd learned that the second in command of the *Familia* Morenos liked to let off steam in the bar across the street, which was flanked by cars filled with armed sentries, as well as several police cars. Juárez was a city where money bought influence, including police guards to diminish the appeal of an assault. *El Rey* knew that there were thousands of soldiers in the town chartered with keeping the peace, but until recently they'd been strangely unable to locate the Sinaloa cartel's outposts. That had all changed when the new regime had come into the government, and now Sinaloa was on the run, forced to keep a low profile. This had helped the Morenos solidify power in what would have been an impossible way just six short months earlier, when Sinaloa had maintained a stranglehold on the streets. Now the Juárez situation was in flux, and the Morenos' ascent had emboldened other groups to come to town and challenge one and all for a piece of territory.

El Rey understood why this was an impossible circumstance for Aranas – it called into question his authority and created competitors in what had been a relatively stable corridor. The entire situation had been exacerbated by the armed forces cracking down on his group, telegraphing the message that it was open season on Sinaloa. In the delicate world of cartel power, any hint of disequilibrium invited in rivals, which was exactly what had happened. Aranas made five million dollars every evening in Juárez alone, so *El Rey* completely understood the reasoning of wanting his Morenos problem taken care of while he was available.

A dark green Escalade rolled up to the bar and stopped in front. Five men got out, all wearing cowboy hats and windbreakers, which hardly concealed their weapons. The smallest of the group was his objective for the evening – the number two man in the Morenos organization, Paco Aceviere. He would know where *Chacho* was hiding out, which would have to be nearby. You didn't try to take over one of the gateways for narcotics smuggling into the U.S. on a remote basis. He had to be close by, so all that remained was to find out where and come up with a plan to exterminate him – a chore *El Rey* was more than confident he could undertake in short order.

He'd been watching the coming and going at the bar, and now that he had visual confirmation that the *Familia* Morenos' captain was going in for a drink or three, it was just a matter of time and patience until the man led him to his boss. He toyed with the key fob in his shirt pocket and glanced down the block at the brown Ford Taurus he'd parked there hours ago. At least nobody had stolen his ride – that was a plus.

El Rey flipped the paper over to the sports section and began reading the coverage of the hotly contested soccer matches that were the nation's fascination. It was a warm evening, and he had all night. Nobody gave him a second glance, other than an occasional older man curious about his wares. *If you only knew, my friend,* he thought to himself and smiled. It was going to be another long evening, he could tell, but the end was in sight.

❧❧

Don Aranas answered the small cell phone the following afternoon and listened impassively as *El Rey* requested several items. He snapped his fingers and gestured, and one of his guards hurried to his side with a pen and sheet of paper. Aranas carefully wrote down the unfamiliar combination of letters, and then agreed that he would call back as soon as he had arranged for the desired items. Aranas lived in a world where anything could be had, for a price, no matter how exotic or esoteric. Still, after he hung up, he studied his note and shook his head.

This wouldn't be easy. Then again, it was only money. The sooner he located the goods, the sooner one of his big headaches would be over.

He considered the errand and then placed another call, to the man who supplied his troops with whatever they needed. He would know where to acquire the assassin's necessary tools. Of that, Aranas was sure. After a few minutes of back and forth, he disconnected. Nothing in life worth doing was cheap, and this had been no exception.

The estimated delivery time was three days, allowing for transatlantic shipment.

Aranas called *El Rey* back and relayed the news. They would arrange for pick up at one of his facilities in Juárez.

When Aranas hung up, it was with a sense of satisfaction. His nemesis would cease to exist before the week was done.

Five million was a bargain.

CHAPTER 12

Music boomed from the patio of the expansive ranch house sixteen miles from the outskirts of Ciudad Juárez. A seven-foot-high wall encircled the large central compound, which held a dozen SUVs, a stable, a trio of guest *casitas*, and the seven thousand square foot central hacienda. Dusk had transitioned inevitably to night, lending the surrounding desert a balmy tranquility after the sun had baked it relentlessly throughout the day.

Armed guards patrolled the perimeter, which was equipped with the latest motion sensing technology, along with pressure sensors and powerful spotlights that could illuminate the area around the ranch for two hundred yards in every direction. It would be impossible to creep up on the location without being detected, if not by the sophisticated electronics, then certainly by the armed police who guarded the road from town as a paid courtesy to the ranch's owner.

The men were more relaxed than usual, their ongoing war against their enemy, the Sinaloa cartel, having taken a turn for the better. Sinaloa had been devastated by a series of clashes with the army over the last week and was licking its wounds. Still, nobody put down their weapons, and the guards held their guns at the ready. While it was unlikely that an attack was imminent, one never knew.

High pitched squeals of drunken female laughter mingled with the festive tune emanating from the house; the nearest sentries exchanged knowing glances. Their boss enjoyed a party as much as anyone, and tonight looked to be another late one. A car with four of the freshest local girls had rolled up an hour earlier, and their patron, *Chacho*, had inspected the talent with approval as they'd strutted towards the house following a cursory frisking by the security detail. The head of the Morenos cartel was renowned for his appetites, and his appreciation for the finer things in life had only increased as he'd gotten older.

Tonight he had reason for celebration. The army units in the area had seized another shipment of Sinaloa cartel methamphetamines bound for the border, delivering another black eye to his competitor, as well as costing it sixteen of its best men in a rout that had ended with all the cartel personnel dead or wounded. At this rate, even the seemingly infinitely powerful Aranas would have to give some ground, enabling *Chacho* to solidify his claim on Juárez and use it as a leverage to further his ambitions in the states to the south. He, better than most, knew you were either eating, or being eaten, and he was determined to emerge as one of the top leaders in the cartels that effectively ruled Mexico.

Chacho playfully spanked one of the young women on the bottom as she squeezed past him into the house. It was good to be king, he thought, taking a swig on the five hundred dollar bottle of tequila he brandished as he slammed the heavy rustic pine door closed.

El Rey pulled cautiously away from the police checkpoint, his silenced Ruger P95PR 9mm pistol still hot from the rapid series of deadly shots required to dispatch the four officers. He knew from the satellite imagery that the ranch was a mile and a half further down the rutted dirt road a hundred yards up on his right. He'd already removed the brake lights from the old Ford so they wouldn't illuminate at an inopportune time, and he shut off the headlights before he made the turn, his eyes quickly adjusting to the gloom as he cautiously stole down the dusty track.

When the lights of the house came into view over a small rise, he calculated the distance and kept driving for another thirty seconds, then pulled silently to a stop after carefully performing a three point turn, so the car was prepared for a fast getaway. He was approximately five hundred yards away, which allowed for a decent margin of error on accuracy. With the music booming from the compound over the desert scrub, he wasn't overly concerned about making noise. He could hear the blare through his open window as he studied the light wind's tugging on a ribbon he'd tied to his antenna. It sounded like quite a *fiesta*. He quickly climbed out of the car and opened the trunk, pausing before removing three compact tubes and setting two of them on the ground. He raised the third to his shoulder and sighted on the front gate, squinting to adjust his focus.

The first rocket streaked to the opening and detonated, destroying everything within forty feet with its thermobaric blast. He dropped the smoking tube and grabbed another. The second projectile detonated inside the house, as did the third, likely killing everyone inside. The pair of five thousand liter steel propane storage tanks adjacent to the house finished the job when they ignited in a massive fireball that erupted several hundred feet into the air, with a boom audible as far away as downtown Juárez.

Pausing for only a moment to watch the house engulfed in flames, *El Rey* carefully placed a tarot card bearing the familiar image of the King of Swords amongst the rocket launching tubes, taking care to wedge it so that it wouldn't blow away in the breeze. Satisfied with the result, he hurried back behind the wheel and tore off down the road in the direction he'd come. By the time any of the surviving guards could give chase he'd be long gone, and he was confident their enthusiasm for pursuit would be short-lived now that the head had been cut off the snake. *Chacho* was nothing more than an oily smudge in the crater that had been his *hacienda*, and with his black soul's journey to hell had also gone his eponymous cartel's fragile dominance.

The Russian-manufactured RSgH-1 rockets hadn't been easy to get in time, but Aranas' contacts had been able to locate several that had somehow walked away from a Russian armory a year earlier. A private jet had transported them from Europe to Mexico, and the rest was simple logistics. He needed every shot to count, and his experience with the RSgH-1 had been that they were accurate at far greater distances than the more common RPG-7, even though the Russian devices were much harder to find. Well worth the extra effort, in his opinion. Normally, he would have gone through one of his regular contacts in southern Mexico, but in the interests of time he'd chartered Aranas with locating them.

He sped down the final hundred yards of the track and took the turn back onto the larger paved road, effectively flying by the dead police at the checkpoint. He wasn't worried about an innocent vehicle discovering the cops – it was a rural highway, and in Ciudad Juárez, there was literally no chance that anyone who didn't have to be on the road would be driving after dark. Still, he knew that it wouldn't be too much longer before they were found by army troops heading to the ranch to see what had caused the explosions. By that time he'd be nearing the dirt airstrip where his escape plan waited. *El Rey* had arranged for a private plane to take him to Ciudad Obregón, where he would lay low for a few days until he could coordinate the logistics for the next phase of his mission – the execution of the Mexican president.

∾∿

Dinah was cooking in the kitchen when Cruz made it through the door, tired after another long day at the office. He was in plainclothes, it being Saturday, and even though he was only supposed to put in a short session he'd quickly gotten buried and nine hours had flown by. It was an occupational hazard that Dinah had grown accustomed to, although she didn't like it. But she knew Cruz wouldn't change, and so had incorporated the routine into their lives.

"I'm sorry, *mi amor*. I don't know how that always happens," he said as he entered the kitchen and planted a kiss on her exposed neck. She was shredding chicken she'd cooked. "What are you making? It smells wonderful."

"*Enchiladas mole*. I've been working on the sauce for hours. I kind of figured when you called at one and said it would only be a little longer that you'd get stuck for the rest of the day. It almost never fails," Dinah said as she moved to the sink to wash her hands.

"I know. I wish I could lay off some of the paperwork on a subordinate, but unfortunately it all requires my signature…"

She turned to him and threw her arms around his neck and drew her to him, kissing him passionately for half a minute. His transgression had clearly been forgiven.

Eventually they came up for air, and he smiled at her.

"You make the best *mole* I've ever tasted. Really. It's always a treat," Cruz said.

"You better say that. You're going to be eating it for a long time. I hope you're telling the truth…"

"I have no reason to lie. Other than self-preservation."

"Damned right. Now go get cleaned up. It'll be ready in fifteen minutes."

Cruz obligingly moved to the bedroom and shrugged out of the dress shirt and slacks he was wearing. After considering his watch, he decided to take a fast shower, and once dry, switched to comfortable old jeans and a sweatshirt. He padded back out into the dining area just as Dinah was placing plates on the table, next to two bottles of *Negra Modelo* beer. He pulled out one of the chairs and took a seat, sniffing appreciatively.

"It smells delicious," he proclaimed.

Dinah smiled. She loved cooking and looked forward to the weekends when she had time to make a meal from scratch. It was one of her hobbies, passed to her from her mother, and she considered herself very good at it. Cruz seemed to like it.

They ate, chatting about their plans for the next day. At Dinah's insistence, he'd stopped working Sundays, and they tried to plan something fun for their time together. Dinah had arranged to have lunch with another couple, friends of hers from the school where she taught second grade. Cruz got on well enough with them, and they'd agreed to meet at noon, and then catch a matinee of a movie Dinah wanted to see. Cruz would wear a baseball hat and sunglasses to lunch – his attempt at a disguise. Although he was known from the obligatory press conferences he was forced to attend when his task force had a major victory, he wasn't particularly distinctive looking, and could have been mistaken for thousands of other men of similar age. There wasn't a lot of risk that he'd be gunned down, especially since his whereabouts were secret and had been ever since the kidnapping incident ten months earlier.

Cruz cleaned his plate of every morsel and rubbed his stomach appreciatively while Dinah cleared the table.

"Have you given any thought to a date?" she asked as she placed the plates in the sink.

"A date?" Too late, Cruz realized his misstep. "Oh, of course. I was thinking maybe September? That will give us time to plan something…"

She gave him a curious look and then nodded. "I don't want anything big. Just a small ceremony, with close friends and family. And we can limit the reception to a few hundred."

Cruz stared at her.

"Kidding." She smiled.

He rose from the table with a look of clear relief on his face and moved past her to the refrigerator for a second beer. They hadn't really discussed the minutiae of the wedding, and he assumed that Dinah would handle things. Perhaps they needed to talk about it in more depth. He remembered from his first marriage that things could rush up on them, and if they didn't start soon, they'd be buried all summer playing catch up.

"Come here, my angel, and let's talk about the where's and how's of this. It's an important event, and I want to make sure it's perfect. As long as you show up, I'll be happy, so tell me what you're thinking and I'll do whatever I can to make it so."

He patted the area next to him on the sofa and admired Dinah as she rounded the kitchen island and came to him, a vision of beauty in his otherwise bleak and brutal world.

CHAPTER 13

Cruz strode through the doors of the CISEN headquarters, recalling the last time he'd been there. That meeting had been disastrous, with the heads of the Mexican intelligence service alternating between treating him like a slow child and laughing him out of the room, after he'd warned them that *El Rey* was targeting the American and Mexican presidents at a high-profile international financial summit.

Since then circumstances had changed because Cruz had been proved correct in his warnings. That had resulted in CISEN looking like incompetents, or worse, and in the wake of the event, Cruz's power and standing had markedly increased at the expense of CISEN, whose supposedly superior information-gathering apparatus had botched it. Missing the most serious assassination attempt in the nation's history would have been bad enough, but having been given clear notice by a ranking federal police captain in charge of the Mexico City cartel task force, and then ignoring it, had ended several careers. To say that bad blood still existed between Cruz and CISEN was an understatement.

Cruz was puzzled as to why he'd been summoned. None of his current operations or investigations were in an area where CISEN, Mexico's equivalent of the CIA and NSA, had any interest that he knew of.

Surprisingly, he was only kept waiting ten minutes before being shown into a conference room, where he was greeted by three high-level officials — none of whom he'd ever seen before, which wasn't surprising given that those he had met with on prior occasions were the same ones that had ignored his warnings about the assassination attempt.

A well-groomed man in his mid-forties, tall, with gleaming black hair and a trimmed goatee, stood and made introductions. Cruz noted the expensive cut of his navy blue suit and calculated that it probably cost a small fortune. He was Renaldo Rodriguez, the new associate director of CISEN, and the other two men were simply Stefan and Hector. By the looks of them, Cruz doubted those were their real names. No matter – he was now genuinely curious as to the meeting's purpose.

Rodriguez sat back and smiled, motioning to a thermos and cups on the table.

"Coffee, *Capitan*? It's some of the best Mexico has to offer."

"I'm sure it is. No, thank you. I'm fine," Cruz said politely.

Rodriguez shrugged, as if to say 'you don't know what you're missing', and poured himself a steaming cup. He didn't offer the other two any, and they didn't seem surprised.

"To what do I owe this unexpected pleasure?" Cruz began.

"You have developed quite a reputation over the last year as the 'go to' guy on anything related to the assassin, *El Rey*. I understand the task force specializing in catching him has been disbanded, correct? With its responsibilities transferred to you?" Rodriguez asked, obviously already sure of the answer.

"That's right. After three years of non-performance, the decision was made to shut them down and the resources shifted to my group," Cruz confirmed.

"And how is that going? Anything you can share with us?"

"The man seems to have disappeared after the event in Baja." Cruz didn't need to belabor what event he was referring to, given that it had caused a seismic shift within CISEN. "There hasn't been a hint of activity in almost a year now. We believe he's gone underground, and likely quit the game. Why?"

Rodriguez slid a folder across the desk to him, gesturing at it with his head. Cruz opened it and studied the brief report inside, then the photographs of the tarot card amidst the rocket launchers. He slowly looked up from the file.

"This was a few days ago. Why wasn't I notified?" he demanded.

"The army came across the card following the complete destruction of a house outside Ciudad Juárez from a rocket attack. The cartel chieftain *Chacho* Morenos was in the house. The army brought us the information, unsure of how to treat it. As soon as we got it, we called you."

Cruz regarded Rodriguez, sensing there was more.

"We also have picked up some disturbing news. There is an unconfirmed rumor from one of our assets that *El Rey* is back on the scene because he plans to assassinate the president," Rodriguez stated.

"Unconfirmed rumor? From where? I need more specifics than an *unconfirmed rumor*. You know that," Cruz admonished him.

'Hector' leaned forward. "*Capitan* Cruz, the asset in question is involved with the affairs of a group you're more than familiar with. The Sinaloa cartel. For his ongoing safety we have to keep the asset's identity confidential, even from you. But I can say that he is well placed in that organization, and we consider his intel to be of the highest quality," he said officiously.

"Can someone tell me why CISEN is involved with the Sinaloa cartel? Perhaps we can start there. I'm especially interested since I'm the head of the task force chartered with dealing with the cartels, and this is the first I've heard about any involvement," Cruz demanded.

Rodriguez shrugged again. "As you know, we have operations and investigations that are international in scope. This came about as a tangent to one of those operations. It's wholly unconnected to your efforts involving the cartels. I can't say anything more – it's classified. The important thing is that we're here, at this table, sharing intelligence about a suspected plot to assassinate the president, to be carried out by the man you are purported to be the expert on."

It came to Cruz in a flash. This was turnaround. Revenge for causing the disastrous reorganization in CISEN. They were saddling Cruz with a formal report of a plot to kill the president, exactly as he had done with them. If it turned out to be true, and he was unsuccessful at stopping it, Cruz would be in the crosshairs as having neglected his duty, not CISEN. It was perfect. Provide virtually no evidence other than a rumor, refuse to corroborate it due to national security concerns, then pass the whole pile off to Cruz, noting scrupulously that he, and only he, was responsible for following up. Cruz had survived countless bureaucratic battles, and he understood instinctively what was being done, as well as why.

Payback.

"I will need everything you have on this. If it's classified, I will need to get an appropriate clearance. I can't operate without all the information, so whatever needs to be done, let's do it."

Rodriguez shook his head. "I'm afraid it isn't that simple, *Capitan* Cruz. We can't hand out top secret clearances to just anyone – not that you are just anyone, or in any way suspect. It's just that our procedure is–"

"I don't care what your procedure is. You invented it, so you can make an exception to it. If you don't feel like doing that, I can just go directly to the president and have him instruct you to do so. Either way, to protect him, I need all the information, so we can do this the civil way, or the adversarial way." Cruz paused. "Considering CISEN's performance on the last presidential assassination attempt, I would have thought that you would have figured as much by now. But it's immaterial to me how we get it done. I've told you what I need."

Rodriguez scowled and leaned to Stefan, murmuring for a few moments. Stefan whispered back to him. Rodriguez straightened up, and then addressed Cruz.

"I'll see what we can do. This is highly irregular, and I can't make a call on it without speaking with the director."

"Either get him on the phone, now, or I'll be calling my superior, who will be calling the president's people. I don't want to waste any more time. For all we know, this could be taking place today. Which reminds me – I'll need a complete list of all the president's scheduled appearances. If you can't get that for me, I can get it from him myself. Frankly, it would look better from your end if you got it, because right now, to me it appears that you're handing me a hot potato with the bare minimum of information – and that's what my report will say. I've gone up against *El Rey* before, and I can assure you that if he's in the country and gunning for the president, that's as real and imminent a threat as if we just found a bomb under the president's bed. Maybe more so. Now make the call, or I will," Cruz demanded.

He'd had about enough of their ploy and didn't have any reason to be nice. He also wanted to let them know he was onto their game and knew how to play it as well or better than they did.

More murmuring ensued, and then Rodriguez stood and excused himself while he made the call. Cruz stared at the two remaining men, who busied themselves scribbling cryptic notes. Five minutes later, Rodriguez returned with a sheaf of papers and a pen.

"You'll need to read all of this, and then sign. It is our official secrets act, which will subject you to prosecution if you divulge the top secret information we give you to anyone. It's mandatory, I'm afraid. Take your time going through it and feel free to ask me any questions that come up. But it can't be modified, so you either sign it, or I can't divulge the info you want. Sorry," Rodriguez said in a tone that clearly suggested he wasn't, and that he hoped Cruz wouldn't sign.

Cruz took the pages and spent the next fifteen minutes poring over them. Finally, he signed.

"All right. Now who did you get this information from, and why do you believe it's credible?" he asked.

"I will have it typed out for you so you have it in writing, and so you can acknowledge receipt of it. Once you've done so by signing a copy, you can ask any questions that come up." Rodriguez nodded at Hector, who left the room.

A few minutes later he returned with two pieces of paper. Cruz signed one, and then read it. Three sentences.

"This is Aranas' main arms dealer! We've been trying to nail him for years. He's working for you?" Cruz asked incredulously.

"I wouldn't say he's working for us. He exchanges information when it is advantageous for him to do so. This was a particularly interesting piece, I think you'll agree. He sourced the rockets used in the Juárez attack, and apparently he's secured a few other items for Aranas that he believed were for the same contractor – *El Rey*. Aranas has known the arms dealer for over twenty years, and apparently let slip that the new president's ongoing persecution of Sinaloa would soon be coming to an end. He believes it's because of the assassin."

"So this is an inference. He's *inferred* that Aranas has hired *El Rey* to kill the president? He wasn't told that he was..." Cruz clarified.

"It is an inference. Aranas didn't come right out and say, 'I've hired *El Rey* to take out the president'. But the arms dealer felt that was a very distinct possibility based on the discussions they'd had," Rodriguez affirmed.

"Do you see the problem here? You have a snitch, who is trying to curry favor with you, who passes on a speculation that is highly suspect. I agree that it bears looking into, but it's a far cry from confirmation of a legitimate threat. And what were the 'items'? I came to you with far more compelling information than this, and you ignored it..." Cruz pointed out.

"Yes. And we were wrong to do so. That's why the gentlemen who ran this operation are no longer in charge. As to the items, besides the three Russian rocket launchers, he got several radio-transmitter triggering devices, two types of plastic explosive, several fragmentation grenades, and a silenced pistol."

"Hmm. The plastique and the radio-transmitters are ominous." He pushed back from the table. "All right. When can I get the president's schedule?" Cruz asked.

"I can e-mail it to you before the end of the day. It will take a few hours for the president's staff to send it over. But you will have it just as soon as I do," Rodriguez promised.

"Let me ask you a personal question. Why are you working with an arms dealer who is supplying weapons to the cartel thugs, when you know they're going to use them to kill police, soldiers and innocent civilians? Help me understand that," Cruz asked Rodriguez.

"I'm afraid I can't answer that – it's not part of your need to know. But if it's any consolation, I find it as repugnant as you do," Rodriguez said.

"I'm sure that's a consolation to the families of those who get killed by the cartels, as well as the innocents who are slaughtered whole cloth." Cruz glared at him. "One last question, and then I'm finished. Did the arms dealer have any idea of timing?"

"No, but based on what he was sensing, Aranas was behaving as though the crackdown on his cartel wouldn't last much longer. I would consider that it is likely to happen sooner than later."

"Have you briefed the president's staff yet?"

"We felt you would be the best person to do so, seeing as your credibility on *El Rey* is high…" Rodriguez admitted.

Cruz folded the classified summary and put it into his shirt pocket, then stood and shook hands. He was still irritated by these spy types' arrogant superiority, but he had to admit these three were better than the last bunch.

His car picked him up outside, and he sat in the back seat, lost in thought. If *El Rey* was gunning for the president, he knew that there was practically nothing on earth that would stop him. He still remembered his failure at the financial summit, and the quirk of fate that had saved the day. He didn't think they'd be that lucky again.

Which meant that Cruz needed to begin a manhunt for *El Rey* and focus on protecting the president at all costs.

His day had just gone from lousy to miserable.

El Rey, back in action, going after the nation's newly elected leader. And only Cruz standing in his way.

It didn't get any worse than that.

CHAPTER 14

"Lieutenant, what do you have for me?" Cruz called to Briones.

"We'll be ready for you in the conference room in five minutes, sir," Briones responded.

"All right."

Cruz had called for daily staff meetings at the end of each day since starting the *El Rey* working group within his task force. He stood up, stretching. It had been a long afternoon, and for every step forward it seemed like they encountered another obstacle. Cruz moved to the coffee pot near the entrance of his office, and after pouring his fifth cup, walked through the maze of cubicles to the meeting room. When he entered, a dozen faces swiveled to greet him with worried looks. He didn't waste any time with preamble.

"Have we narrowed down the possible public appearances? Which looks the most likely to be our man's ideal scenario?" Cruz asked the room in general.

Briones cleared his throat. "For the last four days, we've been working with the president's staff, and there are only two appearances that look good for *El Rey*. The first is a public speech on the steps of congress in two weeks, and the second is Easter Mass at the Mexico City Cathedral in three weeks. Obviously, the congress speech presents far greater danger due to it being open air for a fair amount of time, so that's the one we're focusing on."

"Have we picked up on any buzz on the streets?" Cruz asked.

They had returned to shaking down every snitch they knew, hoping for a lead. It was a long shot, but they had to turn over every stone.

There was no way of knowing which seemingly inconsequential bit of information would prove to be the one that led them to him. That's how it had been the last time they'd been on *El Rey*'s trail, although then, as now, whiffs of him were few and far between.

Eldiarez, a chief in the plainclothes team, shook his head. "Not really. We've been circulating his photo in the hopes that something triggers, but for now, nobody knows anything," he announced glumly.

"What about leaning on our contacts on the periphery of the Sinaloa cartel?"

"Not a whisper," Eldiarez told him. "If Sinaloa is behind an attempt on the president, it's the best kept secret they've got. Which isn't surprising given that it would have come straight from Aranas, who probably wouldn't have broadcast the fact. Every time we arrest one of their men, we give them the third degree, but so far there's not much to report. That isn't surprising considering that anyone rolling on Aranas would be a dead man. Even if someone did know something, it's unlikely they'd volunteer it."

"We're also watching every airport and bus station," Briones offered, "with the photograph being widely circulated, but you know how that goes…"

Cruz did indeed. The likelihood of a professional of *El Rey*'s caliber slipping up and getting caught through the rookie mistake of not altering his appearance so that it didn't match the known photo of him was exceedingly slim, but they didn't have much else to go on, so it was another checklist item. The whole thing smacked of going through the motions, though. Unless they got some kind of a break, all they were doing was taking the predictable steps *El Rey* would expect, bringing their possible success chances close to zero.

Cruz scowled at the room. "We need to do better than this. We're going on five days since the tip came in from CISEN, and we're no further along than we were then. I know you're all doing everything you have been asked to do, but we need to push the envelope and be more aggressive. I'm not sure how to move this along, but my sense is that we're currently dead in the water. Am I wrong?"

Briones tilted his head. "What about the original lead? Can't we put pressure there? That seems to be our only viable option at the moment."

"I'm meeting with some people this evening to discuss exactly that, but for now, consider it a dead end. It was picked up as chatter, so there's nowhere to push. We just have to wait and see if we get anything more," Cruz warned.

He couldn't tell anyone about the true nature of the source, or the identity – hell, he couldn't even hint that there was a source. But Briones had it right – for all CISEN's reticence, they needed to lean on the arms dealer if they were going to get anywhere. Cruz had a six p.m. meeting scheduled to broach that very topic, although he wasn't expecting much to come out of it. Still, it couldn't hurt to tighten the screw on CISEN.

"All right. I need everyone to get creative. If the president gets killed, it will be because we didn't do enough. That's the bottom line. I have our friends at CISEN looking at financial transactions involving known Sinaloa entities on the off chance there's some sort of a money trail, and I have to believe that if we focus enough energy on the two events, we'll figure out how he's planning to make his attempt. Bring me anything, no matter how seemingly inconsequential. Even if it's a gut feel or a hunch. Because, as of now, we've only got a few weeks. That's all I have," Cruz concluded.

He had a sinking feeling as he scanned the resigned faces of his subordinates. He remembered the last time they'd been hunting *El Rey* – it had been a needle in a haystack, regardless that they'd been sure he was going to make his move at the financial summit. This time, they didn't even know when, or even if, he would act.

Cruz shook off the sense of despondency, squaring his shoulders as he stood up. It wouldn't do for his men to see him in despair. A good leader always projected strength and confidence, even he didn't feel it.

Briones joined him as he walked back to his office. "Not much, huh? Is there any chance you'll be able to get CISEN more involved?" he asked.

Cruz shook his head. "I've been on the line with the president's people twice a day, and they feel like they have a good handle on the security aspect, which means nothing to me. And CISEN is being their usual self. They act like we don't matter, which maybe in their universe we don't. Cross your fingers because I'm not expecting a lot of further cooperation," Cruz admitted.

His limp was a little more pronounced today. Even after the physical therapy, when the weather changed it could hurt.

Briones slowed his pace to match Cruz's. "We need to do something, because as it sits, we're stalled, sir."

"Agreed. It seems like this week is going to be a write-off. I'll let you know if anything positive happens." Cruz slurped the now-cold coffee he had been nursing and retreated into his office, dreading the meeting that evening with the state's intelligence service.

❧

San Salvador, El Salvador

Lush fields of coffee plants rolled over the grass-topped hills, their full, leafy finery swaying in gentle time to the caress of the light breeze. Workers dotted the green-hued expanse, harvesting the beans. A smear of white clouds lingered over the mountain top, offering welcome shade for the laborers toiling in the field.

This was one of Aranas' hideaways, in the mountains on the outskirts of the capital city – a working coffee plantation well away from prying eyes, in a country distant enough from Mexico for the cartel chief to be safe from attack or capture. He paid off all the local law enforcement groups, including the government functionaries, so El Salvador, as well as Guatemala and Honduras, were safe havens.

The colonial home had breathtaking views, and only one winding approach road, which was heavily guarded by sentries under orders to shoot first and ask questions later. The locals stayed well away, for good reason, making it one of the most private areas in the region.

Aranas sat on the expansive patio, watching the laborers go about their backbreaking tasks as he sipped rich brew from a Delft china cup. It was a miraculously beautiful day, and he felt strangely at peace – as he always did when at this home.

A man cautiously approached from inside the house, taking care to close the wooden French doors behind him to keep any bugs out as he stepped onto the veranda. "*Don* Aranas, we have more information on the task force that has been set up to hunt *El Rey*. It's being headed up

104

by Romero Cruz, and it has committed significant resources to finding our operative. Photos are everywhere, and they've stepped up activity."

Jacinto Felestero was one of Aranas' trusted deputies, who had been with him for as long as he'd been the head of the cartel – over two decades.

"How did they get on to him? Did we ever discover that?" Aranas asked.

"No. Cruz is playing that very close to his chest. All we know is that they're in a state of high alert and believe he will strike at one of two possible events within the next month."

"That complicates things. Somehow they now know *El Rey* is targeting the president, which is unacceptable. There aren't many places such information could have come from. My inner circle, or *El Rey*'s contacts. I can't believe that one of his people, whoever they are, tipped off the *Federales*. That leaves my group – a disturbing idea, obviously. There are only four among us who knew. Including you, Jacinto."

Jacinto's face darkened. "*Don*, I swear on my mother's grave, I haven't spoken with anyone about it..." The danger of being suspected was obvious.

"I know. I'm not saying I think it was you. I'm saying that the circle who knows is small, and all are trusted beyond any doubt. Perhaps one of them murmured the wrong words to a mistress? Or made a call on a line that has been compromised? It's a shame our source in Cruz's group can't get us better information – I'd like to put a stop to any further leaks," Aranas speculated. "No matter. I think we need to throw a wrench into the government's hunt for *El Rey*. I have an idea. I know this man Cruz, and I've also gathered a fair amount of information about him. I believe he has a weak spot."

Don Aranas pushed his empty coffee cup away from him and glanced up at the thinning clouds as they relented to the piercing rays of the sun. He invited Jacinto to sit, and laid out his plan.

If everything worked out well, Cruz's life would become extremely complicated within a few days, and the search for the assassin would be the last thing he'd be focused on. It was simple, and effective. Create a bigger problem for the man, and he'd shift his energy to solving that one.

It was human nature. And Aranas was a post-grad student of human nature.

Yes, Cruz would soon be otherwise occupied.

࿈

Mexico City, Mexico

Cruz stared across the table at Rodriguez, astounded by what he was hearing. This wouldn't do.

"I don't think I'm being clear," he began. "At the rate we're going, *El Rey* is going to be successful in getting to the president. While I understand that you may have some operation going that involves the arms dealer, I'm telling you that the commander in chief is going to get assassinated if I can't get help from you in putting pressure on him."

"It isn't that easy, *Capitan*. He's integral in an ongoing situation that is bigger than your hunt for *El Rey*. We've been working on it for years. Years, not weeks. And frankly, if we push him or threaten him, he could just go dark on us, and then everything on our operation collapses. It isn't that we don't want to help you. It's that we don't have any way to leverage the man, so we can only politely request more help and see what he delivers," Rodriguez explained.

"How about if you give me his name, and within an hour I'll haul his ass in and throw him into an interrogation cell for a week? That won't require anything from your side and could seem to be completely unrelated to anything you're doing."

"His first phone call would be to us, netting the same end result. If we didn't get him out, he'd never work with us again. If we did, just a whiff of him having been in custody might terminate his usefulness to Aranas, and he'd be found floating in a river somewhere. No, the lousy truth is that this is far too delicate a situation to handle that way. I'm sorry. But he's off the table," Rodriguez concluded.

"I can go to the president."

"If you thought that would help, you already would have. We both know that. And even if you did, once he understood the scope of the operation, he'd shoot you down, and then we'd be right back in this

106

room. So how about we cut to the chase and think constructively?" Rodriguez sat back and steepled his fingers. "Here's what I propose. I can set up a working group within CISEN to coordinate with you, and we'll put our resources to work with yours to see what we come up with. Pick two men from your side to work with ours; we will get them classified clearance, and then we can proceed more productively. We have the ability to do a wide variety of things that you'd require a judge to sign off on. Bugs. Bank record checks. Networking with other international intelligence services. I would imagine that could speed up your investigation considerably…"

Cruz studied him. It wasn't a bad idea, and was more than he'd thought he would walk away with. Much as he hated to admit it, Rodriguez was right. CISEN had a tremendous network and unilateral capabilities Cruz could only dream of as a police agency. Even with the powers of his task force, he could only do so much. CISEN working with his team could be a game changer.

He nodded. "Fair enough. I'm not going to lie to you. We're not seeing the kind of progress I would hope for so far, and could use any help you can offer. Right out of the gate, if you have a more complete list of Aranas' shell companies and attorneys, we could see if there's a payment scheme we've missed. How would you envision this working?" Cruz acceded.

They discussed the logistics of creating an internal task force for the next hour, and by the time Cruz walked out of the building, they had a good framework. He'd assign the men, and hopefully within a few days would see some results.

Rodriguez watched Cruz depart and shook his head almost imperceptibly. The man was a bulldog. It would be valuable to understand what his group was doing, but in the end, there was no way he could jeopardize any of CISEN's operations to help him. A working group would be perfect. It would create the illusion that CISEN was doing everything in its power, while giving them complete access to Cruz's intelligence, which could be useful in Rodriguez's planning.

At no point did he feel remorseful at refusing to pressure the arms dealer. He probably could have given them more than he had, but

Rodriguez wasn't about to risk his other project by pushing him. He'd ask the nice man politely for more intel, but beyond that there wasn't a chance in hell he would do anything to risk the relationship. Some things were bigger than Cruz's concerns over the president's safety. Regardless of who was president, CISEN needed to stay separate from the day-to-day operations of law enforcement. It was one of the harsh realities of the clandestine world – regimes would come and go, but the agencies would remain long after the masters they supposedly served had departed.

CHAPTER 15

Dinah fumbled with her shoes, then grabbed her purse and a pile of homework she'd graded, before returning to the dining room and kissing Cruz.

"Is there any chance you'll be home at a normal hour today, my love? Or should I plan on making another late dinner?" she asked.

Cruz sighed wearily. "I'd like to say yes, but with this latest *El Rey* situation, the truth is that I probably won't. It's added to my workload tremendously, and all the other stuff still needs to get done, too. So, plan on a late one, and I'll call you mid-afternoon with an update..."

She looked at the time. "Shit. I'm barely going to make it. I've got to go. I'll talk to you later today," she said, bolting for the door.

Traffic on the way to the school was terrible, and she sat in her little Ford Focus anxiously glancing at her watch, the radio tuned to the Top 40 Latin pop station to drown out the cacophony of honking horns that was a staple of Mexico City morning rush hour. It normally took her half an hour to reach the school, allowing for the gridlock, but today was worse than usual, and it was looking like she wasn't going to make it.

When she pulled into the parking lot adjacent to the school grounds, most of the usual slots were full, so she had to park at the back, increasing her travel time further. As she got out of the car, she barely registered the two men who approached her from the dark blue van that had double-parked a few spaces away, obstructing her view of the attendant. She had just locked her door and was turning around when her path was blocked by the larger of the pair – a menacing-looking man with heavy acne scars on his deeply-tanned face. Dinah instantly knew she was in trouble – kidnappings in Mexico City were routine, although she'd never been worried about herself because she wasn't wealthy, nor were any of her relatives. Usually it was those from prosperous families that were most in danger.

"Make a sound and I'll kill you," the man growled at her as his partner glanced around the area to confirm they were alone.

"I…please, I don't have any money. I can give you what I have, but it isn't much. I'm a teacher…" she said, shifting her bundle of papers and reaching into her knockoff Coach purse.

"You stupid cow. I don't want your fucking money. Now shut up and turn around."

She debated screaming, but knew it wouldn't do any good. She was alone in the lot, and the security guard was too far away to do anything. The man reached into his pocket and pulled out a pistol, reading the intention in her expression.

"Do it. Scream and I'll blow your head–"

His warning was cut off by a gurgle as a stream of pepper spray hit him full in the face. He thrashed around with his pistol, but his unseeing eyes were already swollen almost shut. His partner reacted quickly, but not fast enough. Dinah had already squeezed past the front bumper of her car and was running between the vehicles for the street entrance. *Thank God I wore flat shoes today*, she thought as she sprinted for the lot attendant's booth, still three hundred yards away. She thought she heard the sound of the van's doors slamming and the roar of its engine. She ducked into another aisle and continued her beeline for the street.

A gunshot erupted from behind her, and the window of a pickup truck a few feet from her head exploded in a cuboid spray of safety glass. She instinctively crouched lower and moved another aisle further away from the one the van was on, putting distance between herself and her assailants. Another shot punched a hole in the rear fender of an old Chevrolet Malibu she'd just run past – the shooter's accuracy was decreasing with distance.

Gasping for breath, she poured on a burst of speed and sighted a break in the walls that ringed the lot. It was just wide enough for her to squeeze through – she hoped. Dashing to the gap, she braved a glance at her pursuers and saw the van thirty yards away, with its passenger door swinging open as one of the men leapt out to chase her on foot.

Her dress caught on a fragment of rebar in the opening, tearing the fabric as well as the skin of her thigh. She involuntarily cried out at the pain from the abrasion and felt a trickle of blood running down her leg, but willed herself to keep moving. Dinah had seen the telltale shape of a pistol in the man's hand as he'd exited the vehicle and knew that she had to make it to the school or some other densely populated place if she was to be safe. She was only seconds now from turning the corner of the block where she knew there would be a crowd of parents and several traffic cops. Even though they didn't have guns, she had to believe that might scare the kidnappers off. And the gunshots would have attracted attention – it was only a matter of minutes before the area would be swarming with police.

Footsteps slamming against the pavement behind her spurred her adrenaline and urged her on, and within twenty seconds she was in the midst of a group of mothers dropping their children off for school. She dared another look back and saw the second man standing hesitantly forty yards away, as if considering whether to continue. Sirens wailed in the distance, and then the van screeched around the block, tires smoking from the momentum as it careened unsteadily. Dinah didn't wait to see the outcome of the man's internal battle and instead raced for the front entrance of the school. She heard screams from behind her and then another gunshot. A chunk of mortar flew off the wall a few inches from her shoulder before she was through the oversized double doors and sprinting down the hallway.

Lungs heaving, Dinah made a left at the second hall and tore down a flight of stairs, now limping as she moved towards her ultimate destination – a steel maintenance room door that was usually unlocked during school hours, but which she knew had a deadbolt on it.

She slammed into it with her shoulder and twisted at the heavy lever knob. It was open. Dinah slid through the opening and heard footsteps from above running down the hall, then she locked the door behind her before extracting her can of pepper spray in preparation to defend herself, if the gunman somehow made it through the door.

Ten agonizing minutes later, her cell phone rang, startling her in the darkness of the small room. It was the principal asking her where she was, and whether she was all right. The police were waiting at the entrance and had surrounded the building, and several of the parents had told the whole story of the chase, gunfire, and her disappearance into the school. There was no sign of the van or the men.

When she unlocked the door and opened it, she realized that her skirt was soaked with blood and that the ceramic tiles where she'd been crouching were slick with it. It was the last thing she saw before she crumpled to the floor, unconscious.

⁂›‸

"Dinah. Can you hear me?"

She opened her eyes, to see a very worried Cruz standing by her side. She tried to sit up, and then registered the IV line and the antiseptic smell. She was in the hospital.

"What...the last thing I remember..." she murmured.

"Take it easy. They have you on a drip. You bled a lot – it's a good thing you came out when you did," Cruz explained. "By the time the ambulance got there, you were in the danger zone."

With a noticeable effort, she focused and became more alert. "All from that little scratch?"

"You nicked an artery, my love. Thank God you didn't sever it. As it was, it was just a very small puncture along with the rest of the tissue, but that was enough."

"Did they find the men?" she asked in a feeble voice.

"No. Even with ten eyewitnesses, it will be hard. They know it was a blue Chevrolet van, DF plates, no markings or memorable detail. And we have a good description of the man who was chasing you..."

"Two men. I got the first one near my car with the pepper spray. He won't be doing much for the next few days – maybe you can put the word out to clinics and ophthalmologists," Dinah suggested.

Cruz looked at her with wonder. "Will do. Can you tell me anything more about him?"

"The first one was big. Maybe six feet tall, and heavy. Moustache, short hair, acne pock marks, around late thirties. Dark complexion. Wearing jeans and a green and yellow horizontally-striped polo shirt." Dinah had committed both assailants' descriptions to memory, even after all she'd been through. She seemed to strengthen. "And he should be about blind right now."

"Did they say anything? Tell me everything you remember."

Dinah spent the next five minutes giving him a detailed blow-by-blow of the attempted kidnapping and chase.

They were both startled by the door opening, and Lieutenant Briones stepping into the room.

"Hello, Dinah. We have to stop meeting in hospital rooms," Briones cautioned, recalling when she'd paid him a visit after he'd been shot ten months earlier.

"I agree," Dinah said.

Cruz waved him off.

"So it definitely wasn't a robbery?" he asked her again.

"No. I offered them money. They wanted me."

Briones and Cruz exchanged glances.

"Your car is in the farthest part of the parking lot from the street. Pretty remote," Briones observed.

"I was way behind schedule. The lot fills up quickly once the parents start arriving to drop off their kids. That's why I hate being late. One of the many reasons," she said, and lay back, closing her eyes. "I don't understand why these animals can operate in places like this, and nobody can do anything about it."

"The real question is whether you were a target of opportunity, or whether they were after you, specifically," Briones said, exchanging another glance with Cruz.

Her eyes popped back open. "Me? Why go after me? I don't really have anything. I'm a schoolteacher..."

Which wasn't entirely true. She'd inherited some money from her father, but she was hardly wealthy. Kidnappers usually went after the relatives of rich business people or politicians – people who could come up with hundreds of thousands, or millions of dollars, at short notice. Although there was a troubling trend of gangs snatching random well-dressed targets in the hopes of extracting tens of thousands for a day's work, or keeping their abductees in a car trunk for a week while they forced them to extract cash from their ATM on a daily basis.

"And, Lieutenant, they were shooting at her. That's fairly rare," Cruz stressed.

"True. That actually smacks of amateur. Someone who hasn't thought through the situation and gets spooked. Maybe when she hit the man's partner in the face with the pepper spray it infuriated the man with the gun. Maybe he's just a nutcase. It doesn't make a lot of sense to attempt to kidnap someone and then try to gun them down. You either want them alive for ransom, or you want to kill them. They could have just shot Dinah by the van if that had been their intent. They didn't. So this seems more like improvisation than anything, which, to me, says they weren't organized," Briones countered.

"There's no way of knowing, unfortunately. I'm going to assign a patrol to trail you for the next week. Just in case," Cruz said to Dinah. "It's one of the perks of being high in the *Federales*, I hear."

"Oh, honey, really, I don't think that's necessary," Dinah protested weakly.

"Probably not, but I'll feel better for it. So humor me."

"How long am I going to have to lie here?" Dinah asked.

"They said twenty-four to forty-eight hours. You lost a lot of blood," Cruz told her.

They continued speculating about the assault, but Dinah quickly tired. The ordeal had taken a lot out of her, and Cruz gestured with his head to Briones to get the door. He said his goodbyes, and once outside the room, walked slowly with Briones to the elevator.

"Does anyone know about Dinah and I besides you, and the other few people at work? Do you think she's being targeted because of me?" Cruz asked.

"I haven't told anyone, and I can't see the others doing so. Your dating life isn't a big topic on the job, frankly. I think that's a longshot. More likely is that she was just in the wrong place at the wrong time, and the shooter is a nutjob, or lost his cool. We've all seen enough of these where they kill the victim whether or not the ransom is paid. The line of work appeals to psychos. That's the likeliest."

"I still want a patrol car on Dinah, and a guard at the hospital. I agree that the likelihood of the attack being specific to her is probably extremely slim, but I'll feel better with an officer here. Maybe just having one on the floor would be enough. Please arrange for one round the clock," Cruz ordered.

Briones complied and was finishing the call by the time the elevator arrived at their floor.

CHAPTER 16

Guatemala City, Guatemala

Don Aranas stormed around the massive great room of his villa near the downtown city center, gesticulating as he reacted to the voice on the phone.

"What the hell are you telling me? You not only missed snatching her, but shot up a school? You couldn't have been more subtle? Maybe stormed into her classroom with machine guns, screaming my name?" He stopped pacing, listening to the explanation. "Don't you get it? There's no way to make this work now. We have nothing. Take the shooter out and dispose of him. Better yet, take the whole team out and dispose of them."

He entertained another few seconds of discussion before cutting in.

"Fine. Then let the driver live. I don't really care. But the two in charge of making this happen? I want them gone by lunchtime."

He stabbed the phone off and slammed it down on the coffee table. A young, beautiful brunette woman knocked on the door, worried about disturbing him. He looked up at her, framed by the late morning light so that her sheer robe was translucent, and waved her away. He needed to think. Pouting, she spun professionally on her six inch heels and sashayed back down the hall, long coffee-colored legs gliding as though on precision bearings.

Aranas plopped down in an overstuffed chair and fumed for several minutes before flipping open an elaborately-carved tabletop humidor and selecting a Cohiba cigar, rolling it between his fingers near his ear approvingly before snipping the end off with a cutter and lighting it. He puffed at it distractedly as he considered his options. What should have been an easy snatch had gone horribly wrong, which meant that he wouldn't get another chance.

He picked up the phone and selected a number from the contacts.

El Rey answered on the third ring.

"Yes?"

"Are you someplace you can talk?" Aranas asked.

"Always."

"There's a complication. I've gotten some disturbing news about a task force I need to share with you," Aranas began, and then tersely described the situation, complaining about that morning's bungled attempt on Dinah.

El Rey took it all in silently. "Nothing has changed," he finally responded.

"I'm glad you're so confident. They apparently got wind of the plan. I would have thought that would give you pause."

"I have always acted as though all facts were known. It changes nothing. The outcome will be the same. That's what you're paying for." *El Rey* hesitated. "Although I have need of an item or two that will require the greatest discretion and will no doubt be expensive."

Aranas' eyebrows rose when he heard the request.

"You're fucking kidding me. I mean, I'm sure I can get it, but in my experience it's not that easy. They tend to keep track of it," the kingpin warned.

"I will need it within a week."

"You still think you can pull this off?"

"Without a doubt. But tell me more about the girl. Have you received any news on where she is now?" *El Rey* asked.

Aranas was surprised. "Are you really interested? I can probably find out in seconds. But that opportunity is over. My men blew it," Aranas admitted bitterly.

"Perhaps. But it would be helpful to me if you could make enquiries. I have an idea."

Aranas called back after twenty minutes and gave him the information. Three hours later, *El Rey* left the apartment he was renting and took the elevator down to the parking garage, toting a brown paper grocery bag in his left hand. He made two stops in downtown Mexico City before proceeding to his ultimate destination, humming to himself. Out of every disaster came opportunity, if one knew how to adapt. This was a perfect example. Now he just needed to be patient, and perhaps he'd convert a negative into an opportunity.

ॐॐ

Mexico City, Mexico

The federal police officer sat at the far end of the hall, studying the nurses moving around the ward with approval. Some duty was desirable, some not. Watching the floor for threats to Dinah was definitely a plum position, even if some of the staff seemed perturbed by him being there. He'd originally sat in the corridor right by the room, but it wasn't wide enough to accommodate him as well as the gurneys and carts, and they'd made a position for him at the nurse's station, forty-five yards away. Over time, some of the cuter, younger nurses had warmed up to him, and by his third hour they were stopping in regularly to chat, there being not much else to do. Unlike intensive care, this was a quiet floor, at least by large hospital standards. A steady hum of physicians and staff buzzed around, doing whatever it was they did, and an occasional patient rolled by.

Around dinner time, a doctor in a white coat moved from room to room, and the officer became alert as he approached the woman's room. One of the nurses assured him that the physician was fine – he checked on the patients every four to six hours, marking off the forms affixed to clipboards outside every room. Satisfied that he had done his duty, the policeman relaxed again and took up his discussion with Yvette, a pretty petite twenty-four year old from Veracruz.

After another few hours the lights on the floor dimmed, and the ward moved into evening rhythm, with dinner gliding down the passageways on rolling carts. The officer was able to convince one of the orderlies to have the kitchen prepare him a meal, and he was ravenous by the time the tray made it to his position. He dug into the chicken enchiladas with gusto and was done within a few minutes, smacking his lips with satisfaction.

Two hours later severe abdominal cramping overcame him, and he sprinted for the restroom at the far end of the ward, barely able to keep from vomiting.

A maintenance man moved steadily down the hall, checking the air-conditioning grids with a laser thermometer. He smiled to himself as he watched the cop rush to the facilities and reasoned that he'd be occupied on and off for the rest of the evening. A little Visine in the man's drink and mixed in with the enchilada sauce had worked miracles – he'd be vomiting for hours.

He hummed as he verified the temperature of the air coming out of the duct and stopped into every room to ensure there were no anomalies. When he reached the woman's room, he checked the hallway and verified that the guard had departed once again for the comfort of the restroom before slipping through the door, closing it behind him.

Dinah looked up from the magazine she was reading and then returned to it when the man apologized and checked the airflow. It was only after a few seconds that something caused her to look up – he was standing closer, smiling at her, but with an expression that chilled the blood in her veins. He had a beard that obscured most of his lower face, but his eyes were disturbing. The first impression that came to mind was that they were dead.

She saw a flicker of something cross his expression, and he seemed to hesitate, and then spoke.

"Dinah. We don't have much time, so I'm going to make this short. I am known as *El Rey*. I am an assassin. The reason I'm here is because I need your help. If you scream or sound any kind of an alarm, you'll be dead within seconds. If you know of me, you know I'm not exaggerating," he said in a reasonable, calm voice.

Her hand crept under the sheet to the nurse call button as she absorbed his statement.

"I thought I just told you that you'll be dead if you do anything foolish. Calling the nurse would qualify. Now if you want to continue breathing, put both your hands where I can see them and listen carefully to me. I have a proposition for you," *El Rey* cautioned.

She froze and then slid her hand where he could see it. The other still clutched the magazine, gripping it automatically.

"Wha…what do you want?" she blurted.

"I want you to live. I want you and your boyfriend – no, fiancé – *Capitan* Cruz, to have a long and healthy life. I want you to be married and happy and have newborn babies you love and care for. All of which I can help you with."

"I…I don't understand…"

"I know you live with Cruz. He's running a task force that's devoted to my deeds. I need you to pass me any and all information you can get – and it'd better be good. I'll know if you're working with him, or if you're holding out on me. Trust me on that – just as I knew what room you were in. And there is nowhere you will be safe if you fuck with me."

"I…there's no way I can do that. I can't betray him, and we don't discuss business." Dinah sounded stronger now. Defiant.

"Start." He studied her. "You seem very brave, so I can imagine that you don't fear that much for yourself. I mean, I'll kill you as well, but before I do, your lover will die an agonizing death. I'll make sure of it. I trust you know my reputation. I don't threaten, and I don't bluff. If you want Cruz to live, and not be tortured in the most horrible manner you can imagine, you'll do as I ask. If you don't, he'll die, and so will you. It's a simple proposal, really. Oh, and if you're thinking that he can protect himself, and you, consider the long list of extremely rich and powerful men who were wrong about their ability to be protected from me. It's not an option."

Dinah shook her head in anguished conflict. She couldn't.

"I know you're thinking that you can't do this, that it's wrong, and that some things are more important than remaining alive. But I can assure you that you're mistaken. I'm in the death business, and I can promise you that when you've seen as many die as I have, you realize that nothing is more important than what remains of your life." He seemed to grow impatient. "It's a choice of either ensuring your man lives, or dies. You get to decide that. Do you kill him with your pride, your arrogant vanity, or do you do what you must so he can live. That is the true test of love. I hope you make the right decision – if you don't help me, it won't change anything, except for you, and him. I'll still do what I do, the world will still turn, but he'll have been maimed and tortured before drowning in his own blood, as will you." He allowed that to sink in. "But that doesn't have to be the future. So decide, Dinah. Choose wisely."

She followed his words and saw the truth in his eyes. He wasn't threatening. He meant every word, and it wouldn't bother him in the least to snuff their lives out.

It was an impossible choice.

He raised his eyebrows.

"You have five seconds, and then I make the decision for you." He smiled. "It was a pleasure meeting you, Dinah," he said and reached into his pocket.

"Wait. What…how do I know I can trust you?"

"Dinah, every day that you breathe from this moment on will be because I've kept my word to you. Every breath will be proof of my trust. And most importantly, nobody is paying me to kill you. This is merely a means to an end – a way to make my life easier. As I said, I'll still do my job, but it would be better for me if I knew what your boyfriend was up to. And I can guarantee that nobody else tries to kidnap you. If you're helping me, however reluctantly, they don't need to kidnap you to get his cooperation. This is a win-win, Dinah. You get what you want – a life with Cruz – he gets what he wants – life with you – and I get what I want. Everybody wins."

Her face collapsed, and her shoulders hunched in humiliated resignation. She'd chosen. Now she would need to live with herself.

"How do I contact you?"

ᕬᕠ

El Rey exited the room and walked to the next air-conditioning vent, dutifully measuring the temperature. The guard took no notice of him, being otherwise occupied trying to contend with his cramps, and within thirty seconds the maintenance man had finished his duties and moved through the doors to the emergency stairs.

El Rey was a little shaken by the similarity between Dinah and his first and only love, Jasmine. They could have been twins, separated at birth. It was uncanny. He'd never seen anything like it. She was older, maybe four or five years, but still – the resemblance was more than striking.

Perhaps it was some sort of an omen? Not that he believed in such things, but the odds against two people looking so...exact...were astronomical. If there were a deeper meaning, what could it be? Was he meant to meet her for some reason?

He quickly dismissed the speculations. They were foolishness and would do nothing but distract him. And he needed to stay focused. The clock was ticking, and his date with the president was rapidly approaching. A date that wouldn't be denied.

Whatever the case with Dinah, who he was and what he did wouldn't change.

He was the reaper, the bringer of death.

And he would be victorious.

CHAPTER 17

Tampico, Mexico

The small cargo ship was tied to the long concrete wharf next to the massive dry dock boatyard on the *Rio* Panuco. The oil refinery next door dwarfed everything else on the ugly waterfront, and huge tankers rested at their berths as they on-loaded oil. It was a muggy evening, one of many for the town, and the river mouth that was the entrance to the port was redolent of decay and pollution, raw sewage and chemicals combining to create a toxic stew. Rust streaked the burgundy steel hull of the hundred-eighty foot ship, from which a Panamanian flag hung limply off the stern. The name was barely legible for the decay. *Toledo.*

Three SUVs swung into the dark parking lot, their headlights off but moving at high speed, and seventeen heavily-armed men leapt from the vehicles once they pulled to a stop, running in a crouch the remaining twenty yards from the lot to the gangplank entrance. After a few moments the barking report of assault rifles greeted them from the gunmen on the vessel, and several of the newcomers uttered distressed grunts as the slugs found home. The attackers returned fire, and soon there was a full-fledged gun battle underway, with bursts of shooting angrily punctuating the dark of night. The bodies of fallen men lay scattered near the trucks, with the ten remaining assailants having taken cover behind several dumpsters on the periphery of the dock.

The whoomp of a grenade exploding on the ship was quickly followed by another. The two men clutching M203 grenade launchers affixed to their M4 rifles peered determinedly from their shelter nearby, surveying the damage they'd inflicted. All but two of the dozen guns firing from the vessel had been silenced, and the grenade launchers sighted carefully at either end of the ship, where the remaining defenders were ensconced. Two detonations sounded nearly simultaneously, momentarily blinding them, and then the old freighter fell silent, straining against its lines from the tow of the current.

The surviving attackers approached the gangplank with grim determination, wary of another salvo from the boat. Just as they were moving up the ramp, two pickup trucks filled with armed men screeched into the lot and sped towards them, the standing men in the truck beds firing into the attackers. A swath of death rattled the sides of the hull, denting the aged metal while leaving trails of blood and flesh on the paint. The fully exposed assailants never stood a chance and were cut down by the latest arrivals in a hail of lead. Two of the SUVs peeled off and tore for the road, hoping to escape the new attackers. One made it, but the other exploded in a brilliant orange fireball as a slug ignited its gas tank, bathing the lot in a fiery glow.

As sirens sounded far in the distance, the men jumped from the trucks and ran for the ship. Within a few minutes they descended again, the leader shaking his head, helping one wounded man to the dock. Two more gunmen started down the gangplank carrying another man from the vessel, who was moaning and bleeding from shrapnel wounds. They were loading the two survivors onto the vehicles when a small convoy of military trucks approached from the road – Humvees with fifty caliber machine guns mounted on turrets, plus four armed personnel carriers followed by three large trucks filled with soldiers.

The army weapons opened up, shredding the bodies of the second group of armed men as they futilely returned fire at the military vehicles. The heavy army guns sounded like anti-aircraft artillery as they boomed across the water. The leader of the men who'd taken the ship by storm sprinted for the nearest vehicle, but he was seconds too late. The driver's head tore apart while he was frantically trying to get the vehicle in gear, and the leader was shredded into a bloody pulp by the relentless shards of death.

Rounds from the ship's defenders tore into the soldiers as the deadly convoy rolled to a stop, and one of the combatants with the grenade launchers successfully drew a bead on the lead Humvee. The vehicle exploded in a burst of debris, the men inside vaporized by the warhead. The second grenade launcher operator prepared to fire his round, but was cut down by a lucky burst from one of the soldiers' M16 assault rifles, his chest riddled with smoking bullet holes. His finger reflexively jerked the trigger of the launcher as he went down, sending the projectile in a smoking arc through the air in the direction of the refinery and the shipyard.

The explosion from the grenade's impact created a minor firestorm in the dry dock when it landed and ignited a pool of oil in the concrete work area. Flames danced in the darkness, illuminating the corpses of the dead and dying lying on the pavement, creating a hellish panorama. The soldiers made quick work of mopping up the rest of the resistance, and within five minutes, silence pervaded the killing field. A total of forty-seven cartel fighters had been slaughtered, with no survivors. Military casualties were six wounded, twenty-one dead.

Four hundred kilos of uncut Colombian cocaine were found ferreted away in the ship's cargo amidst coffee beans and produce. Street value was eleven million dollars, which worked out to be a hundred and sixty four thousand dollars per corpse, not counting the cost of vehicles, equipment and weapons.

The average worker in mainland Mexico earns a hundred and sixty dollars a month.

֍֍

Guadalajara, Mexico

Don Aranas was sitting with two of his captains having breakfast. They were gathered in the smaller of his two dining rooms at a nineteenth century red cedar table in his lavish retreat when the call came in. He listened intently, asked a few questions, and then issued a terse instruction before hanging up. He turned to his men, who had stopped eating once he'd begun his phone conversation.

"Los Zetas cartel attacked one of our shipments in Tampico. We lost four hundred kilos and all our men. Apparently it was a big deal.

Soldiers showed up and it turned into a war," he recited dryly, returning to his food.

"What the fuck? *Don*, this can't be tolerated. We need to hit these pricks hard and fast. They need to learn the price of taking us on," Mauricio, the plumper and younger of the two, blurted.

"I know. I told them to move against Los Zetas today. We know of several of their meth plants in Quintana Roo we can take out. I already gave the order." *Don* Aranas sipped his coffee. "They lost all their men in the attack as well. So nobody benefited from this...except the newspapers."

"These events are becoming too regular for my liking. If it isn't the police or army, it's one of our rivals. There was a time when this would have been unimaginable. Now it's business as usual. We have to do something," Hernandez, the other captain, said, spearing his eggs with his fork for emphasis.

"I think it's safe to say that this is temporary. It's all related. Once the military backs off, the other cartels will get the message and retreat. I'm confident that the push to eradicate our operations will end sooner than later. Call it a hunch," *Don* Aranas assured them with a humorless smile. He waved to the woman at the brightly-tiled kitchen island and motioned for more orange juice. "You're right. This can't continue. But don't worry. Things have a way of working out."

Quintana Roo, Mexico

Fourteen miles outside of Cancun, a dilapidated private ranch sat two miles from the desolate road connecting the Mayan ruins of Chichén Itzá and the highway that ran along the southern coast. A rusty chain secured in place with a padlock hung across the pale dirt track that led to the compound. Two armed men were nestled among the trees, taking shelter from the sweltering rays of the angry sun, bored from months of guard duty where nothing happened. One of them sat on the ground, smoking a hand-rolled cigarette, while the other recounted his weekend in Cancun at one of the strip clubs. It had been a raucous evening, and he was boastful of his prowess. The older man cackled as he exhaled a long plume of smoke into the air, nodding appreciatively at the younger man's exploits.

The storyteller was surprised when a hole appeared in the older man's forehead, mid-exhalation, and he had almost gotten his Kalashnikov AK-47 swung around when two silenced rounds found him, knocking him against one of the scrub trees, dead before he hit the ground.

A lone figure in jeans and a cowboy hat approached through the brush, and when he was a few feet away, fired another round into the second man's head for good measure. He fished a telephone out of his shirt pocket, muttered into it, and peered down the long winding white sand drive. Several vehicles pull up to the barrier a few minutes later. A man hopped out of the back of one of the vans with bolt cutters and expertly severed the lock's shaft. The two vans pulled down the track, and the man re-attached the chain, then trotted after the vehicles to resume his position in the rear cargo area of the second van. The man in the cowboy hat walked to the passenger door of the lead vehicle and hopped in, carrying the two assault rifles he'd retrieved from the dead guards with him.

The vans inched down the track until they were roughly three hundred yards from the ranch, over a small rise and around a bend. They stopped and disgorged twenty men, armed with a smorgasbord of assault rifles – Kalashnikovs, M4s and M16s, Heckler and Koch HK416s. Nobody spoke as they moved carefully off the road and into the surrounding trees. The leader of the group removed his cowboy hat and tied a navy blue bandana around his hair to absorb any sweat, and then motioned to the men to split up in two groups. He prowled closer to the buildings, followed by his group, the second bunch barely visible fifty yards off to the right. Once they made it over the ridge, he counted eight guards loitering around outside the ranch's large rustic barn, weapons slung over their shoulders or leaning up against the wooden ramshackle walls.

The leader made an abrupt gesture with his left hand as he was sighting in with his rifle clenched in his right, and then opened fire. It was no contest – the guards collapsed in bloody heaps onto the dirt, dead before having a chance to shoot back. Once they were all down, the attackers stopped firing and raced to the buildings, the team on the right approaching the ranch house, wary of more sentries.

An old man appeared in the doorway brandishing a battered shotgun and took a potshot at one of the assailants, liquefying his chest with a load of buckshot. He pumped the reloading mechanism to try for another of the attackers, but a bullet caught him in the abdomen, ending his brief resistance. The area went silent again, then three women bolted from the back of the barn, running for their lives. All three were cut down by gunfire before they made it thirty yards.

When the bandana'd leader kicked in the barn door, he was greeted with a few pistol shots from within, one of which tore through his left shoulder. He tumbled to the hard dirt floor, firing even as he dropped, and caught the shooter in the torso, ending the failed defense. His men shouldered through the doorway after him, but all held their fire – the remaining occupants of the barn were unarmed, and mostly female, with a few young men in their twenties interspersed.

The leader stood, and after briefly checking his wound, barked a series of orders. The women shrieked in panic, and one of the young men began sobbing. The armed men rounded them up and herded them outside, while the leader surveyed the methamphetamine laboratory. Large drums of liquid sat to one side, and along the far wall were two large metal reactor containers and assorted processing hardware, including a number of industrial ovens. The liquids were all marked flammable, and the leader knew from practical experience that the entire compound would go up like a natural gas explosion when detonated, leaving toxic residue throughout.

He winced from the pain of the wound and grabbed some matting material off a work table and stuck it inside his shirt, where it would staunch the flow of blood until one of his men could rig a field bandage. It was a crude improvisation, but an effective one. This was not the first time he'd taken a bullet, so he was familiar with the pain. He gauged the amount of bleeding and grunted. He'd make it. This time.

Two shots echoed from the interior of the ranch house, followed by the distinctive chatter of a Kalashnikov, and then the shooting stopped.

His men must have found more people inside. There was to be no quarter given, no mercy shown. Anyone on the grounds was an enemy.

He spun and exited the barn, where nine women and two men were kneeling in front of the house in the harsh morning sun, most of the women crying in terrified gasps. He studied them dispassionately, many of them clearly of Indian extraction, and then nodded to his second in command, who pulled a cell phone from his shirt and made a call. The two vans rolled down the dirt road to the house and skidded to a stop in a cloud of dust. Two of the men moved to the van side doors and slid them open. When they turned from the interior, one held a machete and the other an aluminum baseball bat.

The task was finished within a few minutes, and the men loaded back into the van after carting sixty-two one kilo packages of crystal meth out of the barn and wedging them into the cargo area of the second van, cutting the space for passengers by half. It was a tight fit, but nobody complained. It was just a matter of time until the gunshots attracted the military, even in this rural area, so everyone was anxious to get on the road.

The second in command jogged over to the barn and pulled a pin from a hand grenade. With a grunt, he tossed it through the doorway and then ran for the vans. He made it in seven seconds. The vehicles were pulling away when a huge series of explosions blew the structure apart, a massive fireball billowing into the sky as the drivers accelerated dangerously down the rustic trail in a white haze of dust.

CHAPTER 18

Briones stood in Cruz's office, sorting through reports at the small circular table set up for three and four person meetings. They were expecting their counterparts from CISEN to appear at any moment, and Cruz multi-tasked as they waited, signing documents and creating piles of paper in his outbox. In the larger main room, uniformed men and women circulated between the cubicles, busy with the business of battling the cartels.

"Which do you think he'll hit?" Cruz asked Briones.

"I think the president's security detail has a nightmare with having an open speech on the congress steps. I don't know whose bright idea that was, but it stinks."

"Fortunately, that's not our problem. I don't envy the poor bastards responsible for it."

Briones nodded in accord. "It'll require a massive outlay of manpower to lock down every possible place in the area where an attack could come from. Sniper at up to a thousand yards, bomb threat, a gas attack...it's a lot of ground to cover. I'd recommend to them that they move it inside, like they normally would. This is a reckless risk."

"We've already had that discussion, and they're adamant that the president doesn't want to appear to be skulking around hiding. He's hell bent on being the brave bull in public, no matter how much difficulty it presents."

"Then we do what we can to track down *El Rey*, and pray a lot," Briones said.

The receptionist entered, followed by the two men from CISEN. Cruz motioned for them to take a seat. She closed the door behind them as she left, her offer of soda or coffee rejected by all.

Cruz greeted the pair, Dario Pareto and Solomon Quiniente, of unknown rank. Solomon seemed to be the senior of the two, but as with all the others of their ilk, they weren't big on sharing information, including what office they held. They shook hands with Briones and Cruz, and then Dario set a yellow legal pad on the desk and uncapped his pen.

Cruz launched into a ten minute briefing of their efforts to date, describing the steps that had been taken, and finished with a glance at Briones.

Solomon was the first to speak. "Then you have no leads?"

"No. Nobody has heard or seen anything, and even with extra staff on the streets, we're coming up empty. *El Rey* works alone, so it's not surprising. We've always believed that the best chance we have is another information leak from your side. We simply don't have any way of mounting this sort of a manhunt with any hope of success, given the lack of any new info," Cruz admitted.

"None of the photos or the arrests over the last week have resulted in anything?"

"No. I wish they had. Then we'd have something more material to discuss. As I told you at our last meeting, we could really use any help you can offer."

"I'm afraid nothing has surfaced on our end, either, *Capitan* Cruz. As always, we'll keep you informed, but this isn't an exact science," Dario said with a trace of condescension.

"Why is it that whenever we get together, we do all the reporting and you tell us zip? I mean, what good is our cooperation with CISEN doing us? So far we've gotten nothing but the initial warning, which has done us exactly zero good," Briones pointed out, echoing his earlier discussion with Cruz.

Solomon regarded Briones as though he'd just wiped him off his shoe.

"Well, probably because we have nothing else to report. I mean, that would be the logical explanation, no?" he said.

Cruz decided to defuse the situation before it escalated. He rose from his seat, signaling that the discussion was at an end.

"Gentlemen, it's always a pleasure. Please let us know if you hear anything at all that might be of interest, or if you have any suggestions on how we can be more effective in tracking *El Rey* down. You have considerably greater resources than we do, and no doubt more expertise in sensitive areas." Cruz motioned to the door. "Thanks for coming in."

Once the two CISEN men had left, Cruz fixed Briones with a neutral gaze. "I'd say that went well…"

"This is bullshit, sir. They're just here to get a status report and take it back to their bosses and are giving us nothing in return. How is having them in our hair helping us? It isn't," Briones griped.

"All true, but it won't do us any good to get into a fight with CISEN right now. They gave us the lead, probably to set us up to fail, so just accept it. I'll work with the president's staff to ensure he stays safe. If we can't track *El Rey*, then the least we can do is push the president to do the right thing. Even if he is as stubborn as a burro."

They finished up their routine reports and Briones departed, obviously unhappy with the situation.

Cruz studied his watch and rubbed his burning eyes. He was tired and wanted to leave. He didn't have the patience for these pointless sessions, or for his subordinate's emotional storms. Dinah had recovered and had been discharged from the hospital, and he'd committed to himself to spend more time with her – making them a priority. He'd been a workaholic for too long, and he knew it wouldn't fly, especially once he was married. He had to create boundaries, and one he'd decided on was to be out of the office by six every evening, unless it was an emergency. A real emergency – not one of the routine emergencies that seemed to be a daily occurrence.

He finished his paperwork and hurried out of the office, anxious to see her. She'd taken a few days off on her doctor's advice and was waiting at home. Dinah had seemed different after the incident, and Cruz attributed it to shock. Part of being a decent partner was to be there for her when she needed him, not at work till all hours.

His car took him into the underground parking garage at the condo, and he deliberately made more noise than necessary when he entered, so she'd know he was home. Dinah came out of the bedroom, looking ravishing in a red silk robe. Cruz registered with mild concern that she hadn't gotten dressed all day. That couldn't be good.

"*Hola, mi Corazon*. How's my heroic crime-fighter tonight? Did you conquer the world?" she asked playfully.

"No more than any other day. How are you doing?"

"Oh, you know. Just being lazy, taking it easy. Might as well relax on my days off."

"Why not? Hey, do you want to go out, or eat in? Or I can call for some food…" Cruz asked.

"Let's eat here. I can make something," she replied. Her tone and mannerisms were the old Dinah, but something was different. She seemed preoccupied, her mind elsewhere.

Over dinner, they made small talk, about how Cruz's day went, and the topic of what he was working on came up.

"Same as always, *mi amor*. Struggling to keep the world safe from the cartels," he said.

"Anything really interesting? You had mentioned *El Rey* a while ago. Is there anything happening with that?"

He told her about his progress, and she seemed to finally perk up, engaged and interested. That encouraged him, and he regaled her with the minutiae of the case, taking care to leave out anything classified.

When they finally got ready for bed, he was upbeat. Dinah had bounced back during their interactions during dinner, and now seemed as vital and immediate as ever. *Perhaps she was just depressed or frazzled from the attack and felt left out of his life*. It had to be hard being with a man who was married to the job. He vowed to include her in more of his daily affairs and make her feel more connected to him.

As they drifted off to sleep after making tender love, a solitary tear rolled down Dinah's cheek, unnoticed by Cruz as it absorbed into her pillow.

CHAPTER 19

As the morning wore on, CISEN headquarters in Mexico City was buzzing with activity. Solomon approached Rodriguez's office, tapped discreetly on the door and waited in the harshly illuminated hallway, holding a report. After an appropriate delay, he heard his boss call for him, and he entered, taking care to close the door softly behind him.

The office was large, furnished in a Mexican contemporary style, all angles and lines, fashioned from Danish birch and glass. A collection of modern oil paintings were featured on the main wall, abstract renderings with swatches of color on a dark gray background. Rodriguez sat behind his desk, his suit jacket hung on a hook on the back of the door, blindingly white shirtsleeves rolled up as he typed busily on his computer.

He glanced at the new arrival and indicated with a nod of his head that he should take a seat. Solomon complied, saying nothing.

"Yes, Solomon. What do you have for me?"

"A delicate development on the *El Rey* front, sir. Our asset is scheduled to deliver a package of material to the assassin tomorrow, here in Mexico City."

Rodriguez stopped typing and pushed back from the keyboard.

"That creates a problem for us, doesn't it?"

"I'm not sure I understand, sir."

"If we pass the information on to Cruz, the positive is that he may be able to apprehend the assassin. The negative is that the information couldn't have come from too many places, so it potentially jeopardizes our source – who is crucial to our ongoing operation, as you know," Rodriguez explained.

Solomon shook his head, but chose his words with care. "I don't see it quite that way, sir. I see it as us having information that could prevent a successful attack on the president by an assassin with a miraculous track record of hits. Which, if we didn't pass the info on, would have us looking like traitors – especially if the execution attempt was successful." He hesitated before continuing. "I see it as life in prison, versus doing what we have to." He slid the report across the glass desktop.

Rodriguez took the file, stood up and paced the length of his office, reading the two pages carefully. A few minutes later, finished, he stared at one of the paintings, as if the solution lay in its inscrutable brushstrokes.

"You have a point. But the danger to our ongoing operation is still very real. And the truth is that the likelihood of information leaking about our having this information after the fact is small."

Solomon took a breath, and realizing he was in delicate territory, put his most convincing disinterested expression forward. "So there's *only* a *small* likelihood that everyone who knows about this spends the rest of their lives in prison. That would be you, and I, and two others who have already seen the report – at least two others. I'm sorry, sir, but I don't like those odds. Bad news has a way of breaking at the worst possible time…"

Rodriguez frowned. His subordinate was right, unfortunately.

"Get Cruz on the line. Or better yet, have him come over here." He looked at his watch – a newish Rolex stainless steel Submariner. "Put a rush on it. We don't have much time."

Solomon stood and moved to the door. "I'll let you know if he's available to come in today."

"Do that. Tell him if he delays, it's on his head. That will get him motivated."

"Yes, sir."

❧

When Cruz returned from CISEN headquarters he practically ran from the elevator to his office. Briones spotted him as he crossed the floor, and after one look at his superior's face, stopped what he was doing and followed him in and closed the door.

"Call a meeting. Now," Cruz ordered. "All the *El Rey* task force heads. We just got a major break – this will probably be the best lead we've had on him since this case started."

"When are you available?"

"Five minutes."

Briones trotted back to his cubicle and hastily called the various members of the team who weren't in the field. A few minutes later, they were gathered in the conference room. Cruz entered and moved straight to the head of the table. He surveyed the expectant faces and then launched into a condensed version of the information he'd gotten from CISEN.

"Tomorrow, eleven o'clock, the assassin is to meet a cartel member to take delivery of some explosives and other items, at a machine shop six miles from here. Obviously, we need to take him. We can expect that he'll be disguised, so it's paramount that we be discreet. We can't circle the building with *Federales* until he's confirmed as being inside."

A hand shot up. "I know that area, sir. It's dense, even for Mexico City, and the buildings are packed together. Maybe we can get a few apartments or offices that are proximate and set up surveillance he won't see?"

"Excellent suggestion, Guerrero. But it has to be low key. Get a team to canvass the area once this meeting breaks up. Softy and gently. We don't want the neighbors freaked out, or the contact to get spooked," Cruz warned.

"Maybe we can bug the machine shop tonight while it's closed?" Briones suggested.

"Not a bad idea, but we have no intel on what counter-surveillance gear is in place, so we could give ourselves away if we try. We need this meeting to take place, gentlemen. We can't do anything that would tip off either *El Rey* or his contact. Let's just assume that the shop is a front for illegal activity, and that as such, it is likely wired with security equipment," Cruz advised.

"How do you want us to take him, then?" Guerrero asked, willing to step into the breach, as always.

"I want a team of twenty men in full tactical gear ready to go in on thirty seconds' notice. If we can get a nearby building without attracting attention, perfect. If not, we'll use one of the big transport carriers and wheel up to the shop for a shockwave deployment. But people? We can't screw this up. It has to go off like clockwork. Ruiz? Sandborn? Pick your very best men and ensure they don't blow it."

They spent the next half hour discussing the assault and agreed that they would combine visual observation of some sort with a raid by a lightning strike force. Cruz left it up to his field officers to recommend a final approach once they'd studied the lay of the land. As the men gathered their notes, there was a palpable sense of energy in the room. Finally, after weeks of no progress, there was a break, and they could get into the field and bring their quarry down.

❧

Dinah left the condo, walking in a seemingly aimless manner, window shopping at the upscale shops in the trendy neighborhood she and Cruz had been moved to three weeks earlier. She hated the upheaval every few months, but had come to accept it as a part of staying alive. She understood the need for constant moving, but it still created a hardship on them. At least they were being put up in high-end buildings. There seemed to be no budget limitations when it came to keeping the task force commander alive. For that she was grateful.

She paused at the corner and glanced around to ensure that the two plainclothes officers watching the building were still there, and noted with concern that one had left his position in the car across the street and had begun following her at a discreet distance. She swallowed, her mouth dry from anxiety, and crossed to the far side.

Continuing her walk, she picked up the pace, putting a few yards of valuable distance between herself and her bodyguard. She debated trying to give her protector the slip and then realized that it was an impossibility. His presence would just make things more nerve-racking, but wouldn't alter the outcome of her trip, and trying to lose him could raise difficult questions with Cruz she preferred not to be asked.

She'd gotten a call that morning on the small cell phone the assassin had given her at the hospital, and the man's soft voice had calmly laid out instructions. She was to summarize any information she had gleaned and drop the notes at a pre-ordained spot at a specific time. When he hung up after only a few seconds of instruction, she'd scrambled to pull herself together, her heart pounding in her ears from the tension.

Dinah had done as instructed, methodically detailing the conversations she'd had with Cruz on a single sheet of her note paper, and then set about showering and getting dressed. It was a Saturday, and school was out, so she had half a day before Cruz would return from headquarters. Still, she felt rushed, and guilty – she was selling her future husband down the river.

She forced herself to stop the negative internal dialogue. What she was doing was protecting the one she loved, as well as herself. The assassin was right. The priority was on staying alive and together, not on sacrificing everything over a tenuous ethical belief. Every year thousands of innocent people were slaughtered in the cartel clashes, and many of those people no doubt had laudable morals. But they were still dead, and nothing would bring them back. She took a deep breath and steeled her resolve. It was too late to second-guess her decision now.

Dinah saw the sign for the large department store and made for the entrance, taking care to move quickly into the clothing section. After a few moments of glancing around at the selections, she chose a pair of jeans and two tops and approached the changing rooms, where an attendant showed her to a cubicle.

Five minutes later she emerged and handed the clothes to the girl at the counter with a shake of her head. She didn't really like anything.

Stalling for time, and so as not to be too obvious, she browsed for other items for a little while, straying into the underwear section. Finally, appearing to have exhausted her shopping enthusiasm, Dinah wove her way through the aisles, retrieved the little phone, and pressed redial. Several seconds later the assassin answered.

"It's there."

Shortly thereafter, a middle-aged man with a thick beard and a beret strode to the attendant carrying a pair of slacks. The woman quickly confirmed that he was carrying only the one item and then directed him to take whichever stall he liked – the area was empty, the store having only opened half an hour earlier.

El Rey quickly located the hidden note wedged into the crack he'd created two days before in the flimsy surface of the wall and extracted it using the folding blade of a razor-sharp survival knife. Satisfied that he had gotten everything Dinah had left for him, he waited another minute, and then returned the pants to the attendant before unhurriedly strolling out of the store.

Back at his apartment, he pulled the foam strips out of the bottom of his cheeks, where he'd stuffed it to form the appearance of jowls, and wiped away the makeup that had completed his transformation into a debauched older man. He scratched absently at his beard as he read Dinah's small, precise handwriting and smiled. They knew nothing of consequence. His scheme was working perfectly, and there were no loose ends. The president would be dead in due course, and he would retire again, permanently, a very wealthy fellow with abundant time on his hands.

His arm bumped the mouse connected to his laptop, and the screen blinked to life, revealing a set of blueprints and a schematic for the construction of the device that would terminate the president's stay on the planet. He'd already ordered the necessary item from eBay in the United States, and the shipping company was due to deliver it within seventy-two hours. Some modification would be required, but that was fine. It would give him something to occupy his idle hands with while he waited for the big day to arrive.

Holding his arms above his head, he stretched and then tossed the cotton balls with the greasepaint on them into the trash. No time to lounge about. He had a meeting tomorrow and wanted to be prepared for anything. That was a big part of why he was successful.

He was always prepared.

CHAPTER 20

El Rey drifted through the streets of Mexico City like a ghost, blending in with the crowds and avoiding being in any way conspicuous. The morning rush hour was finally over, in the sense that it was ever over in one of the most populated cities in the world, but the sidewalks in the area of town he was navigating were still jammed, as were the streets. Music blared from storefronts hawking women's clothing, appliances on payment plans, shoes, pets – every imaginable variety of oddity, all to the beat of Shakira at a hundred-plus decibels.

As he strolled past open-air taco stands, to the heady smell of *pastor* and grilled onions lingering in the air, he casually eyed his surroundings for any signs of threat. It was automatic, and he scanned each sector in his vicinity with clinical detachment, even as he appeared to be a man without a care in the world, taking in the sights.

He disliked meeting anyone new, but couldn't see a way to avoid it. He was running up against a deadline and, given the urgency of the situation, he had to rely on Aranas for help in securing the more difficult to acquire goods he'd need for the job. The president's speech was rapidly approaching and he didn't have time to source some of the harder-to-procure materials. It left him with precious little leeway in terms of preparation, but he wasn't worried. He had come up with a plan that, even by his standards, was audacious.

The neighborhood gradually degraded, and the clothing stores transitioned into automobile parts shops and muffler repair bays, interspersed with the odd internet café and small market. Blankets lay on the sidewalk, trinkets and obviously stolen items spread out upon them, the vendors shamelessly offering their goods for fractions of their legitimate worth. He noticed that the foot traffic had grown sparser as the district became rougher, and his nose crinkled at the pervasive odor of garbage wafting from the alleyways.

El Rey resembled a day laborer, with a stained, red baseball hat emblazoned with the Feyco construction supplies logo pulled low across his brow and knockoff Oakley sunglasses he'd bought three blocks back for seven dollars. He wore baggy black cargo pants and a long-sleeved burgundy rayon dress shirt, crumpled and stained as it would be from days of wearing it while pulling wire runs or laying flooring. He'd darkened his complexion with a deep base and trimmed his beard into an elaborate goatee and set of Elvis sideburns, presenting an image of a worker who was desperately trying to proclaim some sort of hipness, but failing miserably. He knew from experience that people would focus on the most memorable attributes, and the unusual facial hair would ensure that's what they remembered – the face behind it would be almost forgotten if anyone tried to describe him.

Three blocks from his rendezvous point he paused in front of a hardware store with racks of toilet seats and shower heads proudly mounted on a board display outside the windows, guarded by a surly, overweight man eating a bag of potato chips. He'd caught a glimpse of a federal police truck moving down one of the parallel streets, which triggered an immediate internal alarm. It might have meant nothing, but his senses moved to high alert. His eyes scrutinized everything with increased intensity from behind the shades, roving over the buildings and vehicles, looking for any signs of surveillance. He didn't detect anything, and after a few minutes of ambling down the block without noticing anything amiss, he turned the corner and made for his destination.

The streets were scarred with potholes and grooves from where the asphalt had worn bare, leaving filthy gravel or pools of odiferous liquid collected in the pits. A dilapidated American sedan adorned with Bondo and primer prowled slowly down the way, street gang thugs glaring from its tinted windows as it rolled past him. Traffic had thinned out, and instead of the manic bumper to bumper morass a few blocks back, only a few cars navigated the increasingly shabby roads.

His anxiety increased again as he glanced at the windows above street level, noting that many were open, their interiors darkened to the point where making out the occupants was an impossibility. The hair on his arms prickled under the synthetic material of the shirt as he felt a sensation of being watched. This was the wrong kind of setup for a meet, at least, according to his preferences, but it would have been a dream come true for a hit.

A cat shot out from behind a dumpster, startling him, and raced off down the street in vain pursuit of a gathering of pigeons it had spied strutting by. He watched as the emaciated feline made its play, failing to snare any of the birds as they flapped effortlessly away to safety. He could sympathize with its disappointment – he'd been there, although thankfully, only once.

With only one block to go, he still didn't see anything overtly alarming. Perhaps he was just over-thinking it. Still, the vague sense of unease lingered, and he'd spent too many years refining his instincts to ignore them. Outwardly, he projected nothing, and if anyone had been watching him there would have been no giveaways. His gait didn't change, nor did he seem in any way on guard, or interested in anything but making his way to whatever drab existence awaited him.

When he arrived at the run-down building that was his rendezvous, he continued walking past it, fishing for his cell phone in his shirt pocket, then shifting the empty black nylon backpack to his other shoulder as he held it to his ear. There were a number of other pedestrians on the block, most of them down on their luck, moving with the sickly shuffle of the perennially downtrodden. Mexico was a hard country, where, if you fell, you didn't get up, and Mexico City was merciless in the way it devoured its weak. Much of the population was poor by any standard, earning a few hundred dollars a month. Districts like the one he was in housed those of sufficient means to avoid the endless shanty towns on its perimeter, but who were only a week's pay from living on dirt floors.

He pretended to make a call, using the ruse as an opportunity to lean his head back to better study the surrounding tenements above. There was nothing of note, but he still had a buzz of disquiet in his stomach. When he reached the end of the block, he rounded the corner and continued down the alley, terminating his simulated call as he did so. His gut told him to abort, but reason failed to find any reason to do so.

As a compromise, he circled the block, noting the layout of the streets leading to and from the machine shop that was his destination. It was one large section of buildings, all two and three story, most with rebar stabbing into the sky; the rusting remnants of unfinished structural columns of future floors that had been aborted – typical for the neighborhood, with a few narrow alleys running between the shabby structures.

When he turned onto the street again, he felt more confident. He glanced at his watch, confirming that he was five minutes late – early by Mexican standards. In Mexico, you were on time if you arrived within half an hour of your appointment, which virtually nobody ever did.

Except *El Rey*.

He approached the opaque glass door and pushed on it, but it was locked. He spotted a buzzer by the handle and jabbed it with his thumb. Footsteps sounded on the concrete floor within the building, and forty-five seconds later, the lock rattled and the door opened. *El Rey* noted two security cameras angled to capture both directions on the street as he nodded at the figure inside – a gaunt, tall, fair-complexioned man, wearing jeans, cowboy boots and a western-styled shirt. The man seemed more on guard than *El Rey* did, which made him feel slightly better.

"What do you want?" he demanded.

"I'm the *Don*'s friend," *El Rey* said, as instructed.

The man gestured for him to come in, eyes roving over the sidewalks as he stood aside, before he locked and bolted the door behind him. *El Rey* saw that there were wrought iron bars on the interior of the door, as well as the front window, both of which had been painted black to defeat prying eyes. As they made their way towards an office at the back of the space, dimly lit by a few weak bulbs dangling from the ceiling above, he registered that the shop was empty, essentially vacant.

The cartel man edged through the office door and motioned to an industrial steelwork desk, upon which sat several cardboard boxes, two hand grenades and a silenced pistol.

"Here's everything."

El Rey carefully inspected each item before placing it into his backpack. He checked the magazine on the Beretta nine millimeter pistol and verified that it had a full clip, and set it back on the table after chambering a round. The final box was fourteen inches by twelve. He opened it and gazed at the two cream-colored rectangles sitting in form-fitted foam before carefully closing the lid and replacing the three oversized rubber bands that secured it in place. The entire inspection took under two minutes.

Once he was loaded up, he turned to his host. "Where are the security camera feeds for the front?"

"In the back. Follow me..."

The man walked out of the dingy little office to the rear of the shop, where a piece of plywood sat on top of two milk crates. On the makeshift support were a computer and two monitors, next to a CD-Rom recording device. He pressed a button, slid the CD out and handed it to *El Rey*, who took it and dropped it into the backpack with the rest. As he did so, his eyes detected movement on both of the screens, one which was the alley in the back, and the other the front entrance cameras on a split screen. A group of heavily-armed federal police were creeping against the wall on both sides of the building.

The man's eyes grew wide with shock.

El Rey instantly sized up the situation and whispered to him, "Is there a roof exit?"

He nodded and motioned at a steel ladder mounted to the back wall running up to a hatch in the ceiling two stories above their heads. *El Rey* joined him in peering up into the gloom, and then in a flash slashed the man's throat with a stiletto he'd palmed while the man had been distracted by the vision on the two screens. He stepped back to avoid the arterial blood spray as the man crumpled to the concrete floor, twitching as his life ran out of him.

Not pausing to wait for the impending battering of the front and rear entrances, *El Rey* ran to the ladder and began climbing.

❧❧

Cruz watched the men deploy from one of the windows down the block, cringing when a woman stifled a scream at the sight of the heavily-armed officers moving into position. They knew the building had cameras, so the first order of business was to knock them out. They'd had no choice but to leave them working until the beginning of the operation – anything else would have alerted whoever was in the building.

The squad arrived at the doorway and stopped. It was out of his hands now. All he could do was wait.

At the shop entrance, Briones held a can of spray paint overhead and quickly hit both lenses with a blast of flat black primer, rendering them instantly dark. He listened in his earpiece as a whisper told him the same had been done at the rear emergency exit. There were no cameras on the roof, so the two men who had gone up a neighboring building's access way to cover the machine shop were safe from observation.

Shifting against the uncomfortable Kevlar bulletproof vest, Briones gave a signal with his left hand and tossed the paint can into the street before un-holstering his service pistol.

Cruz murmured into a radio handset, giving the go-ahead for the team in the rear. He glanced at the time and saw that the assassin had been inside for four minutes. They'd captured him on film, but he knew it wouldn't do them much good – with sunglasses and the baseball hat and all the facial hair, he could have been Cruz's brother after a three day drunk.

Two officers sidled up to the door, slapped explosive charges to the hinge locations and pulled back to the shelter of the wall, where Briones was waiting. Three seconds later the charges detonated with a sharp crack and the assault was on. Two other men slammed through the glass with a cement-filled iron pipe, knocking it inwards, and then the team shouldered its way inside, weapons at the ready, expecting to be fired upon.

Guerrero was first to notice the movement at the rear of the building, and then sunlight streamed in. It was the other team blowing the back door. The rear team spotted the corpse on the floor at the same instant Briones ran for the ladder, not waiting for confirmation that the building was empty. He thumbed on his com earpiece and warned the men on the roof, demanding a confirmation even as he reached the ladder, but got no response. Taking a deep breath, he ascended the steel rungs, Guerrero and another officer following behind him. The wall fastenings creaked ominously under the strain.

"Stay down there until I get to the top. This fucking thing is about to tear off the wall," he hissed through clenched teeth, when only a few rungs from the trapdoor at the top. He craned his neck skyward and caught sight of the lock.

The bolt was open. He had a sinking feeling even as he threw it wide and peered around cautiously, training his gun as best he could. There was nobody on the roof. He pulled himself up and out and saw a boot sticking out from behind a ventilation duct twenty-five feet away. Moving in a crouch, he quickly reached the body. Dead, shot in the face. Ten feet further away, another corpse lay on the hot surface in a pool of blood.

Fresh blood.

He swung around wildly, straining for a glimpse of the assassin, but didn't see anything. Then he heard a thump from behind him, and he spun just in time to spot a figure in the distance leap across the roof to another building on the other side of the alley.

"He's on the roof. Two officers shot dead up here. I'm in pursuit. Heading northwest," he cried into the earpiece, and then sprinted to the roof edge. He jumped across the three foot gap between it and the neighbor, and then repeated the process at the next structure. When he arrived at the alley, he skidded to a stop. It was at least ten feet to the other side, maybe more. Briones glanced across in frustration and saw a blur of movement a hundred yards away. He fired his pistol three times at the area in the hopes of a lucky shot, but knew he hadn't hit anything worthwhile. He realized even as he did so that he'd made a critical mistake in not snatching up one of the dead men's assault rifles – a mistake that would haunt him if the assassin escaped.

"He got across the alley, and he's on the next group of roofs. Can we get a helicopter here? Get the men to cordon off the northwest block, now," he screamed.

His earpiece crackled.

"Can you make it across?" Cruz's voice sounded tinny in his ear.

"Negative. I don't know how he did it. He must be able to fly," Briones said in frustration, straining futilely for a better shot at his quarry.

But *El Rey* was nowhere to be seen.

CHAPTER 21

El Rey locked the door behind him and turned on the air-conditioning before placing the backpack on the coffee table. He'd worked the question of how the police had known about his meeting over and over as he'd made his way back to his apartment, and come to the conclusion that there weren't many possibilities. Either someone in Aranas' camp had talked, or the man he'd killed at the warehouse had sold him out. In the end, it didn't matter. He was safe. But he was also furious. That had been far too close. And it reaffirmed every belief he had about what a bad idea dealing with unknown quantities was.

He paced the length of the living room, calculating how to proceed. The raid had been a big operation, and he'd only escaped by a miracle. But he got the sense that the miracle bank was running low, and he wouldn't be so lucky the next time.

Fucking Cruz. The man was an annoyance and was fast becoming a real impediment. And the woman hadn't told him anything – which had lulled him into complacency. That couldn't stand.

He went into the kitchen and opened a drawer, retrieving a phone from its depths.

Dinah's voice sounded guarded when she answered.

"Hello?"

"Listen very carefully. Don't talk. Your boyfriend just launched an operation to capture me. It failed, of course, but now I'm upset. I feel like you haven't been keeping to your side of the bargain – you didn't warn me. That makes me want to hang him upside down and peel his skin off."

"I…I didn't know anything about it! You have to believe me…"

Dinah sounded like she was telling the truth. No matter.

"Shut up. I said don't talk. Here's what you're going to do if you want him to be breathing this time tomorrow. Get me information. Figure out where the leak came from that alerted them about the meeting. Failure on your part won't be tolerated. Get me something, or our deal is off, and I'll make sure the last thing you ever see is his rotting corpse skewered like a pig."

"But how am I supposed to find that out?"

"I don't know, nor do I care. Just do it. Tear his office apart, or wherever he keeps his papers at home. Tell him you desperately want to know everything about today's operation or he'll never have sex again. Whatever you do, it better be good, because I'm out of patience. You have twenty-four hours."

He hung up and tossed the phone back into the drawer. That might shake something loose. Maybe she was telling the truth, or maybe she had been feeding him inconsequential minutiae. Whatever. She needed to perform, or he'd see to it that the pair of them regretted every moment of their last breaths.

Now he had to make the call he'd been considering since he'd leapt across the buildings like a demented free-runner. He went into the bedroom, emerged with another phone, and pressed a speed dial button. *Don* Aranas answered.

El Rey took him through the morning's events, omitting that he'd killed Aranas' man at the rendezvous. That would be attributed to having happened during the police raid, and he didn't see any reason to rock the boat. Aranas sounded worried – mostly about the viability of the plan moving forward.

"I have no concerns over our arrangement. I'm planning to close the contract in the agreed-upon time," *El Rey* assured him. "I think it's worth probing to see if you can find the source of the leak, though. I don't have to tell you that it's not in your best interests for your confidential information to find its way into the hands of the *Federales*. Even after this is concluded, you still have a problem."

"I'll take steps."

"I'm also working on some avenues. I'll keep you apprised of any progress I make," *El Rey* finished, having delivered the message he wanted to send.

Aranas had to deal with the issue in his house or he'd be in constant jeopardy. He didn't have a reputation for tolerating disloyalty, and *El Rey* had no doubt that he'd do whatever was necessary to find the traitor and silence him permanently.

❧❧

"The man is really superhuman," Briones declared in frustration towards the end of the staff meeting. "I still have no idea how he made it across that alley. I mean, it's obviously possible to do, but I can't imagine throwing myself into the air in the hopes I made it. Two stories is a long way down…"

"No, he's not. He's flesh and blood, just like you and I – like everyone in this room. He simply reacts differently than we do. And that has to stop. I made a critical error by not having more men on the roof. I underestimated *El Rey*. A mistake I will never make again," Cruz spat.

"It was a one in a million chance that he'd discover the assault in time to escape. The odds of alerting him with a dozen officers tromping around on the roof was far greater, sir. It was the correct call," Briones reasoned.

"That is neither here nor there. At this point our only hope of capturing him has gone down the drain. That puts us back on square one. Worse, he's now alerted that we're hunting him. I think it's fair to say that we lost this round. We can't afford to lose any more," Cruz said emphatically. "I want twice as many men on the streets. We know he's in the city, and we have the footage of him we got when he approached the shop. It's unlikely he'll be able to stay incognito if his photo is plastered everywhere. I want the film and the construction photo leaked to the press so his face is on every news station and newspaper in the country. There's no reason to play it quiet any longer."

The meeting broke up a few minutes later, and Cruz motioned to Briones for him to accompany him to his office. Once behind closed doors, he slumped into his chair and stared off into space before focusing his attention on the younger lieutenant.

"The spooks at CISEN are going to lose their minds when I tell them what happened," Cruz complained.

"Probably. They won't be happy, just like we aren't happy. It's a generally unhappy time for everyone right now. They'll get over it, sir," Briones assured him.

"That's not what worries me. No, it's more that they might not share any more information with us after this, or they might pass it to someone else, like the president's staff. If we get too many players on this field, it will only make finding the assassin even harder."

Briones nodded. "I'm sorry I didn't try to jump across the alley, sir," he said in a quiet voice.

Cruz waved it away with a curt gesture. "Don't be ridiculous. The job is dangerous enough without demanding that you try something that would get you killed. I wouldn't have done it, either. That's the difference between being the cornered rat, and being the cat," Cruz said.

They continued the discussion, moving to the practical logistics of getting maximum coverage of the images they had of *El Rey*, but the atmosphere remained uneasy as the afternoon wore on. Neither said anything more about Briones' chance at getting *El Rey*.

Neither had to.

Both knew Cruz would have jumped.

৶৶

When Cruz made it home that evening, Dinah was making pasta for dinner – chicken *piccata* with linguine. He went to the bedroom, changed out of his uniform, and returned a few minutes later wearing sweat pants and a white linen short-sleeved shirt. He obligingly took plates out of the cupboard and set the table, then uncorked a bottle of white wine – after Dinah forbade him a draught of the wine she'd bought to cook with.

He poured them both healthy glasses, and they ate contentedly as he inquired about how her day had gone. She seemed on edge, and Cruz wondered whether it was a return of the anxiety she'd experienced after getting out of the hospital, but it gradually receded as she ate and consumed her wine. He was relieved – even after as many months together as they'd spent, he still didn't have a clue what was going on inside her head most of the time.

The conversation eventually turned to his day, and he gave her a rundown of the operation and its ultimate failure.

"You were that close, and he got away? He sounds like some sort of devil," she commented.

"Tell me about it. Briones is convinced he has wings, like a bat. I went up on the roof myself and looked at the pursuit path, and he made a jump most wouldn't have tried. It's frustrating. I feel just like I did last year, when we were on his trail. He's always three moves ahead of us. If I recall, that didn't end well," Cruz complained.

Dinah knew all about the attempt at the summit.

"I'd say that at least one good thing came out of it. You and I wouldn't be together if not for that."

"Yes, but I don't want to even think that we're a couple because of *El Rey*. Although I suppose I do have him to thank for something…" Cruz acknowledged before sipping more of his wine.

"How did you know he was going to be there?" Dinah asked in a neutral tone, struggling not to show how desperate she was for the information. Her heart ached that she had to mislead him like this, but there was no other option.

Cruz hesitated, and then told her a partial truth.

"It was a tip from one of the other agencies. They'd picked up some chatter, and we got lucky," he dissembled.

"Another agency? Who? I thought you were the *El Rey* experts. Is there more than one group hunting him?"

"CISEN. The intelligence agency. They got the lead and handed it over to us."

"CISEN! What are they doing involved in this?" Dinah fought to keep her voice under control.

Cruz finished his glass of wine and strode into the kitchen to get the bottle, carrying their dishes in and placing them in the sink before he returned and refilled their glasses. He took a large mouthful, swishing it around in appreciation.

"Mmmm. This goes down easy. You may have to lock up the cooking wine. There's no telling what I'll do after two glasses of this stuff," he said, changing the subject.

Dinah smiled. "I'll see if I can think of something," she said suggestively. "But you never finished your story. What about CISEN? I thought they were only international operations…"

"Typically they are. But somehow they tripped onto information about the assassin and a plot to kill the president, so they brought it to me. Mostly to set me up for a big fall if he succeeds, I think. They still seem a little testy over having half their top brass fired." He took another swallow of wine. "This way they can say they passed on everything, and if he's successful, I'm the one who failed."

"But that's not fair! What about the president's guard? His security detail? Surely they would be more accountable for the president's safety than you."

"It's true, but if the assassin manages to kill the president, everyone will be looking for someone to take the blame. CISEN will point the finger at me, and so will the president's staff. All roads will lead to me – the head of the task force that failed to prevent it." Cruz shrugged. "It may not be fair, but the world's not fair. There's no use complaining about it. I simply need to find this invisible man and take him out of commission, with no new information and no leads to go on. Piece of cake." He took another pull on his wine and winked at her playfully.

"Romero, this sounds serious. What are you going to do?" Dinah said with concern.

He sighed. "What can I do? The plan is to get his photo everywhere to turn up the pressure, and hope he slips up or someone recognizes him. We're going to offer a half million dollar reward for information leading to his capture. Hell, for that kind of money most of the city will be mounting a manhunt." He finished his second glass of wine and regarded the empty bottle wistfully. "It hasn't been my favorite day ever, *mi corazon*. I just want to put it behind me."

Dinah reached across the table and took his hand, her eyes moist. She finished her second glass and stood, gently pulling him in the direction of the bedroom.

"I can help."

CHAPTER 22

Dinah called in sick with the flu the next morning and stayed in bed until Cruz had left. After waiting a few minutes to ensure he wasn't going to return for some forgotten item, she did a hasty search of his office and then rushed to the shower and hurriedly rinsed off before gathering her notes and sealing them in a small envelope. She donned jeans and a silk blouse and then called Cruz's office to tell him she was going to run to the pharmacy to get some medicine. She knew he wouldn't be there yet, but wanted him to know she'd gone out in case the officers watching the building mentioned it.

On the ride down the elevator her stomach churned at what she was about to do. It was tearing her apart to pass this kind of information to her fiancé's nemesis, but she could see no other way out. One thing had become apparent from their discussions. *El Rey*'s reputation as the most dangerous man in Mexico, if not the world, was deserved, and she had little doubt that he'd make good on his promise to kill them both if she strayed. It wasn't a risk she could take.

She repeated her trip to the large department store and sighed a breath of relief when she'd stuffed the envelope in the hiding place. As she walked out of the store, she decided she should go to the pharmacy at the end of the block – not that she believed Cruz had an iota of doubt about her, but it was a loose end. She rummaged in her purse for the cell phone *El Rey* had given her and made a furtive call, letting the phone ring three times as agreed and then disconnecting. There was no need to speak. He would know what it meant.

As she walked along the bustling sidewalk, the eyes of her bodyguard boring through her back from a hundred yards behind, she wondered what she had become. The letter she'd hidden contained two items – a single page summary of her discussion with Cruz, and a copy of a top secret document she'd found in the bottom drawer of his desk that morning, under a pile of monthly expense sheets.

After skimming it, she'd powered on the copier and carefully made a duplicate, then replaced it in the exact position she'd found it. A wave of guilt had washed over her as she checked the copy for legibility. If Cruz found out about this, he would be crushed. Then again, Cruz might be willing to tackle *El Rey* head on. But she wasn't.

She bought some decongestant and some vitamins and paid in cash, then returned to her building, taking her time, allowing the sun's gentle rays to warm her as she strolled unhurriedly to the front entrance. It wasn't like she'd voluntarily chosen this path, she reasoned. It was an impossible situation, and if the decision to favor survival was a selfish and bad one, she perhaps would have acted differently had it been only her life on the line. But by threatening Cruz, the assassin had created a situation that could only end with her helping him.

Dinah tried to push the thoughts aside, but they wouldn't leave. How could she marry a man she was willing to deceive in such a fundamental way? What kind of woman was she?

She shook her head in the elevator as though the movement would banish her introspection. *El Rey* was a predator, and moreover, a brilliant and legendary one. Dinah had no doubt that he would be successful in outwitting the authorities. A single motivated individual with skill and commitment usually could prevail over a large, unwieldy bureaucracy. Cruz had complained about that numerous times. The best the police could hope for was to be lucky, and maybe mop up after everything had played out. It was one of the aspects of the job that infuriated him.

When she got back into the condo, she set her purse down and stared vacantly around the space before unwrapping the medicine she'd bought and taking two tablets. The drugs would make her sleepy, allowing her to finally recoup some of the lost hours when she'd lain awake last night, pretending to doze as she listened to Cruz's soft snores. She quickly stripped off her clothes and threw herself onto the bed, her body racked by shuddering sobs as she cried her frustrated rage into the pillow.

Culiacán, Sinaloa

Carlos Herreira gazed out at the exotic granite slabs in the massive stone yard he operated and rubbed his hand over his beard. It had been another extremely profitable day, with a shipment of grenade launchers and assorted assault rifles bringing in eight hundred thousand dollars, three hundred of which was profit. This was his second shipment to Jalisco this week, and he mused silently that the boys in Guadalajara looked like they were gearing up to launch a major offensive against his other big client, the Sinaloa cartel.

Carlos was an equal opportunity arms merchant, beholden to no one. The cartels wanted guns and came with cash, and he was in the business of selling them. It was a simple transaction, and nobody cared that he sold to everyone. Or at least, no one begrudged him his right to do so. He was merely a conduit, a vessel through which the desired implements flowed. Carlos' role was not to take sides, any more than the banks that laundered the cartel funds took sides. It was all green, and while cartels came and went, the money never changed.

He had been in the business for twelve years and was rich beyond his ability to imagine, yet he continued to go to work every day at the stone yard that was his legitimate operation. The constant shipments in and out were perfect cover for his far more profitable sideline, and he'd branched out and created two import/export businesses to facilitate his deadly traffic.

The first five years had been good, but nothing like the last seven, when the cartels had escalated their conflicts and created armed wings that did nothing but wage war against one another. All those new soldiers needed weapons, and when the cash was easy they generally wanted the best they could get. He'd gone from supplying battered, twenty-year-old Kalashnikovs by the crate load from Honduras and Nicaragua to the very latest high tech weaponry from the U.S., with its attendant higher margins. The escalation of violence had been good for business, there was no doubt, and there had been occasions when he'd had to scramble to find suitable trophy pieces.

That had resulted in the most profitable partnership of his life, with the most unexpected counterparty – the CIA.

At first he'd suspected it was a setup, but he'd insulated himself and done one test transaction, and then another, and then finally had crafted a deal where they supplied most of the high-end weapons he bought nowadays – .50 caliber sniper rifles, fully automatic assault rifles, grenades, semi-automatic pistols, sub-machine guns…all at prices that allowed him to make a handy profit without worrying about sourcing the goods. Every few weeks he would aggregate the requests, supply his contact at the American intelligence agency with a list, and presto, it was shopping time.

He'd been amused when he'd read about the scandal involving the Bureau of Alcohol, Tobacco and Firearms allowing weapons from the U.S. to be smuggled into Mexico. Hell, they had been facilitating his business for seven years. His partner to the north would put together the order, and then the goods would miraculously appear on his side of the border, with the ATF turning a blind eye. When the American Congress had held hearings on the trade – the notorious 'gun walking' everyone knew about but pretended was a surprise – he'd gotten worried, but had been assured that it was business as usual, and that the hearings would go nowhere.

The problem was that some of the American-manufactured weapons had turned up in slayings of border patrol officers on the U.S. side, sparking an outcry. His contacts had told him that things would work very much like Mexico – there would be protestations that everyone was shocked, shocked indeed, that anything like routine traffic of guns south of the border took place while the watchdog in charge of preventing it pretended to be deaf, blind and mute. Days of grilling in congress would be met with stonewalling, and perhaps a few functionaries would have to take token falls to appease the public. They would be well compensated, so it wasn't rough duty. There would be vows to continue the investigation to its bitter end, which would die as soon as the cameras were turned off. Meanwhile, everything would continue to work as it had, the supply of instruments of death un-slowed.

The tunnels that were as regular in Tijuana as subway stations in New York had served him well, enabling him to get anything he needed from San Diego without having to worry about bribing customs agents in Mexico to look the other way – a profit-sucking annoyance he preferred to forego. Homes, warehouses and shops would receive shipments from gun dealer middlemen, and the crates would seamlessly move beneath the border to TJ, where they would be transported southeast. He had a similar arrangement in Ciudad Juárez and El Paso. It was a lucrative, risk free way for the cartels that ran the tunnel scheme to make extra money helping him help them. And after all, it wasn't as though they had to pay a toll – the tunnels were already dug, so it was just a few hours of ferrying guns and explosives on a return trip from the cocaine, heroin, marijuana and meth trips. Same underground rail systems, just moving south instead of north.

The CIA had also proved very efficient at introducing him to Russian and Iranian syndicates that could source the more difficult to obtain items he was sometimes requested to get. Anti-tank weapons, specialized explosives like C-4 or the newer variants…whatever, they could get anything for a price. That was how he'd gotten involved with CISEN. His Russian and American contacts had introduced him to their Mexican equivalent, which had been paid to help ensure that the real traffic didn't run into problems. Sure, token shipments were intercepted periodically for the media, but for the most part, the CIA helped get the drugs into the U.S. and the weapons out. It was perfect, really, and the only ones none the wiser were the American and Mexican public. He'd been assured that the great unwashed would believe whatever the television pronounced as the truth, so he wasn't worried about the trade ending any time soon. It had been going on ever since the Colombians had severed their partnership with the agency, and the heads had 'gone to prison' – jails they controlled being the only place they were safe from agency hit men taking them out to ensure their permanent silence.

He'd always wondered why Escobar and crew had one day turned themselves in, at a time when they were among the richest men on the planet. Although the official story was that the Colombian military, augmented by the Americans, had eventually won the struggle against the Colombian cartels, the true facts were simple. There was nowhere they could be safe, except behind maximum security walls guarded around the clock. He knew for a fact that all the Cali and Medellin cartel chieftains lived in unparalleled luxury while serving life sentences, and once his contact had spilled the beans over shots of tequila one night, everything had fallen into place.

The Colombians getting out of the trafficking trade and sticking to production in-country had created an opportunity for the Mexican cartels, which had forged similar arrangements with their neighbor's intelligence service in return for protection. The relationship was simply good business. Dope north, weapons south, with their 'friends' taking a cut of each, presumably to fund their less savory operations. There were many things Congress couldn't or wouldn't fund, and as early as the Sixties, the CIA had moved to augment its budget with narcotics trafficking. That had proved a wise move, and soon the agency was acting as conduit for drugs from Vietnam and Afghanistan, oil and cash from Iran, and eventually cocaine and heroin from Colombia and Mexico.

The phone on his desk jangled; he grabbed at it.

"Boss. You have visitors. Angel and a driver," his number two man alerted him.

He watched as a white Cadillac Escalade rolled through the gate leading from the retail yard and pulled to a stop outside his office. The passenger side door swung wide and a familiar figure stepped out.

It was Angel Talvez, one of *Don* Aranas' lieutenants. He always liked to see Angel. It meant one thing. Another big order.

Carlos moved to the screen door that kept the bugs at bay and opened it, spreading his arms in welcome.

"Angel! It's been too long. What? Three months, since we hit the clubs in Mazatlán?" Carlos enthused. He was a connoisseur of young strippers, the closer to their teen years, the better. Angel shared the passion for his hobby, and they'd spent many a night sampling the wares a few hours west.

"*Compadre*. Always good to see you," Angel replied with a smile.

Carlos motioned to him to enter and take a seat.

"Tequila?" Carlos asked, and then without waiting for an answer, moved to the small bar he had set up in a corner of the expansive office and poured two shots of Don Julio 1942. He turned to face Angel, glass outstretched, and found himself staring down the barrel of a silenced semi-automatic pistol.

Carlos' eyes grew wide when he saw the look on Angel's face. Angel shrugged a halfhearted apology for what was to come.

"Why, Carlos? Why did you fuck the *Don*? You've made your money. Why give up information on *El Rey*? Why do it?" Angel asked, curious as to why his friend would put himself in this position, requiring him to do something as unpleasant as killing him.

"I...I don't know what you're talking about," Carlos stammered, his voice suddenly tremulous.

Angel shook his head. They always lied in the end. Human nature. With his free hand, he removed a piece of paper from his pocket and placed it on the desk.

"Sit down and read that. Oh, and best have both of those yourself. It's good tequila," Angel said, motioning with the gun.

Carlos did as instructed and swallowed both shots as he stood, and then turned, placing them on the bar. He swung back in a blur of speed, aiming the heavy, tall tequila bottle at Angel's head.

Angel had anticipated the move and stepped back, easily dodging the blow, and calmly fired a round into Carlos' skull through his right eye. The .22 target pistol he favored was laughably small in caliber, but he'd never had any problems putting down his victims with it. Carlos proved no different, and his body went rigid as the small flat-headed slug careened through his brain, tearing the gray matter to a scramble. The arms dealer buckled at the knees and fell forward. Angel moved to the side to avoid any messy splatter, having done this many times before. The tequila bottle crashed to the travertine floor, splintering into shards amidst a splash of precious nectar that pooled next to the slowly spreading blood.

Angel leaned over and put another bullet into the back of Carlos' skull from three inches away. He paused over his friend's corpse and inspected his handiwork, and then, satisfied that the job was done, walked to the desk and retrieved the piece of paper, glancing disinterestedly at the Top Secret stamp across the top. He folded it and slipped it into his pants pocket, and then returned the pistol to its place in a custom made shoulder holster as he made his way to the door.

A few moments later, the Escalade roared off in a cloud of dust.

Nobody would report having seen anything. Apparently the granite counter business was a dangerous one in Culiacán, Sinaloa.

Most businesses were.

CHAPTER 23

Mexico City, Mexico

Sun streaked through the filthy windows of the workshop; a cloud of dust motes hung lazily in the air like snowflakes frozen on a Christmas calendar. The space was small, twenty by twenty, with a roll-up door and a few electrical outlets – plus the worktable at which *El Rey* stood, patiently adjusting his project with a toolkit that lay spread across most of the top. A heavy, green vise was mounted to the edge, and he'd wedged two neoprene mouse pad remnants on either side of its jaws, to soften its grip on the metal canister he had just finished fabricating.

He flipped the welding mask up and wiped away the sweat that had accumulated on his brow. He would have loved to open the windows for ventilation, but discretion won out. *El Rey* glanced up at the row of two-foot-wide glass squares framed by rusting metal, each with iron bars spaced every eight inches, and resigned himself to live with the stifling heat. It came with the territory.

He pulled his T-shirt over his head and absently blotted the defined muscles of his chest, testament to three hour a day workouts that had never ceased, even in retirement. A tattoo of a crow on his left pectoral glistened with perspiration as he leaned over his handiwork, studying the cylinder with satisfaction. He painstakingly threaded a stainless steel plunger into one end, taking care to avoid damaging the spring and, once finished, stretched his lower back by reaching to grab his toes so as to avoid cramping.

The detonator would be armed just before it was show time, but this sort of detailed preparation was essential. As with all things, being meticulous ensured a superior result, and *El Rey* trusted no one with this work. He wasn't about to spend months planning a sanction and have something fail at the moment of truth – he'd farmed out the explosives end only once before and that had been the only hit that had been unsuccessful. He had learned his lesson, and he hummed to himself as he patiently filed away the burs from the seam he had created, stopping to brush perspiration out of his eyes every few minutes.

Eventually satisfied with that piece, he unscrewed the vise and moved the metal tube to the side. Pausing for a few minutes to drink a half liter of water, he considered his next task.

He'd never built one of these before. The instructions had seemed straightforward, if a little convoluted, and he estimated it would take about thirty hours to completely assemble it. Then he'd need to test it and get comfortable with the technology, and calculate effective blast radiuses and ranges.

Leaning across the table, he unfolded the schematic for the device and moved the epoxy containers and paint off to the far end of the table, where they wouldn't get in his way as he undertook the mechanical and electrical part of the job. Reconciled to a long afternoon, he slid a high stool to the work area and sat down, pulling the larger pieces of his contrivance towards him. The main body was simple enough, but he could already see that the necessary modifications would take some time. And he would have to adjust for the trigger and create space for it without throwing the balance off. Perhaps with a small amount of weight on the opposite end to offset the explosive charge.

Three hours later, the first piece was assembled, and he took a lunch break, unwrapping a sandwich he'd bought at one of the family-operated shops by his apartment. Mexico City made the best *tortas*, hands down. It was one of the things he'd missed while out of the country. Argentina had brilliant beef and Italian food, but if you wanted a good old-fashioned *torta* with everything on it, there was only one place to go.

He absently thumbed the ridges of his abdomen, where the muscles could have been the model for photos of washboard abs. His exercise regimen included three hundred chin ups and three hundred sit ups per day, in addition to the same number of pushups, a weight training course, an hour of martial arts stretches and drills, and an hour of hard cardio. He'd been addicted to his routine since a teenager and was Spartan in his existence. Other than *tortas*.

Finished with his break, he studied his project, and then nodded to himself. It was perfect. Now he would need to create a foolproof cavity for the detonator to fit. He plugged a digital scale into the wall, and then set the triggering device he'd made earlier on it. Five ounces. He'd weighed the explosive earlier, and it had come in at nine ounces. He'd considered more explosive, but based on his research into the material, that would be enough to ensure a death zone of twenty feet. More than enough for what he had in mind.

Next, he set the first part of the contraption he'd built on the scale, and then set to creating a cavity for the trigger. It was slow going, but eventually he was done, and he placed it back on the scale. Five ounces eliminated, for a net addition of nine ounces once the explosive and trigger were in place. He returned to reading the specifications, and soon concluded that the new, improved device would work. He'd know soon enough.

He moved to the far end of the workbench and set about assembling the specialized electronics for the unit, which occupied much of the rest of the day. By the time he was finished, it was getting dark, and after swigging his third liter of water, he moved his work and re-packed his tools. He would be back tomorrow, and in a few more days would start experimenting. But the hard part was done. He'd built the hardest part of his president-killer.

El Rey donned his shirt and rubbed his hand over the two day stubble on his head. He'd opted for a new look and had shaved his head and facial hair to the same length. The difference was remarkable. He looked more like a Latin rap star now than a laborer, which was immaterial to him – aesthetics had never been important. It was all about the final result, which was invariably more about planning than looks. That, and execution.

He smiled to himself.

Execution, indeed.

❧❦

Briones knocked twice but entered the office without waiting for a response. Cruz looked up from his computer screen, where he was going over budget and personnel requests. The task force was burning money on the *El Rey* hunt, but it couldn't be helped. Just the payments to informants in the hopes of securing a meaningful lead were now up over a hundred thousand dollars – with nothing to show for it. That was a lot of petty cash in a month. Fortunately, or unfortunately, the following month they wouldn't have that burn. The most dangerous public presidential appearances would be over. If they were successful in stopping *El Rey*, the money was noise. If not, Cruz wouldn't have to worry about it. He'd be out of a job.

"Yes, Lieutenant. What can I do for you?" he asked.

"We've got a lead. An anonymous call came in yesterday asking about the reward – wanting to know more details about it. We've had our share of these, but this one seemed genuine. One of the desk guys fielded it and talked the caller into coming in to headquarters. She'll be here in twenty minutes," Briones reported.

Cruz looked at his watch. Twelve fifteen. "She? Who is *she*? What do we know about her?"

"Not much. She was guarded on the line, sir. Wanted to understand how the payment would be paid, and whether it would be subject to tax," Briones said.

"Tax? Interesting. That's someone who believes she's going to be collecting..." Cruz smiled.

"That's what I was thinking. Which is why I'm excited."

"What's her name?"

"All she would give us was a first name. Gabriela," Briones said.

"Put her in one of the interrogation rooms on the main floor when she arrives. I want to tape our discussion."

Cruz's building had two floors of interrogation rooms. The main floor was for friendly questioning of low priority suspects. The basement chambers were more discreet, and there were no recorders or observation rooms – only drains in the floor and electric outlets.

Briones nodded and left, a noticeable spring in his step. He'd taken the hunt for *El Rey* personally ever since the assassin had given them the slip on the rooftop. Truthfully, he'd been emotionally invested before that – *El Rey* had, after all, shot and almost killed him ten months earlier. So the lieutenant had skin in the game, as well as blood. The prospect of information leading to his capture had noticeably improved his disposition.

Half an hour later, Cruz's phone rang. The woman, Gabriela, was waiting downstairs.

He strode to the restroom and ran cold water over his face, using some to smooth his hair, then dried himself with a paper towel. His eyes stared back at him, and he couldn't help but notice the shadows beneath them. The hunt for the super-assassin was taking a toll on everyone but *El Rey*, apparently.

Briones waited outside of meeting room two, his hip holster empty. Cruz wasn't wearing a gun – it was locked in his office. He didn't plan on going outside.

"What have we got here?" he asked perfunctorily.

"Fifty-eight, anxious, greedy eyes. I gave her a soda and told her I couldn't answer any questions, that the leader of the task force would be with her in a few minutes."

Cruz smiled. Briones was learning.

"Let's go meet our mystery woman, shall we? Gabriela, right?"

Briones nodded and opened the door. Cruz strode in with all the self-importance he could muster, Briones trailing him before closing the heavy steel slab behind him. The two *Federales* took seats next to each other, facing the woman, who seemed nervous and fidgety. Behind them, a one-way mirror reflected the harsh fluorescent lighting.

"I'm Captain Romero Cruz, the director of the DF anti-cartel and *El Rey* task force. I understand you've come with some information for us?" Cruz asked in as official a voice as he could summon.

Gabriela seemed suitably impressed. She looked like she'd had a harsh existence and was clearly not from the wealthy side of the tracks. She was missing several teeth, and her hands were gnarled from a lifetime of manual labor.

"I'm here to find out about the money," she announced with a voice ravaged by hardship.

"Ah, yes. The money. The reward. For information leading to the apprehension of the suspect."

"I saw his photo on the television. It looked different, but it was him. I'm sure of it."

"Yes? Why don't you tell us about it?" Cruz suggested.

"How do I collect the money? Is it in cash? Will I have to pay taxes on it?" she demanded guardedly.

Cruz sat back, allowing a moment of impatience to flash across his face.

"Good questions. It will be paid by check following the successful capture of our quarry. And no, you won't have to pay taxes. But you don't need to worry about any of this if you don't have information that results in us finding him," Cruz explained.

"How long after you capture him?"

Cruz was now very interested in whatever information the woman had. She obviously already believed the money was hers. The only impediment would be logistical. You could almost see the hunger for it on her face.

"We would have the check ready within forty-eight hours. Payable to whoever you like."

"And how do I know you won't go back on it once you have him?" she asked, the distrust evident in her eyes, borne from years of being screwed by authority.

"We would execute a contract. You get a copy. It would lay out the conditions clearly, and I would sign it," Cruz said. "But again. To collect, you would need to tell us what you know. And it assumes that we catch him. The chances of which go down the longer we sit here…"

Gabriela fixed him with an intent stare and then grunted.

"Get the contract."

Ten minutes later, Briones returned with two single-spaced pages the district attorney had prepared at their request when they'd offered the reward, which Cruz signed with a theatrical flourish in duplicate, handing both copies to her for signature. She pored over the document, obviously struggling with the reading, and then signed it with a scrawl that was almost childlike, her tongue poking out of the corner of her mouth from the effort of making her mark.

"You keep one copy. The other is for me," Cruz said. "Now tell me everything you have so we can catch this bastard and make you rich."

Both Gabriela and Cruz smiled at that, and her eyes twinkled for a brief instant.

She sat back in her chair and sipped her soda.

"I'm the caretaker – the custodian – of an apartment building near the main cathedral, seven blocks from the square. Anyway, there's a new tenant, moved in a month ago, who's your man. I'm sure of it. He looks different, with a beard…and the face is a little longer and thinner – but it's him. The eyes are the same." She took another swig and continued. "I've been like that ever since I was a child. I can remember anything. It's like taking a picture with your brain. I can do it with calendars and phone numbers, but especially with faces. And your man now lives in my building."

Cruz and Briones exchanged glances.

"In your building?" Cruz said quietly.

She nodded decisively. "Unit 6C."

"How big is your building, Gabriela?"

"Forty-two units. Seven stories."

"And when did you last see him there?" Briones asked, speaking for the first time.

"Yesterday morning. I see everyone that comes and goes from my office downstairs off the lobby, except at night. He goes out every morning at around ten, and then comes back in the evening around nine. The rest of the time he's in."

"But you didn't see him today?" Cruz asked.

"That would be kind of hard, since I'm here and had to take the bus to get here. I took the day off today to do this because it's easier to call in sick for a full day than to leave early. But I saw him yesterday. That's why I called. I figured it out after seeing the photo on the news. Took me a little while, but I'm sure."

After a few more minutes of questioning, Cruz was sure, too. Fate had smiled on them. They had another shot at nailing *El Rey*, and this time they wouldn't let him get away.

჻჻

When Cruz returned to his office, he had three messages, all from Rodriguez at CISEN, asking him to call immediately. He really didn't have time for this, but in the interests of maintaining the fragile political equilibrium between the agencies, he reluctantly dialed the number. His secretary answered, and after keeping him waiting for three minutes, his voice came on the line.

"I need you to get down here – now," Rodriguez demanded.

Cruz held the handset away from his ear for a moment, staring at it in disbelief.

"I beg your pardon?"

"You heard me. We need to talk. Now."

Cruz took a few deep breaths to calm himself before responding.

"As much as I enjoy eating half my day driving to and from your building, I'm afraid I can't today. We've got a lead on our favorite killer, and it's time sensitive," Cruz explained.

There was hesitation on the other end.

"A lead?" Rodriguez couldn't help himself. CISEN, like every other intelligence agency in the world, was mostly about knowing things. A drive to know things overruled most other concerns, and apparently this was no different.

"Yes. I can't go into it, but we're scrambling. Just tell me what's going on over the phone. I don't have time to take away from this to meet with you face to face."

Rodriguez paused again. "There's been a leak on the matter of the top secret lead we gave you, and it had to come from your end," Rodriguez accused.

Cruz barked out a humorless laugh. "Impossible. I haven't told anyone, and nobody has access to the report. If there was a leak, it wasn't from me. But tell me what happened. What's going on?" Cruz demanded.

Rodriguez didn't seem to know how to respond, but then cleared his throat.

"Our contact was murdered yesterday. By the Sinaloa cartel. That's what we were able to glean."

"So the arms dealer got snuffed by his criminal client. Why does that translate into me giving up top secret information? Do you honestly think I feed information to the largest, most dangerous criminal enterprise in the world? And to what end?" Cruz asked.

"We had listening devices in his office. We heard the execution. A high level enforcer from Aranas' gang, called Angel Talvez, went into his office and made clear before he killed him that it was because of the information he provided about *El Rey*," Rodriguez said.

"Well, that may be, but I haven't breathed a word about it to anyone, so the leak had to come from somewhere on your side. I'd start turning over rocks internally, or from whoever the contact person was with the dealer, because it wasn't me," Cruz repeated with an edge to his voice. He was rapidly tiring of being accused of treason by this smug prick.

"There is no way anyone in my group gave this information to Aranas," Rodriguez stated flatly.

"Right. So we have a mystery…like virgin birth." Cruz collected himself. "You guys are in the spy game. I'd suggest you apply some of that craftiness and figure out who in your camp sold you out. Now, if you'll excuse me, I have to go stop the man who's hell bent on killing the president – much as I enjoy our little chats," Cruz spat.

"This isn't the las– "

Cruz hung up, shaking his head. *Who did these assholes think they were?* He ran the most important police task force group in Mexico. And he wasn't even sure what the hell Rodriguez did, or what CISEN was working on. It was all too secret to discuss.

Shaking his head, he stabbed at the keypad of the telephone and dialed a number. He needed to coordinate another all-out strike to get *El Rey*. That took precedence over Rodriguez's difficulties because a lowlife gun smuggler had gotten killed – hopefully, with one of his own bullets. The line answered.

"Meeting in ten minutes with all the group heads. It's going to be a late one."

CHAPTER 24

Four dilapidated vans with tinted windows encircled the block where *El Rey's* building was darkened in the two a.m. gloom. Only three apartments had faint lights on, where insomniac or partying residents burned the midnight oil. The insides of the vans were a marked contrast from their innocuous exteriors – sophisticated electronic eavesdropping equipment sat in racks in the back, feeding visual and audio to headquarters in a real-time stream. Tiny, cutting-edge military cameras were mounted among the cracked fog lights on the roof, and one had a directional microphone pointed at the assassin's bedroom through a grimy half-lowered passenger side window.

The surveillance teams had been on watch since six that evening, but hadn't detected any sign of him. It was possible that he had spent the evening out, or slept in the interior bedroom – Gabriela had drawn a crude blueprint of the layout, and there was a study/guest bedroom that had no windows, just off the living room. They couldn't make out anything in the living room. Heavy drapes over the small windows rendered it permanently dark, as was the kitchen. They had asked about the curtains, and the woman had told them that they were new – the place hadn't come with them, only the blinds in the kitchen. *El Rey* must have valued his privacy enough to install them himself.

Putting a female officer in with Gabriela had been discussed, but Cruz had rejected the idea. He didn't want anything to tip off the assassin, and he was erring on the side of caution. Gabriela had been instructed to go in at her usual time in the morning and to call if she saw him. She was more than willing to play along.

A block away, Cruz and Briones sat in a condo they were using as the command center for the operation. Their field techs had set up the com lines and an auxiliary feed from the vans, and the four screens flickered with an eerie light in the darkened space. Another block beyond, two tactical assault personnel transports waited patiently, the men inside accustomed to hours of wakeful inactivity before they were thrown into the fray.

As the hours ticked by, fatigue set in, and the coffee maker one of Cruz's subordinates had thoughtfully brought for them got a workout. These sorts of stakeouts were the worst, and Cruz would ordinarily not have been on site, but given the unpredictable nature of their assignment, he and Briones had chosen to stay up and supervise. At three a.m. a soft knock sounded at the door, and two officers entered carrying folding cots; blue canvas supported by aluminum tubular frames.

Cruz had always hated the field beds, but had to admit they came in handy on all-nighters. The officers in the assault teams weren't so lucky. He picked up a radio handset and murmured instructions into it – the men could stand down for four hours and grab some shut-eye while they could. He wanted them ready for action at seven.

Gabriela had told them that *El Rey* usually didn't go anywhere before ten in the morning, but he didn't completely trust her judgment. She started work at nine, so for all she knew he could have been out from midnight to six every night at the clubs. She routinely stayed in her little office until ten at night, so he was fairly confident she had his daily schedule down pat.

Although, right now he was seriously questioning the entire affair. He knew it was the boredom and lack of sleep that had him pessimistic, but he couldn't shake the feeling that this was a non-starter. The discussion with CISEN had come back to nag at him. What if *El Rey* somehow had eyes and ears in the *Federales*? In his own squad? It wasn't impossible. Nothing was impossible, including that CISEN may have been penetrated.

He was a long way from when he'd joined the force, with high hopes and ideas about changing Mexico for the better. After the better part of twenty-five years in the federal police, he'd shed any illusions about his fellow man. The country, *his* country, ran on graft and corruption. As did most, he supposed. Some had civilized veneers and pretensions of honesty, but when it came to money, everywhere was the same. It just was a question of how much. The only difference in Mexico was that it was cheaper than in the U.S. because they'd eliminated the middle men – there were no lobbyists or influence peddlers, just wires to offshore bank accounts or briefcases of cash.

"You want to take the first watch, or should I?" Cruz asked Briones.

"Go ahead and get some rest, sir. I can monitor things until, what, five? That's two hours of sleep apiece if we're going to regroup at seven, but it's better than nothing."

"Are you sure?" Cruz asked, eyeing the cot.

"Absolutely. Too much coffee," Briones said, although they both knew that wasn't the truth.

"All right, then. Wake me if the slightest thing happens," Cruz said, with a doubtful glance at the monitors.

අංගුණ

Ciudad Juárez, Mexico

The sun was already heating up the air temperature, even though it had only been light for fifty-five minutes. Traffic was just starting to hit with full force for rush hour, which made the congestion caused by the assembled police, military and television vans a major bottleneck on one of the main thoroughfares. The soldiers were visibly agitated, their weapons at the ready as they formed a protective perimeter around the cops and the reporters, who were chatting as though they were at a sporting event, waiting for the big match to begin. Two uniformed officers waved traffic around a roadblock, directing the cars to an alternative route, and the combination of having to loop around, coupled with rubberneckers straining to see what the fuss was about, had caused a vicious snarl.

The captain of the Juárez office of the federal police approached the ranking officer of the army detachment, Major Trujillo, carrying a cup of

OXXO coffee in a polystyrene cup. The major grinned when he saw his friend, Captain Pompa, up early for once.

"This must be very inconvenient for a late sleeper like you, eh?" he offered by way of hello.

"You have no idea. I was just getting to bed when I got the call," Pompa fired back.

The men smiled and took in the creeping procession of annoyed motorists. "What do you think it means? Another round of retribution killings going to start?"

"No, I don't think so. Although this is worrisome. They usually don't target the press. Then again, why should journalists be any different than us? We all bleed the same," Pompa observed.

"What's his name?" Major Trujillo asked.

"Eligio Nerevez. Worked the crime beat at one of the local rags. Seems like he pissed off the wrong people. Dangerous line of work." Pompa took another sip of coffee. "I don't have to tell you that nobody saw anything last night. This was called in by someone driving, who didn't want to identify himself. Imagine that. Wanted to remain anonymous..."

"Nerevez? That's him? Huh. I recognize the name. He just did that series on the bloggers who were outing politicians on the take. I thought it was an ambitious project, but you're right. Hazardous...obviously," Major Trujillo agreed.

"He could have just printed a list of every elected official in the state. That would have saved time," Pompa said, and both men laughed.

"You want to cut him down, or should we?" the major inquired, eyeing Pompa's coffee. He wished he'd had the foresight to get a cup before taking up his station. It was too late now, but the smell was intoxicating.

They turned and considered the body of the young man, hanging upside down, suspended from the steel guardrail by a yellow nylon rope around his ankles. The blood on his face was coagulated and brown, already dried. A small amount had stained the road beneath him, its rust-colored puddle a contrast to the filthy gray. His hands were bound behind him, and half his head was gone from where a large caliber round had entered his mouth, blowing the top of his skull off. Next to him, a bed sheet with the distinctive markings of the Juárez cartel hung, issuing a warning to any good citizens who wanted to shorten their lives by focusing on the cartel's misdeeds. It was a crude, but effective communication tool. Everyone got the point: taking on the cartels was bad for your health.

Pompa shook his head. "Nah. We'll do it."

❧

At seven o'clock there was still no sign of activity in the apartment. Cruz slurped an oversized mug of coffee and ate an energy bar while watching the feed from the vans, and Briones used the bathroom. They'd just gotten confirmation that the tactical teams were back in place, awaiting instruction, but Cruz was unsure how to proceed. He felt better after the glorified nap, but not nearly at peak performance, and while he wanted this to be over he also didn't want to blow their only chance at *El Rey*. He battled internally for a few minutes and then decided to have everyone stand down until they spotted their quarry. Better to keep the surveillance going than to rush in as they had at the machine shop. On that one, in retrospect, they should have hung back and waited for the assassin to exit the building and then taken him. He didn't want to make a similar miscalculation on this one.

Cruz radioed the tactical team and relayed his orders. Remain in place. Next, he contacted the van operators and instructed them to do the same. They were also likely exhausted by now, but that was the job and it came with the territory. At worst, the two man teams could sleep in short shifts, as he had. It wasn't his problem, but he still felt sorry for the men.

The morning dragged by, and at noon Cruz made a judgment call. They would go in, but stealthily, only three plainclothes officers using a passkey provided by the soon-to-be-wealthy Gabriela. If *El Rey* was in there, he'd managed to shield the apartment from their best surveillance efforts, but that didn't surprise Cruz.

Cruz turned to brief the men he had selected, who had arrived a few minutes earlier.

"Guerrero, you, Simon and Roberto do the entry. Use whatever force is necessary. You have my permission. And make sure you have vests on under your jackets. I don't want to have to call anyone's family and tell them daddy's not coming home."

Guerrero pounded his chest with his fist, thumping the Kevlar panels of the bulletproof vest for emphasis. They were ready.

The men made their way to the apartment complex, scanning the sidewalk reflexively. They stopped in the well-kept lobby and got the key from Gabriela, then took the elevator to the sixth floor. The building was a medium luxury property, where the rent on a two bedroom apartment would run three month's salary of any of the officers; when they exited the elevator they stepped onto marble tiles polished to a glassy finish.

El Rey's apartment was the last on the left. The officers moved soundlessly on rubber soles, pistols ready, safeties off. Guerrero, as usual, was in the lead, and he moved to the far side of the doorway, with his two partners taking the opposite wall. He gingerly slipped the key into the lock and turned it with the delicacy of a neurosurgeon. Their ears strained for any hint of movement inside, but heard nothing. Guerrero nodded at Simon and Roberto, holding each man's gaze, and then with a deep breath, he turned the knob and eased the door open. Under Guerrero's protective cover, Simon lunged into the foyer, doing a lightning scan of the small entryway with his weapon but detecting no threat.

Roberto and Guerrero followed him, guns sweeping, and they moved as one into the darkened space beyond the entry. As their eyes adjusted to the paucity of light they could make out a kitchen on the right and a larger area straight ahead. Guerrero moved past them into the living room, his Beretta M9A1 now pointing at the master bedroom doorway, and then he stopped, sniffing the air.

What the hell?

He turned to Roberto, who was reaching for the wall switch to give them some light, and screamed, "Nooo…!"

It was too late.

A blast erupted through the apartment door, blowing out all the windows, showering the street below with glass and debris as the fireball shot through the apertures. The crude five gallon gas can had been augmented by leaving the stove propane running with the pilot light off and the automatic shutoff disabled, creating a massive bomb. Rigging a simple electrically-activated detonator had been laughably simple. The three men were instantly incinerated, the air sucked out of their lungs almost as quickly as their skin melted and their bones seared.

Cruz watched the firestorm erupt through the apartment's façade on the monitors and realized immediately that somehow, the assassin had trumped them.

He threw back his chair and slammed his coffee cup down against the table, shattering it with a crash. Briones pushed away from his vantage point and moved to help, and then thought better of it when he saw the look in the captain's eyes.

Cruz licked away a rivulet of blood from his hand and wrapped a paper towel from the coffee tray around it, seemingly oblivious to the pain. He collected himself with a shudder and then took another glance at the screens, watching black smoke belch from the front of the structure. He didn't need to wait for the report from the team that was rushing towards the building.

That afternoon, he would be making the visits he dreaded to the three spouses.

CHAPTER 25

Cruz exited the conference room where he'd been meeting with the president's security people, frustrated at their conviction that *El Rey* couldn't get to him. He understood that they believed they were good at their jobs, but he knew that the assassin was better – which wasn't to say that the president's detail wasn't dedicated or good, they just weren't *El Rey*. He'd already proved he could get past them once. And not only them, but also the American Secret Service, considered the best in the world.

He'd said as much at their get-together, but met with blank stares and polite assurances, except for the president's chief of staff, who had seemed to get it. Then again, his career was predicated on his boss continuing to breathe, so he was probably more motivated than the rest. He'd taken Cruz aside on the way out and slipped him his card, and asked him to call whenever he had more information or any breakthrough ideas on how to handle the mess. That had given Cruz hope, even if it was a slim reed upon which to rest optimism.

He walked to his car, waiting in the secure lot, and thought to himself that they were in serious trouble. If it had been him, he would simply cancel any appearance that could create an opportunity to execute the president. He really didn't understand how these men's minds worked. They'd blithely told him that they had every confidence in his abilities, had listened politely as he'd detailed the story of the threat, as well as the latest series of miraculous escapes, and then thanked him for his time. It was like everyone was in denial – like *El Rey*'s existence, if they acknowledged it, challenged their competence, and so it was better to ignore him.

And there was the question of how the assassin had escaped, which still lingered in Cruz's mind – as well as how the Sinaloans had known that the arms dealer had been the leak.

Cruz mentally went down the list of everyone who had been privy to the task force's moves and dismissed them one at a time as potential traitors. Briones had proved his loyalty with blood, as had many of his group chiefs. They put their lives on the line every day to combat the cartels and had all lost more than their fair share of men to the bastards. There was no way they would sell him out for money. Even if some of them were corruptible, and he didn't deceive himself that they were altar boys, passing information to *El Rey* went beyond anything they would risk. It was high treason, especially if it resulted in the death of the president. Even the most larcenous and greedy man drew the line somewhere, and that was not a line – it was a twenty-meter-high wall.

His driver opened his door for him, and he gratefully sank into the seat, feeling exhausted by the presentation as well as the course of the last few days. He'd attended a memorial service for the men he'd lost at the apartment – there was literally nothing left of them after the explosion, so it was the best they could do – and had tried to comfort the wives and children of men he'd known only in a professional sense, and even then, not particularly well. His words had sounded hollow to him even as he'd uttered all the usual clichés. It was disheartening – the assassin was winning every round. Which meant that the trend wasn't Cruz's friend.

As much as it pained him, he would need to begin a quiet investigation into his group leaders, to see if anyone had recently come into some inexplicable money or had bought a car or home outside of their pay range. He couldn't just discount the possibility someone had rolled, as improbable as it was to him. Harsh experience had long ago taught him to expect the worst, and then be happy if the outcome turned out anything less than horrible. While he was now happy with his new life with Dinah, there were still nights where he awoke in a cold sweat, dreaming of his family's final moments, or reliving the day he'd opened the special delivery box to find the heads of his wife and young daughter in it, with a scorpion in each of their mouths. He hoped that eventually he could keep the horror at bay, but during times of stress their ghosts came back to haunt him.

Thank God for Dinah. They were building a life from nothing, and she was a perfect partner. He felt guilty talking shop with her – he'd never told her that *El Rey* had been responsible for her father's death, preferring to leave the fiction in place that it had been some sort of crazy, or a robbery gone horribly wrong. Better to let the dead slumber in peace than allow them to ruin the lives of the living. Knowing the truth wouldn't have helped Dinah get over the heartbreak of a murdered parent, so there was no point to sharing it with her.

As the car wound its way through traffic on the way back to headquarters, Cruz remained silent, lost in his thoughts. They only had a few days to go until the president's speech, and he didn't like their chances. Barring a miracle, Cruz dejectedly realized that he wouldn't be able to catch the assassin in time, which meant that the only thing that stood in the way of *El Rey* murdering the president was his security detail.

That wouldn't end well.

෴

El Rey put the final touches on the device he had so painstakingly assembled and smiled at the thought of the seemingly near escape from his apartment. He'd caught the cleaning woman paying just a little too much attention to him, and she'd been a hair too quick to avert her gaze when he'd noticed her. The effort to appear uninterested had appeared almost comical to him, and he'd quickly determined that his days in the apartment were over. That night he'd moved his few belongings out under cover of darkness and had rigged things to provide a nasty surprise for anyone breaking into his place. Which he had no doubt would be the police.

He'd seen the news coverage of his old photo and had thought that he'd sufficiently altered his appearance to be in the clear, but the woman had somehow matched him. It happened, occasionally, and rather than dwell on it he'd cleared out. But he wasn't worried. It had been a fluke, plain and simple.

He stepped back from the work table and inspected his project with pride of craftsmanship. It would do.

Now all that remained was to get it within range of the president, and the rest would be history in the making. Then he could go back into retirement and savor the life of a rich man in South America – a future that in no way seemed bad. It would all be concluded soon enough, and then he would disappear, never to be heard from again.

❧❦

Don Aranas greeted his guest, Estaban Mareli, and offered him a seat at a small table in the open air of the courtyard. This particular home was built in a typical hacienda fashion, around a private central court with a fountain, with terracotta tile underfoot and rustic sponge painting in bright orange and purple hues splashing color on the walls. The water tinkled in a pleasing way, creating a kind of Latin Zen effect.

"Coffee?" Aranas offered to Mareli, gesturing at the white clad man waiting in the wings by the dark alder and stained glass French doors.

"Please."

Aranas held up two fingers; the man nodded before turning to enter the house.

Mareli studied Aranas' face for a few moments. "How are you, my friend?" he asked.

"Ah, you know. Things could be better. We've lost a number of shipments on the Mexican side of the border over the last few months. An irritant, although in the end, not material," Aranas replied.

"Yes, I've seen the numbers. I agree it's unfortunate. But sometimes a necessary cost of doing business, *eh?*"

"Perhaps. But I liked our luck better under the last two regimes. This one seems to be favoring groups that aren't aligned with our interests, and that's causing complications." Aranas rubbed his chin. "I thought we had it taken care of, but it appears not."

"Well, the only thing that is sure is that nothing will remain the same. Change is everywhere. We adapt or we perish," Mareli offered.

The coffee arrived, and neither man spoke until the steward was out of earshot again.

"Yes. Change. Speaking of which, we had another regrettable occurrence recently. Our mutual acquaintance, Carlos Herreira, was passing information to the Mexican authorities. Steps had to be taken," Aranas said.

Mareli feigned surprise. "The authorities? Jesus. What are people thinking these days? I don't understand it. He was always dependable, and then one day he goes and does something like this…?" He put one hand on the table and studied his nails, as if for guidance. "What is there to say? When a dog goes rabid, you have to put him down, even if you love him. I'm sure you only did what was necessary."

Mareli had known this was going to be the subject of the discussion, but figured a show of indignation was obligatory. He lifted his fine china cup and took an appreciative sip of the rich brew.

"You introduced us."

"Seven years ago. And the man was as reliable as a Swiss watch until now."

"Hmm. He was indeed. I do not hold it against you. He was honest, until he wasn't. And he paid the ultimate price for his treachery," Aranas said.

Mareli showed no emotion, but internally he was relieved. One never knew how the cartel chiefs would react, although Aranas was one of the most stable of the bunch. *What the fuck had the idiot been into that he'd crossed the Don?* It didn't take a genius to understand that was suicide.

"So how can I help you today? How can I be of service?" Mareli asked, wondering what the drug lord wanted. He suspected he knew, but didn't want to presume.

"Our arrangement is still working well – once the drugs hit the border, we've had minimal problems, which is good for everyone. I'm grateful for the protection, as always, even if I do think it comes at a steep price," Aranas observed. The fifteen percent of the profit he paid Mareli's group for safe passage into the U.S. and assistance with distribution always came up, but there was no negotiation. And in truth, it was worth it. In the old days, they could expect at least ten percent losses due to law enforcement and sometimes more. It netted out to be roughly the same, but there was peace of mind with Mareli. "I only wish our Mexican officials were as honest as you are. You do a deal with them, and then they stab you in the back as you're getting up from the negotiating table. A pity, and unforeseeable, but it is what it is."

"Our arrangement has survived the test of time," Mareli agreed.

"Carlos' untimely demise has put me in an uncomfortable situation. I need you to find me someone to replace him. Someone you can vouch for, who will be dependable. I think this year and next will be banner years in the arms trade for Mexico, and my demand is strong. I'm asking you to help me with this. I don't like dealing with the freelancers that come and go. Yet another headache I can do without."

Finally. The real reason for the summons. Aranas needed another conduit for weapons. Not unexpected, considering the conflict he was involved in, or the abrupt termination of his last vendor.

"I will ask for a recommendation. There might be an existing entity, or someone who wants to get into the business. We can take care of the supply issue on our end, but he's largely on his own with the Mexican side. Let me talk to my people and see what we can come up with," Mareli assured him. "Is this an urgent matter?"

"No, but I don't want to wind up in a situation where I have to go into the open market when I'm having other difficulties. As you know, word travels fast, and if rumors of my group being unable to secure necessary arms were to circulate, it would embolden my enemies."

"I see. I'll make this a priority. You have nothing to worry about," Mareli said, returning to his coffee.

They discussed the economics of the trade, and the shifting product mix – heroin was down with the worldwide glut since the U.S. had invaded Afghanistan and production was booming. Cocaine demand was down five percent, but methamphetamines were up fifteen. It was a volatile market, but one they understood innately.

Mareli provided more than simple protection. He was also instrumental in cementing the banking relations that allowed Aranas to launder his funds. He'd set up several companies in Panama to handle cash deposits moved through their casino operations and had interests in numerous banks in the region, as well as in Texas and Miami. It was a seamless mechanism, where the cash that didn't hit Mexico would get deposited in his banks in the States, and the Mexican money moved to

Panama. From there, it was scrubbed and could be converted into legitimate funds – for a ten percent fee, of course.

An hour after he arrived, their meeting was over, and Mareli sank into the soft leather of his Mercedes limousine's rear seat with relief. Once they were underway, he made a series of calls, arranging for his jet to be ready to take him to the U.S. that afternoon. He'd stop at his hotel for his passport and to close out the bill, and then be on his way.

The final call was to a U.S. number, using a different phone – with a state-of-the-art attachment that would scramble it with military-level encryption, rendering it indecipherable to eavesdroppers. The odds of a call being intercepted were remote, however it was protocol and, as such, not to be ignored.

The odd ring of the secure line in Virginia sounded, and after switching through a series of relays, a familiar voice answered.

"How did it go?" Kent Fredericks asked, sounding like he was two feet away.

"Good, good. It was as expected. He needs another gun runner."

"Maybe he shouldn't have put a bullet through the head of the last one," Kent observed. His division in the CIA had gotten a report on the killing almost in real time.

"Apparently, our boy was playing both sides of the field. The man found out and took action."

"I thought he was selling to everyone? What's the big deal?" Kent asked.

"He double-crossed the wrong guy, is what happened. Now we need another reliable source. I'm hopping on the plane and will be there in time for dinner. You free?"

"For you? I'm always free. Pick you up at the airport?"

"You bet. I'll fill you in on the rest when I get in."

"10-4."

CHAPTER 26

Ramirez stood with his hands on his hips, his dirty coveralls stained with mystery fluids, a cigarette twitching between his lips as he stared at a bank of red clay planters and debated his options with his assistant, Paolo.

"How the hell would I know what happened? Sometimes the damned things die. That's how nature works. You live, you die," he exclaimed, drawing a lung full of smoke.

"It looks like something killed them. Maybe pollution?" Paolo speculated.

"I doubt it was the smog. They're Mexican plants. They were raised on this stuff," Ramirez rasped, before succumbing to a phlegmy coughing fit for thirty seconds. When he was done, he dabbed his eyes and resumed smoking, with a wary glance at the offending cigarette.

"So what do we do?"

"We call someone, and they bring new ones. These have had it."

Ramirez glared at the dead shrubs as though they'd committed suicide for the sole purpose of complicating his life. This couldn't have happened at a worse time. They were only two days away from the president's speech, and the plants on either side of the east doors to the legislative meeting hall, at the top of the massive stairs leading up to the distinctive façade, with its huge mural depicting an eagle clutching a snake, had chosen this moment to give up the ghost. It wouldn't do to have dead vegetation marring the entrance of the Mexican congress and spoiling the photo opportunity. Wouldn't do at all.

That evening, workers appeared with hand trucks and dutifully hauled away the planters that housed the palms, replacing them with healthy new examples. One of the employees, in particular, seemed especially enthusiastic about the duty – no doubt because he was new and somewhat of a dimwit. The others griped about having to work late with no overtime pay, but he just smiled his idiotic grin and adjusted the flat-brimmed company baseball hat he'd been issued as he whistled, rolling the heavy planters up the ramp on the side of the stairs.

When they were finished, the workers' supervisor approached once the crew chief had made a call, and the small group of laborers stood by the delivery truck as the boss inspected their work.

"This one is crooked," he said, pointing to a planter on the right side of the door. The crew chief waved for the men, and two of them trotted up. "Straighten it out," he ordered.

A few minutes later, the supervisor nodded, and the task was completed.

The men piled into the back of the truck, happy to finally be going home after another hard day of earning their living with their backs and their hands.

❧

Cruz got the call the next morning as he was settling in behind his desk at headquarters.

"They found a bomb," Briones announced.

"Where are you? Who found a bomb, and where?"

"I'll be right in. Give me two minutes," Briones said and hung up.

Cruz fixed him with a curious stare when he sauntered in five minutes later, munching on a muffin. He took one of the seats at the meeting table and leaned back before speaking.

"Bad day for *Señor El Rey*. The bomb dogs found his device this morning on a sweep of the building."

"What? At the congress?" Cruz exclaimed. The president's speech was that afternoon.

Briones nodded. "One of the planters by the mural, not thirty feet from where they were setting up the podium. It was buried in it, with a triggering device. Remote controlled. Enough Semtex to take out everything for a hundred yards. He'd wrapped it in ball bearings inside a protective plastic sheet to keep it from being damaged if they watered the plants. Clever. About the size of a small microwave oven. It would have killed everyone on the platform."

"The same basic approach as he used the last time," Cruz mused.

"Yes. That's what I was thinking. But thanks to a sedulous beagle, he's been foiled," Briones said with glee.

Cruz got up and poured himself a cup of coffee and then sat opposite Briones at the table.

"Doesn't that seem kind of sloppy to you?" Cruz asked.

"Not necessarily. They were lucky to have found it. He probably figured it would be the typical lackadaisical approach, and nobody would notice. As it was, it took them three tries to figure it out. One of my buddies was on duty there doing backup security for the president's advance detail, and he said the handler thought the dog was interested in the planter because he had to go."

They both chuckled at that, and then Cruz became serious again.

"It just seems too easy. When have we ever dealt with anything related to *El Rey* where it was easy?"

"But it wasn't. That's what I'm trying to tell you. The odds favored him getting away with it. He might well have. It was just lucky that the dog was persistent, and that we put the president's staff on high alert. Maybe if they hadn't been, the bomb squad would have pulled the dog away and never thought twice about it. I think this was a victory for the good guys, sir," Briones concluded.

"I hope so. But I'm skeptical. Nothing he's ever done has made it easy for us," Cruz said stubbornly. "No matter. Maybe you're right. Today is a win."

❧❧

That afternoon, Cruz and Briones signed in and went through the security cordon around the congress site, where they watched the combined efforts of the soldiers and the president's guard to sanitize the area. Cruz had to admit that the display of force presented an impressive deterrent. Still, Cruz and Briones were on alert, second-guessing every precaution and watching for any possible weaknesses in the security. They walked around the entire compound, noting that all the steps they would have taken, had been. The park across the way from where the president would issue his state of the union address had been closed to all but spectators who were being methodically searched, and the apartments beyond it were under watch. The freeway would be closed a few minutes before the president arrived, and kept closed for a half mile in each direction until it had concluded. Cruz had to concede that there seemed to be little chance for an assassin to try for the president, although he still had a nagging feeling that they'd gotten off too light.

He'd called the head of security and suggested that the president give his speech from the much easier to protect inner courtyard of the building, but had been shut down. Even when he'd pressed and pointed out that a motivated sniper could pick the president off if he was able to be accurate from over eight hundred yards, his advice had been greeted with disinterest. They'd found the bomb. That was that.

At precisely five p.m. the sound of the president's arrival drowned out the clamor of traffic and the crowd that was being held at bay by barricades. The presidential helicopter set down on the large yellow circle designated for it in the long rectangular parking lot at the southern side of the building. As the spinning blades slowed, the alert level of the sentries noticeably increased, and they shifted restlessly. Cruz watched as the door swung open and the Mexican plainclothes equivalent of the Secret Service got out of the aircraft, forming a loose protective half ring around the aircraft door, and then the president's distinctive form stepped onto the asphalt. He waved at the crowd and the gathered media, then proceeded with his entourage up the steps to the building, where he was scheduled to move to the east side and give his speech in front of the huge stone mural that was the emblem of national pride.

Cruz scanned the surrounding buildings for any sign of danger, but spotted nothing. Snipers watched for anything unusual from their perch on the roof of the congress, their field of vision constantly moving, looking for telltales. The structures within range of a shooter had all been searched and cleared. Traffic had been diverted to streets that posed no possible problems. Even the metro trains had been paused during the scheduled time for the speech so they wouldn't drown out the president's words. Everything appeared to be under control.

The president moved to the podium and cleared his throat. The assembled dignitaries sat down in unison after a round of lackluster applause. Nobody was expecting anything groundbreaking from a head of state that had only been on the job a few short months, other than the inevitable retraction of the campaign promises he'd made to win the vote. It was almost an obligatory formality – the admission that things were more complicated than he'd thought when he'd been on the election trail, and that it would be foolish to make any hasty moves while things were in such a delicate state of flux, and so on. Every president was forced to abandon his pre-election commitments. It was a rite of passage. The only mildly interesting part would be whether he blamed fate, the opposition party, or the economy. Perhaps today would be all three.

In the end, not much changed but the name on the door. Everyone knew the game. It was the same everywhere.

El Rey watched the proceedings with interest. The security was close to comprehensive, unlike the customary routine he'd studied, no doubt due to the bomb that had been found. That had been a masterstroke of misdirection, well worth the two days of drudgery at the landscaping company as a flunky. The hardest part had actually been poisoning the existing plants so they would need to be replaced – the neighborhood wasn't the best in town, and he'd had to do it at three in the morning, dodging the patrols of guards who kept the building free of graffiti and vandalism.

Part of him was annoyed that they'd found the bomb, and another was happy. His alternative plan was so much more innovative. Not that he wouldn't have gladly pushed the button and terminated his target while making the speech. That would have been good. But in his experience few things worth doing were ever easy, and the truth was that it had always been likely that the congress bomb would be spotted, given the heightened threat awareness. Now that it had been neutralized, the hope was that everyone would breathe a sigh of relief, and underestimate him. Just a little.

He switched off the television and put his feet up on the sofa of his new digs. There was nothing more to see, unless he really felt like hearing a speech filled with lies and recriminations. He had better things to do.

With any luck, all the president's men would relax and make his job easier.

If not, no matter.

The president was still as good as dead.

CHAPTER 27

Nuevo Laredo, Tamaulipas, Mexico

As the sun dipped deeper into the horizon, heat waves rippled off the scorched earth, distorting geometry and creating an otherworldly impression of the whitewashed buildings. Eighteen-foot-high concrete walls enclosed the compound, with a twelve-foot-high chain link fence outside that, topped with gleaming razor wire. Guards sat in the turrets that jutted high above, watching the massive interior courtyard where prisoners roamed, some congregating in cliques at the farthest reaches. Duty at the prison was a plum posting due to the under-the-table payments virtually every guard saw from the cartels to allow access for contraband, as well as to turn a blind eye when called upon.

The Nuevo Laredo Detention Center housed some of the most violent criminals in Mexico – every type of psychopathic killer and miscreant imaginable. Not surprisingly, a substantial portion of the prison population was cartel members, and it had long been rumored that Los Zetas were the de facto operators of the place. Located just south of the Texas border in a troubled state widely regarded as out of government control and under the rule of the cartels, the prison was considered to be a veritable vacation getaway for Los Zetas members sentenced to spend their lives there.

Los Zetas had originally started as the armed wing of the tremendously powerful Gulf cartel, when a group of thirty former special forces commandos and police deserted and took up employment with that syndicate. The cartel drew its name from the radio call signal of the leader of the deserters – the letter Z, or Zeta in Spanish. Over time, Los Zetas grew to dwarf the Gulf cartel, and after a split several years back became a feared rival, its power having eclipsed that of its parent. Los Zetas was notorious even by the ultra-violent and brutal cartel standards, and had earned a reputation as the most vicious criminal group in the world. That had been underscored countless times, with massacres a routine part of its operations.

In 2011, one hundred and ninety-three people were killed in what became infamous as the Tamaulipas massacre, and that same year, two hundred and forty-nine people were slaughtered in the Durango massacre. And the burgeoning organized crime syndicate's operations were now international in scope, as illustrated by the slaughter of thirty in Guatemala, where the group had partnered with paramilitary groups for personnel and specialized weapons training.

Federal troops had been moved to the troubled Mexican border region in an effort to maintain control, but the violence continued, and over time intensified in ferocity. This ongoing state of war resulted in a high number of cartel casualties, placing strain on Los Zetas' organization demand for skilled hands, even as it simultaneously battled its adversary, the Sinaloa cartel. Over the last two years, it had succeeded in taking territory away from its enemy, but at a high cost. Concurrent wars with the Gulf cartel, Sinaloa and the Mexican military had taken their toll, and even as its power grew, Los Zetas began experiencing a manpower shortage. Unskilled labor in the form of deserting police and regular army troops swelled the ranks, but the specialized training offered to the marines and commando squads was prized. Due to the attrition, skilled soldiers who had the requisite experience had been in short supply of late. Even the most hardened and avaricious thought twice about taking the high paying, but lethal, duty.

Once it was dark, the prison population was called to dinner with the clamor of a bell, which prompted the surly men to form ragged lines outside the commissary. Only, tonight was different than most evenings. Tonight would be when a carefully planned escape took place, hopefully freeing a large number of Zetas. Word had circulated among the group, and they were ready. But before leaving, there were errands to attend to.

Manuel Ortiz was a lieutenant in the Gulf cartel, sentenced to forty years for organized crime charges relating to murder, drug trafficking, kidnapping and assault. His heavy features belied a peasant lineage, and his squat physique was accentuated by hours of prison weight training, which served to make him seem shorter than his five-foot-seven height. He had a large entourage of bodyguards in the facility – his vast fortune from being a key component of the cartel's Texas trafficking route enabled him to afford the best. Every day in the facility was a potential bloodbath for him, with Los Zetas just on the far side of the prison yard, and Ortiz lived in a constant state of readiness.

When the attack came, it was sudden and brutal. Scores of inmates ran at his contingent and began stabbing them with homemade shanks – sharpened metal shards or pieces of rebar, patiently honed to razor sharp points over countless hours in darkened cells. His men fought back, but they were no match for the overwhelming number of assailants. The entire skirmish occurred in a muted silence, the only noise the wet thwacking of the blades stabbing into flesh, again and again, and the thudding of bodies falling to the ground, blood spreading beneath them. Forty seconds after it started, Ortiz and his seven Gulf cartel brethren lay dead or dying, and another fifteen bodyguards were wounded, as well as twelve of the attackers.

Once the massacre was over, two uniformed guards appeared near the security offices and signaled to the waiting Los Zetas prisoners. They moved as a unit into the interior, the double security doors wedged open thoughtfully for maximum traffic flow. Inside, three more guards unlocked the multiple barred doors designed to keep prisoners contained, and within minutes the stream of killers made its way out to the street, where the men quickly dispersed to the surrounding side streets and climbed into pickup trucks and vans that sat with engines running. None of the guards in the turrets noticed anything, preferring to occupy their time on more healthy pursuits than getting in the middle of a cartel-organized prison break. The vehicles sped off in a cloud of exhaust and dust, and in moments the area was empty.

Ten minutes later, the alarm was sounded, and within an hour the streets around the prison were filled with soldiers, police and media. One hundred and sixty prisoners, each a hardened murderer in the enforcement wing of the Los Zetas syndicate, had escaped. Nobody could explain why the federal troops who had been stationed outside the prison to prevent exactly this kind of breakout had been called away, nor by whom, but they had been. A regrettable incident that would be investigated at some future point. Like so many that seemed to occur when money and power were in play.

Likewise, nobody could explain how the dozens of guards on duty in the towers had missed a mass exodus of prisoners after a pitched battle and mass slaughter near the commissary. Nobody recalled having seen anything. It was one of the many commonplace miracles at the prison – three other mass escapes had taken place over the last two years, each a complete surprise to the warden and his staff. The running joke was that the Zetas used the prison as an inexpensive hotel where the guards and army were there to ensure nobody could get in to harm them. Stories abounded of inmates who disappeared for a day, then reappeared like magic, one of their rivals in town mysteriously gone missing. It was hard not to see the punch line, even if the humor was of a black variety.

The five guards who had disappeared were never heard from again. The rumor was that each man had seen five hundred thousand dollars for his role in the debacle – more than enough to live a full and untroubled life of leisure in one of the many small fishing hamlets along the coast.

Newspaper and television coverage expressed outrage at the escape, and the president ordered more troops to the region, effectively closing the barn door after the mare had bolted. The prior administration had warned the prison system to tighten its security numerous times, and yet Tamaulipas saw more prison breaks per year than many restaurants saw customers. It was further evidence that the state was a rogue one, much like the fifty percent of Colombia that was under rebel or paramilitary control – where the government dared not go and had no effective jurisdiction.

On the U.S. side of the border, local law enforcement warned the federal government that the cartel-driven violence and lawlessness was spilling over into the U.S., but the Feds took the stance that all was well. Speeches were made about how the borders were safe, in spite of the easily observable fact that countless tons of marijuana, cocaine, meth and heroin made it through every week, along with a steady stream of undocumented immigrants, many of them fleeing from the violence in their border states in Mexico, and some of them cartel soldiers migrating the criminality north.

The American government reassured its population that no emergency existed, even as police and state government demanded National Guard troops to bolster what was obvious to them as a porous border.

As far as the Feds were concerned, there was no problem.

಼ೊ಼

Cruz's meeting with the president's chief of staff had gone better than he'd expected. The man had seemed very interested in the recommendations he'd made for safeguarding the president's safety. The head of the security detail had been there with them, and then, towards the end, to Cruz's considerable surprise, after a hushed discussion on a cell phone, the president had stepped into the conference room to hear a synopsis.

Cruz had recited the entire story, including his experiences on the last assassination attempt, his impressions on this one, and the myriad times *El Rey* had outfoxed them. All three men had listened intently, but the real fireworks had started when he'd finished with his presentation and the president had asked him for his recommendation. The head of security's mouth had literally dropped open when he'd told them what he thought was the prudent course of action, even as the chief of staff had nodded. The president's normally impassive expression had broken, just for a moment, and the trace of a smile had played at the corners of his mouth.

Now that it was over, he wondered whether it had all been an episode of temporary insanity. He'd met the last president briefly after the G-20 Summit and had shaken hands with him as he'd thanked Cruz for his efforts, but that was different than sitting in a room across from the seat of power itself and arguing for an unthinkable course of action.

Whatever his life had become, it certainly wasn't boring.

That evening, when he got home, Dinah seemed in better spirits than she had been in for weeks, and they decided to go to one of her favorite restaurants. Over a wonderful meal of slow-cooked *cochinita pibil* and margaritas, he'd given her the abbreviated version of his day, including the meeting with the president.

Even though she seemed interested, he left out the nitty-gritty of his recommendation. Some things were too weird to say out loud, and his surrealistic impromptu suggestion was one of them. Bad enough he had floated it past the great man himself and two of the most influential men in the cabinet. That didn't mean he needed to also embarrass himself with his wife-to-be.

When they arrived at their new condo, bodyguards safely ensconced downstairs, they left a trail of clothes in the hall as they made their way to the bedroom.

For the first time in months, Cruz had the feeling that it was all going to turn out fine.

CHAPTER 28

The morning of the Easter mass at *Catedral Metropolitana de la Asuncion de Maria*, the streets surrounding the church were a nightmare. The cathedral – the largest on the continent – was located in the heart of Mexico City and was ringed on three sides by huge boulevards, which were closed off to traffic for the hour duration of the mass. The presidential helicopter would arrive on the south side of the cathedral, where there was eighty feet of open space for it to touch down. The decision had been made to close the streets for fifteen minutes prior to its landing until after it took off, in the interests of avoiding the complications that thousands of vehicles could introduce into the security scenario – a valid precaution, but one that played hell with downtown traffic.

Likewise, spectators were limited to the huge square across the street, where the citizenry would be confined to an area that was barricaded off at the far edge of the six lane street that fronted the main entrance on the south side. Already, a crowd of almost twenty thousand had gathered, waiting for the spectacle to begin. Soldiers formed a perimeter around the church grounds, and the president's security forces were deployed along the sidewalks of the buildings adjacent to and facing it. Snipers were nestled in the cathedral's towering bell towers, scanning the rooftops of the numerous buildings surrounding the church for threats.

Cruz watched the proceedings from his vantage point near the front entrance of the cathedral, Briones in tow. The president was due in ten minutes, and as usual Cruz was anxious. *El Rey* had vanished, having apparently given up once his bomb had been discovered at the congress, but Cruz didn't buy it. The man wasn't the type to just quit. For all his reprehensible qualities, he had a hell of a work ethic Cruz understood in a very odd and dysfunctional way. *El Rey* was committed and singularly focused. Qualities he knew only too well. For all his distaste of the killer's occupation, he had to concede that he'd never seen anything like his ability to pull off the impossible.

Vendors meandered through the crowd of onlookers hawking *churros* and cotton candy, and a fair number of both uniformed and plainclothes police were interspersed in the throng to watch for pickpockets or possible assailants. A security gateway had been erected at the far end of the square near the ice rink, where *Chilangos*, as the residents of Mexico City were known, normally passed the time on skates, improbable as that might seem to visitors from other countries. The popular view of Mexico was cactus and peasants wearing *serapes* and *sombreros*, walking their burros through dust and scrub with a mission bell tolling in the background, not cosmopolitan middle class business people and their children skating around like they were in New York's Central Park.

Given the crowd, it was impossible to have the area completely buttoned down. Multi-story buildings everywhere, tens of thousands of people gathered, countless pedestrians moving through the far edges going about their business. It was every security planner's worst nightmare. Thankfully, the president would only be exposed for a short while, as he made his way from the presidential helicopter to the massive front doors of the cathedral. Then it became a different matter.

Cruz had accompanied the president's security head as the team had set up the security checkpoint metal detector inside the church, and chained all entries but the main one and the one leading to the vestry. Armed guards monitored the clergy entrance, subjecting the priests and altar boys to the same pat down and search as the general public. In addition to the president, virtually every dignitary in Mexico City was going to be in attendance, so if a terrorist wanted to eliminate the government in a single stroke, a well-timed attack during the service would achieve this with ease.

A team of explosive specialists had gone over the interior of the church all morning with bomb-sniffing dogs, inspecting every nook and cranny for suspicious items. After five hours of intensive searching, they'd turned up nothing. Cruz would almost have felt better if they'd located a device. The anxiety in the pit of his stomach had been building, although he had to admit that there was no evidence of an assassination attempt in play. Now the church was packed, with a hum of murmuring reverential voices vying with the organ music. There was little they could do inside at this point – the mass was imminent.

Briones and he stepped back through security and into the sun, shielding their eyes while surveying the crowd across the empty boulevard. One of the security detail approached them and tapped his watch. They would need to move to the perimeter. The president was due to land in three minutes.

Cruz and Briones walked across the cobblestones to the far edge and waited, Cruz studying the four and five story buildings at the sides of the massive square distrustfully. As he waited for the great man's arrival, he looked up at the church's ornate portico, grimy from exhaust and soot, but still impressive. Built on the site of the main temple of the Aztec city of Tenochtitlan in the mid-1500s, it had been enlarged over the years and was now easily one of the most impressive sights in the city, as well as being a reminder of the Spanish role in the history of the country.

As Cruz resumed scanning the surroundings, his eye caught a glint in a distant window on the top floor of the Gran Hotel de Mexico, across the street from the most distant corner of the square. Simultaneously, the distinctive sound of a large helicopter battering the air above them intruded into the expanse, echoing off the church and momentarily drowning out the din of the crowd. He squinted and tried to make out what he'd seen at the hotel, but it was no good. Then the downdraft from the chopper blew a dust cloud from the cobblestones surrounding the landing area, causing him to cough and close his eyes to fend off the grit. The aircraft touched down and the rotation of the long blades gradually slowed, enabling Cruz to resume his surveillance. He eyed the hotel's windows and then spotted it again.

There.

Cruz elbowed Briones and leaned in to him.

"Binoculars. Now."

Briones hesitated for a moment, then lifted the leather strap that held the glasses over his neck and handed them to Cruz. He raised the lenses to his eyes and studied the window that had caught his interest and then handed them to Briones before racing to where the head of security was standing, in preparation for the president's exit from the aircraft. He cupped his hand over the man's ear and yelled something, and then the security chief moved his handheld radio to his lips and issued a terse order. The helicopter remained in place, but the doors didn't open.

Cruz sprinted across the empty boulevard to the sidewalk in front of the hotel, Briones panting in his wake as he struggled to keep up. Three serious-looking men with ear buds and suits carefully tailored to hide their shoulder holsters dovetailed from their positions near the barricades to meet them, and within a minute they were in the lobby of the hotel.

Ignoring the surprised stares from the guests in the sumptuous, centuries-old lobby, Cruz hurriedly approached the reception desk and gave a command to the young uniformed woman. She looked unsure of herself for a moment and then nodded and picked up the phone. After a few hasty sentences, she hung up and regarded him.

"Miguel, the head of maintenance, will meet you on the top floor in two minutes with a passkey. Do you know which room you want?" she asked.

"It's the fourth from the corner, facing the cathedral," Cruz answered.

She tapped on her keyboard and pulled up the information.

"Registered to *Señor* Ricardo Gomez, from San Luis Potosí. Checked in two days ago," she told him.

Cruz had already motioned to the men and strode to the large, ornate wrought iron elevator that was the showpiece of the spectacular ground floor, its green and gold trim glancing off the sunlight that poured in through the intricate stained-glass roof over the lobby. The hotel was a rough rectangle built around the lobby, with the walkways and room doors facing the atrium.

The elevator creaked to a stop and they got on, with one of the men soundlessly taking the stairs in case their quarry got wind of their arrival and tried to make a stealthy escape.

When they reached the top floor, the maintenance man arrived, having followed the security man up the stairs. They counted the doors, and when they arrived at the suspect one, the group drew their guns. Cruz heard a collective gasp from the crowd in the lobby beneath them, which was now following the unfolding drama with interest. He took three steps over to the railing and held a finger to his lips, his pistol clutched in his other hand. The people below scattered at the sight of the weapon and made for the exits, which was just as well, he reasoned. If there was going to be a gun battle, it would be best if civilians weren't in the line of fire.

He returned to his position by the side of the door and indicated for the maintenance man to open it using his universal card key. The man slid the coded rectangle into the card reader, and the light on the lock flicked to green. Cruz motioned for him to move aside, which he didn't need much encouragement to do, and then quietly gripped the lever and turned it. Once in the open position, he abruptly swung it wide and rolled into the room, gun searching for a target. The rest of the men followed him in, with Briones taking up the rear.

A telescope sat on a tripod, aimed at the cathedral. Next to it, on a chair, lay a laser range finder and an M110 SASS rifle with a custom high-powered scope. An empty golf bag sat in one corner of the room. Cruz gestured to the men to check the bathroom and held his breath while the lead man darted in, pistol first, and then emerged a few seconds later, shaking his head. Briones pulled the door of the eight-foot-tall armoire open, but it was empty except for an overnight bag and a shirt. The assassin had fled.

Cruz unclipped the radio from his belt and gave a quick summary to the security chief, and watched through the telescope as the president and his bodyguards exited the helicopter and made their way into the church.

"Don't touch anything. I want a forensics team in here as soon as possible. It looks like we interrupted *El Rey* and made him scramble, which means that there's a chance we'll pick up some valuable evidence," he ordered. Briones fished his cell phone out of his shirt pocket and made a hushed call.

He hung up after a short discussion. "Twenty minutes, and they'll be here."

"Guard the room. I don't want anyone in here until they arrive. Is that clear?" Cruz demanded.

Everyone nodded, and he stalked out. They had prevented a shooting, but missed their quarry yet again.

The elevator ride down was mercifully brief, and when he got to the ground floor he advised the front desk girl that the room was a crime scene and then interrogated her on when she had last seen the elusive *Señor* Gomez, as well as probed for a description. She didn't have a lot of detail she could offer, and she hadn't seen Gomez since yesterday afternoon. Which did them no good at all.

Cruz left Briones to finish the questions and exited the hotel, making a beeline back to where the helicopter sat.

❧

El Rey watched the flurry of activity at the main entrance of the hotel, as the crowd of guests emptied out through the exits with looks of fear on their faces. It would just be a matter of minutes until the police discovered the weapon, and then the fun would start. He had planned a nice diversion to keep everyone occupied, and they had fallen for the bait. Now they would be less vigilant for the remainder of the mass, concentrating on their shocking new find instead. Word of the assassination attempt would spread through the gathered security, and they would ratchet their guard down, just a little. Of course, as he knew, that was when it was most dangerous – the moment everyone decided it wasn't.

A small boy bumped his leg, jostling the long blue robe, and he looked down at him and smiled. The little tike smiled back uncertainly, and then grabbed his father's hand. The pair continued their trip down the sidewalk, away from the church, a hundred and fifty yards across the square.

El Rey moved to his pre-planned point at a sidewalk coffee shop and took a seat, placing the briefcase he was carrying on the table. When the waitress approached him, he asked for something out of the sun, so she moved one of the tables to a position right by the building. He thanked her and ordered a sparkling water as he pulled his chair against the concrete so his back was to the wall, and he was facing the packed square.

She returned with his bottle and a glass, and he cheerfully paid her, telling her to keep the change. Happy with his generosity, she departed and went back inside the shop, leaving him to his thoughts.

He watched the crowd across the street in the square, already losing interest given there was nothing to see now that the president had gone inside the church, and easily picked out the plainclothes security men. It was always childishly simple to do so.

Seeing no immediate threat and satisfied that they had their hands full with the mob of humanity, he opened the briefcase and connected the cable inside to a jack on the case lid, which he'd run wire through, making the entire top an antenna. Glancing at his watch, he calculated he had another twenty minutes before the mass would be over. He softly closed the briefcase, leaving it unlatched and connected, and reconciled himself to waiting.

Reaching through a slit in the side of the heavy robe, he rummaged in the pocket of his shorts for a small smart phone, extracted it and placed it on the table. He looked around and, detecting no interested observers, pressed a series of keys.

The screen illuminated, and he was suddenly watching the ceremony taking place inside the church – an aerial view. He reached into another pocket and pulled out a cord with an earplug and plugged it into the audio jack so he could enjoy the show.

CHAPTER 29

The interior of the cathedral was flamboyantly ornate; a showpiece of opulence as a tribute to the place the Catholic Church had held in the hearts of the populace over the centuries. The bishop of Mexico City was saying the mass, his deep voice reverberating off the walls and the high, arched ceiling.

The president sat in the front pew, a bodyguard on either side, his wife still recovering from surgery a week before and resting easily at home. He listened attentively to the sermon, a treatise on the power of perseverance in the face of overwhelming odds and of the Lord's unconditional love for those who accepted Jesus into their hearts. It was certainly not a new idea, but the bishop was able to infuse it with sufficient enthusiasm and poignancy to make it interesting enough to keep the faithful awake.

An occasional cough or baby's burble echoed through the church, and clothes rustled and shoes scraped the floor as the congregation kneeled, stood and sat at the appropriate times. At least twenty security men stood on either side of the long hall, with several in the center aisle, where they could head off any hazard.

Eventually it was time for communion, and the crowd lined up behind the president at the head of the queue. Nine minutes later everyone had returned to their pews, and the bishop said his closing piece, asking the congregation to remain seated while the president made his way down the aisle and out through the front doors.

ॐ☙

El Rey watched as the ceremony drew to a close, and the president and his group stood and began moving down the aisle. He waited a few more seconds, and then opened the briefcase and pushed a button, immediately fiddling with the joystick and other controls of the panel he'd recessed into the case.

ॐॐ

The president was three quarters of the way down the aisle when something made a snapping sound in the chandelier above him, and part of it fell towards him, dropping onto the cold stone floor a few feet away. The unmistakable shape of a hand grenade clattered to a stop next to one of the pews nearest the entrance doors, causing instant panic as those seated nearest it screamed and scrambled to get away.

Two of the security men grabbed the president by both arms and ran at full speed for the entry, while another threw himself on the grenade, willingly giving his life to spare the president and the crowd horrific carnage. Pandemonium erupted as the congregation stampeded towards the altar, as far from the grenade as space would allow. Women tripped and men dragged them along as they rushed to safety. A few climbed over the pews before throwing themselves flat on the benches in the hopes that the heavy, ancient wood could protect them.

Within a matter of seconds the president was at the heavy wooden doors. His men shouldered them open, racing against time to get him out before the grenade detonated and the house of worship became a slaughterhouse.

ॐॐ

El Rey pulled the earphone out and placed it on the table next to the phone as he watched the chaos in the church. Satisfied with the panic, he turned his attention to the hotel and craned his neck to see above the building. A lone crow stood at the edge of the hotel roof, peering curiously down at the scene below. Startled by something moving behind it, the bird took flight, spreading its wings and flapping off over the top of the cathedral. *El Rey* watched its trajectory with a vague sense of unease, and then returned his focus to the roof, where he couldn't see anything but the building's façade.

Frustrated, he stood, still maneuvering the levers in the briefcase, and then caught sight of the president bursting out of the church and moving at flank speed to his waiting aircraft. The pilot hadn't had time to start the engine again; startled by the abrupt exodus, he began flipping switches in preparation to power up.

A muffled explosion sounded from inside the cathedral. The grenade had detonated, causing unknown casualties and damage. El Rey couldn't take his eyes off the unfolding drama in front of the church to check the result on the phone screen.

Halfway to the chopper, the president stumbled; his bodyguards lifted him from where he'd fallen painfully against the cobblestones. Whatever it was that was taking place in the church, they were safe. They hauled him upright without ceremony. He bent down and patted his knee, where the fabric of his Canali suit pants had torn, and his hand came away with blood. One of his detail barked a few words, and he began limping to the copter, one arm around the closest bodyguard.

El Rey glanced skyward again and his eyes caught the distinctive shape of the four foot remote controlled helicopter hovering over the roof of the Gran Hotel, fifty feet above the street. He thrust one of the joysticks forward, and it made a course for the front of the church, accelerating until it covered the distance in under fifteen seconds. He twisted a knob to increase the blade pitch for maximum speed and had to adjust for a light wind gusting off the square, but quickly corrected as he brought the craft to bear.

The president was nearly at his chopper's door when his bodyguard at the church doors screamed a warning. The president and his two men swung around in puzzlement, trying to spot the danger, and then with a look of terror the president pointed into the sky, where he'd caught movement in the periphery of his vision. One of the men tried to pull him out of the way, but it was too late. A bright fireball exploded a few feet from where he stood, obliterating everything for a twenty foot radius and peppering the fuselage of the presidential helicopter with shrapnel and bloody bits of flesh.

The crowd went crazy and rushed the barricades, knocking back the steel frames and causing a near riot. Screaming and cries of panic filled the air as *El Rey* stood and closed the briefcase, then slid by the chair and began walking down the sidewalk in the opposite direction from the church, the phone and case abandoned now that they had done their job.

∽∾

Cruz had watched in impotent horror from his vantage point on the empty boulevard as the oversized model helicopter zoomed silently across the square and went into a high speed dive at the church. When the detonation came, he knew instinctively it was too late to save anyone. The police helicopters hovering overhead weren't any good against something that small and nimble, even if given time to react.

He spun around, studying the huge square and the people panicking, eyes searching for *El Rey*. He had to be there. Remote controlled airplanes and cars always required the antenna for the control box to be in direct line of sight, and they were generally limited to a hundred and fifty yards of effective range. That meant the assassin had to be within a hundred and fifty yards of both the hotel and the church. Cruz did a quick mental calculation and determined that he either had to be on his side of the square midway down the block, or on the far side of the square in roughly the same area, midway between the hotel and the cathedral.

Cruz peered along his side of the square first, but didn't see anything significant. All the windows were closed on the surrounding buildings, and there was nobody suspicious on the sidewalk. He quickly surveyed the crowd chaotically milling around the square, trying to avoid being crushed by their own panicked behavior, but it was a mess and he couldn't make anyone out. It was unlikely the assassin was in the multitude, given that everyone had been searched and the control device would be too large to use without being detected, so he quickly dismissed the possibility.

His eyes roamed over the sidewalk on the far side of the square, looking for any anomalies. *There.* Cruz spotted movement. Everyone else on the sidewalk was hurrying in the direction of the cathedral, anxious to see what had happened, except for one figure, who was making a measured move in the opposite direction. He initially dismissed his instinct and then did a double take.

It had to be *El Rey*.

Cruz called out to Briones to get a car and stay on his radio, then ran down the boulevard in the direction of the figure, which was quickly closing in on the corner where the hotel sat. He increased his speed, his leg muscles burning as the healed bullet wound shot spikes of pain each time he landed on his right foot. He radioed to the men in the hotel as he went, but everyone was upstairs guarding the room they'd discovered. It was no good. The assassin would be well past the hotel by the time anyone made it down to the street level.

The figure turned the corner and disappeared from sight. Cruz estimated he was now a little more than a hundred yards behind. He gasped for air and increased his effort.

∾∾

El Rey registered the federal policeman running down the middle of the boulevard in his direction, but figured that by the time he turned the corner to follow, it would be over. Once he rounded it he increased his pace to a run and sprinted for an alley thirty feet up on the right. Several of the pedestrians who were hurrying towards the square leaped out of his way in surprise, giving him momentary pleasure.

After all, how often did they see a nun running the four minute mile down a busy sidewalk in the historic district?

The decision to carry out the assassination posing as a nun had been a natural, and to him, brilliant bit of subterfuge. In the square, any young or middle-aged men would have drawn attention given the manhunt in place for *El Rey*. And there was no way to take the president out with a shot – not with as many eyes on the windows as he'd expected, which had been borne out by the hotel fire drill. That left either a bomb or gas in the cathedral, which would have been impossible to reliably conceal given the size required to ensure the job got done. So he'd needed a method of conveyance that would deliver oblivion to the president at

208

high speed, that was unstoppable and too small to bring down with ground fire.

He'd initially toyed with a number of other possibilities, including contact poison on the front row pew the president would take, or some sort of toxin on the communion hosts, but had dismissed the alternatives as too prone to failure. Even his grenade gambit had been iffy. He'd posed as a repairman two weeks earlier and appeared with a work order to replace the lights in the massive chandeliers and repair anything that was broken, enabling him to conceal the grenade, a small fiber optic camera, and a radio-controlled release mechanism in its heart, but he'd actually been surprised that they hadn't been found. It had never been intended to kill the president – too many variables, and it wasn't nearly powerful enough to guarantee that the job got done. But it had promised to be effective in dividing his security detail and forcing him out into the open.

The remote control helicopter had been an intriguing possibility, and when he'd bought it on eBay before having it shipped to a freight forwarder in Mexico, he was certain he had found the solution to his problem. He'd sneaked up onto the hotel roof at five a.m. and placed the craft at the far end behind a ventilation duct, where it wouldn't be discovered if an errant maintenance man went up for some reason. He knew that the roof would be locked the day of the president's visit, and leaving the helicopter in place overnight in standby mode was a calculated risk he'd had to take – one that had paid off, in the end.

From that point it had been simple. The modifications he'd made to the remote console had increased the effective range to a hundred and seventy yards, which was more than enough for his purposes. He'd taken it out and practiced with it for a week in a deserted area outside Puebla, and had gotten so good with the controls he could fly it with his eyes closed. Effective flight time was under ten minutes before the battery ran down, but he'd calculated that three minutes was sufficient. Even with it sitting in standby mode overnight, he'd had five minutes of power left. More than enough for his purposes.

The explosive had been key. A concentrated, extremely powerful variation of C-4 manufactured in Iran; it had double the explosive power, which meant that six to eight ounces would create the desired lethal blast zone. All he needed was to get it within fifteen feet of the president to vaporize him. Mission accomplished.

With a little makeup and special attention to a close shave that morning, he could pass for a woman, albeit not a beauty. Then again, nuns didn't typically win pageants, so he felt that he'd fit right in.

El Rey ducked into the alley and jumped on a Vespa motor scooter, straddling it with the nun's garb now pulled up around his waist. The engine turned over with a puff of blue smoke, and he gunned the gas, then slammed the scooter into gear and roared off in the opposite direction from where his pursuer would inevitably appear. As he approached the far end a police car pulled across the alley, blocking his way. Without hesitation he did a fast turn and set off, full speed in the direction he'd come. Better a cop on foot than two in a car, probably with shotguns.

He slowed as he reached the alley mouth and then executed a tight right turn, catching a glimpse of the pursuing police captain just now pounding around the corner. *El Rey* opened the throttle wide, putting distance between himself and *Capitan* Cruz, who had his gun drawn.

A navy blue car came swerving out of the next street, sending the Vespa skittering from underneath him as he bounced off the hood and then crashed headfirst into the windshield.

The last thing he saw as he blacked out was a vaguely familiar face nearly obscured by the white balloon of an airbag – the officer he'd shot at the summit – gripping the steering wheel with one hand as he stared in shock at the nun he'd just run down, blood streaming freely from his nose.

CHAPTER 30

"I don't give a shit. I want my men here, twenty-four seven. Two in the room, two outside, and if he tries anything, they shoot," Cruz said to the doctor, who was obviously annoyed with the quasi-military presence of the tactical squad members in full assault gear, toting sub-machine guns and looking menacing. "And he'll remain cuffed to the bed. Both hands. And his feet shackled to the rail. This man is easily the most dangerous in Mexico, so I want no more discussion about what is or isn't good for his convalescence or pain management."

"Captain, I understand, but this is most irregular. He's got a concussion, and a cerebral hemorrhage we're managing now, after the surgery, and two fractured vertebrae, as well as several broken ribs. He won't be going anywhere or trying anything. I really think this is unnecessary..." the doctor complained.

"That may well be, but you don't know him like I do. He's a magician, not to mention that he's killed dozens, if not hundreds of people in cold blood. I wouldn't put it past him to chew his own arms off to escape, so there will be no negotiation. If I need to call the hospital administrator, I'll be more than happy to do so. What's it going to be?" Cruz threatened.

The doctor backed down. Fighting for his patients only went so far, and he didn't need any additional grief in his life.

"Well, I don't like it," he lamented pugnaciously and then stalked off down the hall, shaking his head.

Cruz turned to the four heavily armed officers. "I want you on high alert. No fraternizing with the nurses. Don't eat anything, and only drink bottled water. You'll be replaced in eight hours. Expect a full-scale assault to free this man, and also expect him to try to kill any and all of you with anything he can get his hands on. Don't let down your guard under any circumstances," he warned them. "If you screw this up, anyone that doesn't get killed by the assassin or his rescue committee can expect me to do so. Are we clear?"

The men nodded dutifully at their commander, who was glaring at them as though he was dead serious about his promise.

The elevator at the end of the hall opened, and Briones approached, his nose swollen, with a bandage across it holding a piece of gauze in place.

"Broken, *eh?*" Cruz asked.

Briones nodded. "Damned air bag hit it just the right way. A fluke. It actually blew my hand off the wheel into my face, and my hand broke it."

"So...wait a minute. You punched yourself in the nose?"

Cruz started chuckling, as did Briones. It was a little funny, and the dark humor helped relieve the accumulated tension.

"Yeah, but you should have seen the other guy..."

Cruz grinned, and then described the security precautions in place at the hospital. Briones listened intently and then nodded.

"The doctor just told me that he's come to," Cruz informed him. "They spent five hours operating on his skull, trying to drain the blood and fix the damage. He says the prognosis is good. I wish he'd stuck a pair of forceps into his brain and ended this, but that's not how the Hippocratic Oath works, apparently. So *El Rey*'s still with us," Cruz explained. "I'm going in to interrogate him. You want to be a fly on the wall?" he asked Briones.

"I wouldn't miss it for the world."

The pair opened the door and walked into the room. *El Rey* was handcuffed and chained to the steel frame, and held down with restraint straps for good measure. His eyes followed Cruz and Briones from beneath a bandage enveloping his head as they walked to the foot of his bed. Cruz noticed that he had remarkable eyes. Bright, intelligent, but chillingly devoid of any emotion.

"What's your name?" Cruz asked.

The man smiled almost shyly. "You can call me Romero."

Cruz recognized that the assassin was mocking him by choosing his first name.

"Very amusing, indeed. You're quite a card, *eh*?" Cruz leaned over the bed and lowered his voice. "You've pulled your last stunt, my friend. It's over. You'll spend the rest of your life rotting in prison for your reward. I hope it was worth it…"

El Rey didn't say anything; just stared at them both with a disinterested gaze before closing his eyes.

"You'll never be able to keep me prisoner. No prison will be able to hold me. Enjoy your moment of triumph. You deserve it," *El Rey* said in a hoarse whisper directed to the ceiling.

"Oh, I think you underestimate my resolve. I agree, under normal circumstances you'd have a good chance at escape. But you, my little bird, are going to be kept in solitary in a special facility that houses the worst of the worst – under twenty-four hour guard. If you're lucky they'll give you solid food once in a while, and not make you eat through a straw. Assuming you can even chew, and the doctor that did the surgery on your brain didn't scramble it."

El Rey opened one eye. "Do what you have to do."

"Oh, I intend to. Believe me. But I do have one question. Who hired you to kill the president? Who put you up to it?" Cruz asked.

"It was pro bono. Call it my charitable contribution to the great nation of Mexico."

"I don't believe that for a second. But no matter. I suspect whoever did it will want their money back, or will be looking for you harder than we did. You'll be praying the prison is secure every night as you cry yourself to sleep," Cruz said, smiling humorlessly.

"Right. You're delusional. I watched the president being blown into a million pieces. Nice try, though."

"Maybe you thought you did, but I'm afraid all you accomplished was to kill a few more innocent men. Seems like your reputation is a little bigger than your actual effectiveness. Par for the course with blowhards," Cruz said.

"I'm sure that's the last thing your men were thinking when they disintegrated in flames at the apartment. I read about it in the paper. Sad, really. You don't train them very well, do you?" *El Rey* offered, eyes closed again, reclining against his pillow.

Cruz nodded at Briones. He walked over to the television suspended in the right corner of the room and switched it on. Looking at his watch, he flipped through the stations until he got to a news program. The newscaster was reporting on the morning's attack on the cathedral, and then cut to footage of the president speaking about it. The camera cut back to the announcer, who concluded with the statement that the president had been involved in a near-miss assassination attempt, but was unhurt.

El Rey's eyes had opened at the sound of the broadcast and now narrowed.

"I saw it myself."

"What you saw was an artifice. You failed. Both times you tried to kill a president, you failed miserably. You're a loser. Maybe you got a reputation as hot stuff snuffing out drug lords and local politicians, but in the big leagues, you've been tested and found wanting. And you'll be spending the rest of your life in a hole, the laughingstock of the prison. That's your future, you cockroach."

El Rey stared at him with that dead gaze, and then closed his eyes again. For him, the discussion was over.

Cruz spoke for a few more minutes, taunting him, but got no response. Eventually he tired of it, and he and Briones moved out into the hallway, being replaced in the room by two of the four armed guards.

They walked easily towards the elevator, and Briones turned to Cruz.

"I saw it, too."

"What you saw was a very brave man – no, several brave men – give their lives for their country. One of which was an impersonator. A lookalike."

Briones stopped. "Not the president?"

"No. When I met with his chief of staff, I was able to convince him that *El Rey* was likely to succeed, and that if the president insisted on being seen at public events while he was at risk, that they should find a stand-in for the events where he didn't have to give a speech – much like many of the Middle Eastern despots have. This was the first time he used one, which turned out to be fortunate. Or unfortunate, depending upon who you ask."

"Well, I'll be damned," Briones exclaimed, touching his battered nose gingerly with his fingers.

"Yes, I suspect we both will. It seems to go with the territory."

"At least the hours are good."

They both chuckled again.

The elevator opened and they stepped inside, an odd couple who looked like they were carrying the weight of the world on their shoulders. Cruz pushed the lobby button, and as the doors closed he glanced at Briones again and sighed.

Sometimes the good guys won a round.

Today was one of those days.

CHAPTER 31

"We got the information from the freight forwarder and traced it to a shipping company here. They gave us the address, so whenever you're ready, we'll go in," Briones reported.

It had been two days since the attack at the cathedral, and they had traced down the manufacturer of the helicopter in the U.S. and gotten the information on the address where it had been sent. It wasn't hard – there weren't that many companies making four-foot-long electric remote controlled helicopters that could accommodate substantial modifications. Once they had located the builder, they were able to find the freight forwarder in San Ysidro, California who had imported it into the country. From there it had just been grunt work to track it to Mexico City, where yet another local company had delivered it.

Briones approached Cruz's desk and put a slip of paper on it bearing a street name and address. Cruz studied it briefly, glanced at the mountain of paperwork on his desk, and then shrugged before rising to his feet.

"I've got nothing to do. Let's go take a look at Santa's workshop," Cruz said

The address was in a borderline area of town, mostly industrial buildings covered with graffiti and a few pedestrians, obviously either on their last legs, or overtly dangerous. Briones was driving – it wasn't the kind of neighborhood to take a high-end BMW, and the federal police cruiser would keep most of the miscreants away while they were inside.

Briones had warned the landlord not to enter the premises, cautioning that they could be booby-trapped.

"What are we looking for, exactly, sir?" Briones asked as he navigated around the deep potholes.

"I don't know. Anything that can be used for additional evidence. Maybe a clue as to who hired him to kill the president. Maybe some indication of who he really is. Information."

"He's going to be sentenced to hundreds of years in prison. There's no chance of him ever getting out," Briones said with satisfaction. "Whoever he is, he's going to be staring at the gray walls of a twelve-by-eight cell for the rest of his life."

The prints had come back under the name of a former marine with special operations certification, who had deserted a decade earlier. But further digging into the navy's documentation had quickly showed the birth certificate and voter's registration card he had used to enlist was a forgery. It was mystifying – they had no idea who the man they had under guard awaiting trial really was and were no closer to understanding him than they had been a year before.

Mexico didn't have the death penalty because it considered state-sponsored execution barbaric. *El Rey* would get multiple life sentences with no possibility of parole – the harshest penalty under Mexican law. The district attorney had already spoken with Cruz, and they were going to make a spectacle of the assassin's trial, sending the message that no matter who you were, crime didn't pay. After sentencing, he would go to one of the few truly dependable maximum security prisons in Mexico – Federal Social Readaptation Center Number One, 'Altiplano', near Mexico City, which housed a who's who of drug kingpins. He would be sequestered from the general population and locked down twenty-four hours a day, having no contact with anyone but his guards, who would be regularly rotated from among the most senior and incorruptible in the system.

They rolled to the curb in front of a battered brick building with six metal entry doors, one of which stood with its protective outer grating opened. The owner fidgeted by it jangling a set of keys as he glanced nervously up and down the street. It was late afternoon, but this wasn't an area you wanted to be in after dark.

"Captain Cruz? Hidalgo Sanchez. Nice to meet you," the man said, sizing Cruz up as he offered his hand in greeting.

"Likewise. This is Lieutenant Briones," Cruz said, which prompted the man to shake hands with Briones.

"Have you been inside?" Cruz asked pointedly.

"Of course not. I followed your instructions to the letter. I waited until you got here. Look, I don't want any trouble from anyone. If a criminal was using one of my workshops, I had no way of knowing. I want it understood I'm cooperating with the police," Sanchez insisted.

"Good. And don't worry. You're not suspected of anything." Cruz hadn't told him who the criminal was or what he had done. Some things were better left out of the conversation.

Sanchez exhaled a noticeable sigh of relief and then walked back to the door and ceremoniously opened the deadbolt. He turned the knob and heaved the steel door open, then gestured to the two officers.

"I'll just wait out here. Take your time, gentlemen."

Cruz entered first, his eyes adjusting to the gloom, and then both he and Briones ignited their flashlights – after the incident at the apartment, neither of them was in a mood to try the light switches. A long rectangular work table stood at the far end of the room, near a bank of grimy windows a few feet below the ceiling.

They moved to the table, where Briones began taking photos of the various tools and chemicals. Cruz gave it all a quick glance and then walked over to a black backpack resting against the far wall. He picked it up, but it felt empty. With one eye on Briones carrying out his inventory of the assassin's wares, he methodically checked the zip-up pockets of the sack and found a crumpled envelope.

Briones continued his inventory and after a few minutes announced he was done.

"Looks like this is where he assembled the bombs and the helicopter. You could rebuild an engine with the number of tools in this place. And there are some traces of plastic explosive in a plastic bag. I think it's time to call in the crime scene people," Briones said.

Cruz appeared not to have heard him and then slowly turned to the table.

"Yeah. Call them. Let's get a crew in here and go over the place with a fine-toothed comb. Maybe there's something we can use that will lead us to his employer," Cruz said, his voice tight.

Briones regarded him carefully. "Are you all right?"

He sighed. "Sure I'm all right. I've just been battling a cold for the last day. I think it's wearing me down," Cruz explained. "Make the call and tell the landlord we'll probably have people here for at least six to eight hours. I want to get the prints of every person who's ever been in here, or handled any of the tools or other items." Cruz tossed the backpack onto the floor.

"Anything in it?" Briones asked, drawing his phone from his shirt pocket.

"No. It was empty."

❧

Cruz arrived home at the condo after midnight, exhausted to his core. He locked the door behind him, taking care not to make noise as he padded through the foyer into the living room. A trail of alcohol vapor lingered in his wake, but he moved with surety, no hint of inebriation.

Dinah was asleep on the couch, a half full glass of white wine resting on the coffee table next to a stack of homework she had graded. He considered her, slumbering peacefully, looking angelic in her untroubled dream state, and then brushed past to the bedroom.

Ten minutes later, he emerged with one of his small duffle bags and an extra uniform on a hanger. He placed the bag by the front door and laid the uniform on top of it. Returning to the kitchen, he opened the refrigerator and pulled out a can of Modelo beer. When he popped the top open, it snapped with an audible crack, and Dinah jolted awake. She appeared disoriented for a few seconds, punchy from sleep, and she swung her head around until she saw Cruz. She smiled sleepily, and then her mood faded when she registered his expression.

"*Corazon*. What time is it? God, it's almost one. Where were you? I tried to wait up, but I couldn't..." She stopped – he was staring impassively at her, a hard look in his eyes she didn't recognize. "*Amor*...what's wrong? Is everything okay?"

219

Cruz reached into his shirt pocket with his left hand and withdrew the letter he'd retrieved that afternoon from the backpack. He flipped it at her, the small rectangle slicing a dizzy course through the tense air before it landed at her feet. Her eyes locked on it, and then her face collapsed.

"*Amor*. Romero. I can explain…"

"Can you? Can you really? That would be good to hear. Tell me why my fiancée is passing detailed information to the world's most dangerous assassin, and the subject of my task force's every waking moment of effort is lovingly memorialized for him. Tell me why the man who killed my officers, who wades in blood and lives to murder, benefits from your notes, like a lover sneaking kisses in the night. Explain it to me. Because I'd really like to understand."

"It's not what you think. I did it for us…"

"For us? *Really*. How is that, exactly? How is betraying me, betraying everything I've worked for, good for us? Because I'm confused. I don't get it. I don't see how my wife-to-be could lie to me every day, and be handing my innermost secrets to my sworn enemy, yet really be doing it for my own good. Christ. Do you know what kind of an animal this man is?" Cruz took a long swig of beer, finishing the can in three swallows. He stared at it, and then tossed it into the garbage before opening the refrigerator and grabbing another. He turned back to her and frowned. "This parasite, this psychopath, has killed hundreds of people – and you have been handing him my game plan. Explain that to me because I'm missing some big pieces."

"He…he found me three weeks ago…after the kidnapping, he came into my room at the hospital, and he threatened to kill me. To kill you. To murder us both…" Dinah hesitated, and then told him everything. The dead drops in the store. *El Rey*'s demands. The threats.

Cruz listened wordlessly, taking occasional swallows of his beer, and waited for her to finish. When she had, he shook his head, and walked around the breakfast bar to retrieve the envelope before returning to the kitchen. He took his time in formulating his response and fought to keep the anger out of his voice.

"You could have come to me. Told me. I could have helped. I could have saved you."

"No, you couldn't. The man is a monster, capable of anything. And he's beaten everyone he's ever gone up against."

"All but one. Me. I beat him. He's in custody because of me. So you were wrong. You could have…" he slammed his beer down on the tile counter, "you *should have* come to me. But you didn't. Instead, you passed information to this killer that cost people their lives. To a murderer. A thug. The man who killed your father." Cruz regretted saying it even as the words left his mouth, and he instantly registered the shock and pain in Dinah's eyes. And then a part of him didn't care. *Screw it – let her live with the truth.*

She was speechless as she processed what he had just revealed. Finally, she spoke in a quiet voice, the betrayal in her eyes matching his own.

"He killed my father? And you knew? All this time, every day, you knew?"

He put his almost empty second beer down on the counter and shook his head.

"Your father was his agent – he handled the money for him. He killed your dad when he planned his retirement. It was a loose end."

Dinah had nothing to say to that.

"You gave him a top secret document that could get me put into prison if it had been discovered. You committed treason. It's much more serious than a lover's quarrel. You betrayed me, destroyed our trust, and committed a high crime that carries a horrible penalty," he said, and then turned his back on her, walking towards the front door. "The penalty for treason, for doing what you did, is life in prison. It's that serious. This isn't a joke or a game."

Dinah sprang to her feet and followed, but stopped at the kitchen, standing with her arms down, palms outstretched, taking in the bag and uniform in a split second.

"Romero. Please. What are you doing?"

"I don't want to be here anymore with you. I'm leaving." He turned towards the door and leaned down, shouldering his bag and holding the uniform while he reached for the knob with his free hand.

Dinah's eyes suddenly flashed with fury. "And was it the right thing to send your ill-prepared men up against such a dangerous man? Would Lupita Guerrero deem it right?"

Cruz blinked back at her. What the hell was she talking about?

"Lupita who?"

"Lupita is a pupil of mine – you sent her father up to that apartment to tackle *El Rey* – now she doesn't have one. Can't you see, Romero…you couldn't even safeguard your own men against such a force and yet you expected me–"

"I expected you to trust me. To have faith in me, Dinah…" he said, twisting the lock.

Her anger faded as quickly as it had flared to the surface. Her voice became quiet as she read his face.

"But…Romero. What are you going to do?"

He held up the envelope with her notes and the top secret document in it, then put it into his shirt pocket. With a twist, he opened the door, and then looked at the tears rolling down her cheeks as she sobbed, heartbroken and afraid. He fixed her with a gaze that spoke of sadness, and fatigue, and broken dreams, and then he turned, stepping over the threshold into the long hall.

"The right thing, Dinah." He sighed wearily. "I'm going to do the right thing."

ABOUT THE AUTHOR

Russell Blake lives full time on the Pacific coast of Mexico. He is the acclaimed author of the thrillers: *Fatal Exchange, The Geronimo Breach, Zero Sum, The Delphi Chronicle* trilogy (*The Manuscript, The Tortoise and the Hare, and Phoenix Rising*), *King of Swords, Night of the Assassin, The Voynich Cypher, Revenge of the Assassin, Return of the Assassin, Blood of the Assassin, Silver Justice, JET, JET II – Betrayal, JET III – Vengeance, JET IV – Reckoning, JET V - Legacy, Upon a Pale Horse, BLACK,* and *BLACK is Back.*

Non-fiction novels include the international bestseller *An Angel With Fur* (animal biography) and *How To Sell A Gazillion eBooks (while drunk, high or incarcerated)* – a joyfully vicious parody of all things writing and self-publishing related.

"Capt." Russell enjoys writing, fishing, playing with his dogs, collecting and sampling tequila, and waging an ongoing battle against world domination by clowns.

Sign up for e-mail updates about new Russell Blake releases

http://russellblake.com/contact/mailing-list

7718611R00134

Made in the USA
San Bernardino, CA
17 January 2014